PRAISE FOR *HOPE* BY LORI COPELAND

"Hope is another fun, inspirational outing from seasoned writer
Lori Copeland. Who else but Lori would include among her characters
an ornery goat, a stolen pig, a mule called Cinder, and a man named Frog?
It's easy to see why romance readers are circling their wagons around
the Brides of the West series!"

› **Liz Curtis Higgs** ‹
author of Mixed Signals

"I just loved this book! Only Lori Copeland could weave a knee-slapping
tale with such a beautifully redemptive message. Her characters are
delightfully funny and unpredictable, and her plot is full of refreshing
twists and turns. I can't wait for her next book!"

› **Terri Blackstock** ‹
best-selling author

"Lori Copeland concocts just the right mix of faith, romance, and humor
in *Hope.* I started chuckling right away and didn't stop till the end.
A cheering, uplifting story of God's wisdom and love."

› **Lyn Cote** ‹
author of Whispers of Love

"Lori Copeland's third book in the Brides of the West series, *Hope,* is such
a delight! I laughed, I cried, but most of all I thrilled to see how spiritual
truths could be woven into a rollicking good story! Lori's light and lively
voice makes for good storytelling! This one's a keeper!"

› **Angela Elwell Hunt** ‹
author of The Silver Sword

"This tender and funny page-turner will tug at your heart from start
to finish. Hope's journey to love kept me cheering, sighing, and chuckling
as I read. *Hope* is Lori Copeland at her very best!"

› **Diane Noble** ‹
author of When the Far Hills Bloom

WHAT READERS ARE SAYING ABOUT
BRIDES OF THE WEST

"Faith is one romance that will sit on my limited shelf space and be read over and over."

‹ **L. C.** ›

"Your new book in the Brides of the West series is wonderful! Keep up the fantastic work!"

‹ **P. G.** ›

"I love stories that are both uplifting and realistic, and *Faith* and *June* really fit the bill. God bless you, and may you continue to brighten people's lives with your God-given talent!"

‹ **K. L. M.** ›

"Thanks for a quality story, well written and uplifting! I'll spread the word and recommend this book to others. I'll also check into the other HeartQuest books with anticipation."

‹ **J. B.** ›

"I truly enjoyed your books *Faith* and *June*. I am looking forward to more of your books. My husband (a bookworm) is impressed that I have actually read two books in three weeks!"

‹ **S. T.** ›

"Absolutely magnificent! The stories are fresh and exciting and inspire me to greater faith and service for God. God has anointed you for a mighty work through your wonderful novels."

‹ **K. M.** ›

HEART QUEST®

romance the way it's meant to be

HeartQuest brings you romantic fiction
with a foundation of biblical truth.
Adventure, mystery, intrigue, and suspense
mingle in these heartwarming stories of
men and women of faith striving to build
a love that will last a lifetime.

May HeartQuest books sweep you
into the arms of God, who longs for you
and pursues you always.

ROSES WILL BLOOM AGAIN

LORI COPELAND

Romance fiction from
Tyndale House Publishers, Inc., Wheaton, Illinois
www.heartquest.com

Visit Tyndale's exciting Web site at www.tyndale.com

Check out the latest about HeartQuest Books at www.heartquest.com

Edited by Diane Eble

Designed by Jacqueline Noe

Library of Congress Cataloging-in-Publication Data

Copeland, Lori.
  Roses will bloom again / Lori Copeland.
    p. cm. — (HeartQuest)
  ISBN 0-8423-1936-0
  1. Women pioneers—Fiction. 2. Colorado—Fiction. 3. Sheriffs—Fiction. I. Title. II. Series.
PS3553.06336 R67 2002
813'.54—dc21   2001008344

Printed in the United States of America

07 06 05 04 03
9   8   7   6   5   4   3

To E. W. and Linda Woolley and Chuck and Jane Woolley

Let us be grateful to people who make us happy;
they are the charming gardeners who make our souls blossom.
—Marcel Proust (1871–1922)

Trust in the Lord with all your heart; do not depend on your own understanding. Seek his will in all you do, and he will direct your paths.

PROVERBS 3:5-6

In all relationships, regardless of their nature, there comes the moment when you understand that there are some things you will never understand. When you are standing in that moment, just be right with it.

IYANLA VANZANT

chapter
ONE

THE PHONE shrilled, piercing her sleep.

Emma stirred, vaguely aware now of a dog barking in the distance. She dragged the second pillow across her head to shut out the sounds. The phone jangled again and she groaned at the annoyance. Outside it was still dark. Tossing the pillow off her head, Emma reached out, walking her fingertips up the base of her bedside lamp. One eye opened to peer at the clock: 6:10 A.M. *Who on earth?*

She fumbled for the receiver. "Hello?" Her voice was a croak.

"Miss Mansi?"

Emma didn't recognize the gruff voice on the other end of the line. She fell back onto the pillow, holding the phone to her ear.

"Miss Emma Mansi?"

"Yes."

"I'm sorry, ma'am."

The solemnity in the man's tone suddenly brought her wide awake. Something was wrong somewhere. Sitting upright, Emma ran one hand through a tangled mane of thick, auburn hair.

"What's happened?"

Work? Had something gone wrong at work? Had the heaters quit in the greenhouses? Seattle temperatures had been predicted to drop into the low twenties. The small bedding plants could have been hurt.

"This is the sheriff's office in Serenity, Colorado. I'm sorry to be the one to tell you this . . ."

Serenity? She hadn't been to Serenity in fifteen years.

"It's your sister, Miss Mansi."

"Lully?"

"I'm sorry. There's no easy way to say this. She was found dead this morning."

The words struck Emma like needled ice pellets. Lully? Dead? That was impossible. Lully was only thirty-five years old. Thirty-five-year-old women didn't just die.

"How?"

"We don't know, ma'am. Right now there doesn't appear to have been any foul play involved. An autopsy will be conducted later this morning."

"An autopsy." The words weren't making sense.

"You need to come to Serenity. As soon as possible."

"Today?" She couldn't think straight. Her bedroom took on a surreal atmosphere. The furniture, the white wicker—everything familiar blurred.

"Yes, Miss Mansi. Today, if possible."

"I–I don't know." There were so many arrangements to be made—

"Someone will need to identify and claim the body." The man's voice softened. "I'm sorry. This is always difficult."

Claim Lully's body? Yes, someone would have to do that. There was no one else but Emma. An image of a room filled with stainless-steel drawers and cream-colored walls flashed through her mind. Shadowy corridors. She'd seen morgues on television. The scenes had always given her the willies.

"I'm sorry," said the voice on the phone.

"I'll be there by evening—as soon as I can get a flight."

Emma's thoughts swirled after she hung up. She had to call Sue Rawlings, her employee at the greenhouse Emma owned. Most of the bedding plants would be okay. Nothing her caretaker Ed couldn't handle for a while. It was late fall, so most of the growing season was behind her. The poinsettias were set for the Christmas season. Emma covered her eyes as tears spilled over. *Lully. Oh, Lully.* Her beautiful sister. Dead? It wasn't possible.

Emma slid out of bed, wincing when her feet touched the icy hardwood. Flannel leggings bunched at her knees; a long-tailed white shirt caught at her legs as she stumbled across the floor, bumping into the wing chair that sat beside the bed. *Lully. Lully. Dead.*

The last person she loved. The last—gone. Too young. She was abandoned again. No, she'd heard a radio preacher sermonize just yesterday morning that death was never premature; it was always God's timing.

She hadn't talked to Lully in years, but she always knew her sister was there. She could reach out to her if she wanted. It seemed only yesterday that they had been children—laughing, playing, drinking tea from miniature china cups in the shaded tree house Dad had built behind Mother's perennial garden.

Faint light seeped beneath the bathroom shade. Emma's hand fumbled for the faucet. Water splashed onto the front of her shirt. She stared at the widening blotches with morbid fascination. She was only vaguely aware of tears running down her cheeks. Tears. She hated to cry. She couldn't remember the last time she'd cried. Wait, yes, she did. The last time was when Sam had abandoned her. She'd vowed then to never cry again, but now Lully was gone. Lully had abandoned her too.

Straightening, she dashed water on her face and then turned on the hot water full blast. *No more crying, Emma Mansi. Never again. Understand? You are truly on your own now. You have to act like a big girl.*

No more crying.

Emma's eyes were red when she arrived at the greenhouse. She was the first there, first to put on the coffeepot and turn up the heat in the small office.

Sue Rawlings would be the next to arrive. She was more than an employee; she was a friend whom Emma cherished. Sue was a fifty-year-old mother of two who seemed to be in perpetual motion. Medium height, a little plump, brown hair streaked with gray at the temples—stripes she said she'd earned honestly with two teenage boys.

When Emma, new diploma in hand, had been hired for a position at The Cottage Greenhouse & Gifts, Sue had welcomed her like an old friend. Later, Sue wanted more time for family and furthering her education, so she made Emma part owner, and eventually sold her the whole business. Sue liked to keep her hands in the nursery business so she worked two days a week.

Active in her church, Sue had invited Emma to services many times but was never upset when Emma had one reason or another for not going. God wasn't someone with whom Emma had a relationship. God hadn't answered her prayers when her mother died nor when Dad had disappeared. And he certainly hadn't brought Sam back to her. Obviously God didn't concern himself with Emma Mansi, so Emma hadn't concerned herself with him for the past fifteen years.

Emma unlocked the greenhouse and stepped into the familiar space that was more home than any place she'd ever been. The smell of damp earth and leaves greening teased her senses. She automatically checked the plants as she moved down the rows, snipping a brown leaf here and there. At the end of a row she dug her forefingers into earth and rubbed it between her fingers.

How she loved her work, the care and growing of beautiful plants. She enjoyed planning and executing the landscaping of a new home or commercial building, but it was the miracle of a flower or bush or tree grown from a sprig or cutting that she loved.

"Emma." Sue's voice came to her from the door leading into the gift shop. "You're even earlier than usual."

Emma turned, wishing she'd had more time to think about going to Serenity. Going home after fifteen years. How could she do it?

"I wanted to check on a few things." Emma wiped her hands on a cloth. "Sue?"

"Yes?"

"I need to talk to you."

Sue's smile faded as Emma entered the gift shop. "What's wrong?"

"I need a few days off."

"This isn't a vacation, is it?" Sue asked, her look penetrating.

"No."

Setting a flowerpot aside, Sue smiled. "I'll pour the coffee. It sounds serious."

The combined greenhouse and gift shop was half of a converted World War II barracks—each room dedicated to a different type of gift or décor: clothing, cards and stationery, crystal and china, scents, creams and bath salts. The greenhouse added a nice touch with green plants and perennials in the spring. A variety of aromas permeated the shop as Emma and Sue walked to the tiny space that was Sue's office. The aroma of freshly brewed coffee met them. Emma suddenly remembered that she'd forgotten to eat breakfast.

Sue poured a mug of coffee for Emma and handed her a glazed donut. "Here. Sit and tell me what's going on."

Emma set the donut aside and wrapped cold fingers around the mug. She sipped gingerly, hoping the hot coffee would warm her inside. "I got a call this morning. My sister has died."

Sue's hand automatically reached out to cover Emma's. "Oh, Emma. I'm so sorry! What happened?"

"They don't know. The sheriff's office called." Emma sipped her coffee again. Whose voice had that been? Familiar—yet not. "She was found sitting in her porch swing."

"She lived in Colorado, right?"

"Yes. I haven't been home in a long time. We haven't been close—" Emma's voice caught at the thought of all the wasted years.

"I'm so sorry."

Guilt washed over Emma. She had resented Lully's interference in her life, her sister's part in destroying her dreams. But in spite of that, she'd always known there was at least someone who cared about her. Now death had claimed the last link to family.

"She was only thirty-five. Why would a woman of thirty-five just . . . die?" Tears stung Emma's eyes. *I'm not going to cry*, she reminded herself.

"You need to go and find out," Sue said quietly. "Family is family. It doesn't matter that you haven't been close."

Emma choked back a sob. "Lully was all I had."

"Then you go." Sue waved a hand in the air. "Heaven knows I can run this place while you're gone. You've hardly taken a day in the eight years you've worked here. Take whatever time you need. We'll hold down the fort while you're gone."

"Yes," Emma conceded, "I need to do that." Though her sister's death was the last thing she wanted to confront.

"What can I do for you?" Sue gently helped Emma to her feet.

"There's nothing to do. I have a flight booked for noon."

"Are you packed?"

"No. I thought I'd do a few things here—"

"You are invaluable to us, but everything here can survive a little while without your attention. Ed can handle the greenhouse; I'll hire a temp to help me in the gift shop. You've taught Ed well, Emma. Trust him."

Trust didn't come easy for Emma. She could trust only herself. Experience had proven that.

"Go," Sue said. "Go pack, then come back here. I'll take you to the airport."

Emma knew Seattle fairly well, but in the fifteen years she'd lived here she hadn't taken a flight. "You don't need to—"

Sue set her mug aside with a thump. "Yes, I do. For me. I need to do something. Go." She took Emma's hands in hers. "Go do what needs to be done—for your sister and for yourself."

Emma went. Half of her wanted to go to Serenity to learn what had happened to Lully. But the other half wanted to stay in Seattle and pretend nothing had happened. Pretend that her life went on . . .

6

On the way home she stopped at the halfway house that had become her pet project after Sue had almost twisted her arm to visit the women there. Over the years Sue had taught the women about caring for plants and home gardens. These were women who had run afoul of the law in some fashion and needed education on how to do a number of things that most women took for granted—how to dress and apply for a job, how to plan goals and work toward them. Part of that education included how to create a pleasant atmosphere in the home, which is where Sue had insisted Emma fit in.

While Emma had gone reluctantly at first, soon she became involved in spite of herself. One of the women she'd been drawn to was Janice Carter, a small, fair, blue-eyed, flaxen-haired woman who didn't have a clue about men.

Janice had been with a boyfriend who robbed a convenience store. She had waited in the car, unaware of what the man was doing, until the police stopped them. The prosecutor's office had charged her as an accomplice. Fortunately, her boyfriend had corroborated her story that she hadn't known what he was doing, and the judge believed her. Still, Janice was sentenced to two years probation, which were to be spent at the halfway house, and she was to make a concerted effort to turn her life around. Janice had agreed readily to the terms. She had, she'd told Emma, always chosen the wrong kind of man. Now thirty years old, she was ready to get her life in order.

Janice's story touched Emma. A friendship had sprung up between them, and now Emma visited Janice every week. She needed to let Janice know she was going to be gone for a few days.

"It must be awful, losing your sister like that. I don't have any brothers or sisters. Wish I did." Janice took Emma's hand between hers.

Emma smiled. If only she had been as close to Lully as she was to Janice. "I'm okay. I'll be back in a few days."

Emma hated leaving when Janice was making progress in

gaining self-confidence. She looked and acted like an entirely different woman than when Emma had first met her. She'd taken all the classes Sue had given on makeup, how to dress, how to eat in a restaurant—things Emma had to teach herself. Perhaps that's why she was drawn to Janice; Emma had had to learn how to make her way through life on her own, just as Janice was now attempting to do.

Emma had read aloud—at Sue's insistence—the list of Scriptures Sue had given Janice, trying to make sense of the words. But all that stuff about God's love didn't register with Emma. The meaning of the divine messages seemed more relevant to the women at the shelter than to her.

In a few months Janice would be able to leave the halfway house and begin life anew. Emma hoped she could get her life on the right track and not fall for the wrong man again.

It didn't take long to pack enough personal items for three or four days. Emma was back at The Cottage in plenty of time to head for the airport and check in for the noon flight.

"You don't have to do this," Emma repeated as Sue hurried her to the company van.

"Thought we'd settled that."

Emma stared out the window as Sue maneuvered the van over the freeway to Sea-Tac. Traffic was heavy this time of day.

"You haven't seen your sister in a long time?"

"Not for fifteen years." Emma was grateful that Sue had never pried into her background. She was reluctant to talk about Lully, or Serenity, or why she'd never intended to go back there. "I never thought about Lully dying."

"No one likes to think about death. But we should. Not as a thing to be feared but as the beginning of an eternity, if we have a relationship with God. Was your sister a Christian?"

Emma thought back to those days right after their father had disappeared, leaving only a note on the kitchen table and twenty-five hundred dollars in a bank account in Lully's and Emma's names.

Though at the time the two girls were scared, fifteen-year-old Lully had been sure God would take care of them. Lully's concept of God came from Mother, who had taught them some Scriptures. Lully didn't seem to have a clear idea of who God was, but she'd clung to the idea that he cared about them. Emma hadn't been so certain God even knew who they were. But they somehow made it by scrimping and selling produce from their garden and Emma's dried-flower arrangements from Mother's perennial and rose gardens. The arrangements were simple, but Emma's talent had shown even as a teenager.

"In her own way, she believed," Emma finally answered Sue. "She couldn't make herself go to church because she didn't like people, didn't like being out among them. But she prayed and believed."

"That's a comfort."

Was it? Emma wasn't sure about that, either. Nothing had been a comfort to her. The only thing she was certain about was that she didn't want to return to Serenity without Lully being there.

Sue parked the van and walked with her to the security gate. "You take care." Sue hugged Emma tightly. "Call if you need anything."

"Thank you for the ride and for taking over for me." Emma blinked back tears, swallowing sentimentality, something she hated. "And for your friendship."

Sue hugged her again, patting her back. "Deal with this, kiddo—it won't go away."

Emma doubted that too. Everything she'd ever loved had gone away in one form or another.

"I wish you weren't doing this alone," Sue fretted. "If there's anything I can do to help—I mean it. Sometimes we have to accept help."

Emma mustered a smile. Sue knew her independence well. "I know. Thanks."

"And you'll be in my prayers."

Emma didn't know what to say to that. Prayer was foreign to her lately. She was convinced that the only thing you could depend on was yourself, not some pie-in-the-sky benevolent person who watched over everything you did and cared—really cared—about your needs and hurts and disappointments. God surely didn't care about joys because there had been so few in Emma's life.

Sue pulled a handful of magazines from her large purse. "Something to occupy your flight time."

"Oh, I didn't even think—"

"I know. Now, go. Don't worry about anything here. Just take care of things at home, and Emma?"

"Yes?"

"Just remember. Without the valleys, how could we ever be confident God is always with us?"

Without the valleys.

After a final glance back at Sue, Emma passed through the security system. Her flight was being boarded, and she entered the Jetway. She found her seat and stowed her carry-on, then sat looking out the window until the plane taxied down the runway and lifted off. She closed her eyes. Sue had said to take care of things at "home." Technically, Serenity wasn't home. It hadn't been for a long time. Emma wasn't sure what she'd find there, and that made her stomach clench. Home. She really didn't know what that was anymore. But soon—too soon—she'd be back in Serenity, and she would know what had happened to take Lully's life. Tears pricked her eyes again and she closed them, willing the tears not to fall.

Would Sam be there? She hoped not. Surely God wouldn't do that to her—would he?

Serenity, Colorado, was in the four corners region of southwestern Colorado, 31.6 miles from Durango—far enough from the visiting tourists attracted by Durango and the Silverton Narrow Gauge

Railroad, a scenic trail that runs along the old route to the silver mines, developed by the Denver and Rio Grande Western.

While the old city of Durango, with its history and cultures of the early settlers, was now a tourist, educational, and agricultural center, Serenity was a small community with few attractions other than its natural beauty. Even as a teenager Emma had recognized that. Tucked in the foothills of the Rocky Mountains where silver and gold had once been mined, the streams were cold and clear, the mountains tall, majestic, and snowcapped most of the year.

Long before Emma was ready, the plane landed at La Plata County Airport, a few miles outside of Durango. She rented a car, oriented herself with a map the rental agency provided, and got on Highway 160 west to Durango. Maneuvering the compact through the last of the tourist traffic in Durango, she turned on Highway 550 north to the Serenity cutoff, then drove, admiring the beauty of the rough hill country. The Animas River sparkled beneath late October sunshine.

Aspens that had already peaked in color once again captured her heart. This had been home for the first seventeen years of her life. When she'd left, she wasn't thinking of the rugged beauty she was leaving behind; all she'd thought of was the heartache she hoped to shed. To some degree it had worked, but now she was reminded of both the beauty of her home and the heartache that had driven her away from it.

Emma had forgotten to ask the sheriff's deputy where to go when she reached Serenity. She stood beside the rental car, staring at the old courthouse as a ball of red fire backlit the historic two-story building. *Fall sunsets are still the greatest*, she thought. Amber tones wrapped around the red-brick building, painting it in muted browns and gold against the blue of the snow-topped mountains in the distance. The scent of woodsmoke hung in the air, stirring memories she'd buried a long time ago.

Emma hoped the attorney who had been helpful when their

father had left was still Lully's attorney. Merle Montgomery would know what to do about making arrangements for services, about the house, about Lully's personal effects.

Leaves covered the ground, and squirrels darted about, tucking nuts away for the coming winter. Walking slowly up the concrete walk, Emma focused on the five-and-dime variety store on the corner of the square to the left of the courthouse. Still there after all these years.

She and Lully had saved their pennies and nickels, and every six months they'd walk to the dime store to buy something special. A treat. Emma got a new doll one year. Lully bought colorful beads and embroidery thread for her special jewelry projects, even though money was tight.

They'd felt the stares following them, the whispers about "those crazy Mansi girls," but they'd gotten adept at ignoring them. Lully was rumored to be a witch—ironic, since nothing could be further from the truth. She was eccentric, even as a young girl, drawing a fair amount of curious stares by the way she dressed. Flamboy-ant—weird, Emma conceded. Clothing in those days after Dad left had come from what they could scavenge from the Salvation Army bins. Lully picked the most colorful and dramatic garb she could put together.

On their way home, they'd stop by Lott's Restaurant and order two chocolate–chocolate chip, single-dip ice cream cones, carefully sort out the change, and after selecting one paper napkin each from the dispenser, they left the store, closing the door carefully behind them.

Old man Lott would step to the window and watch the girls making their way down the sidewalk, side by side, licking their cones. "It ain't right," the big Swede would say, crossing his arms over his ample stomach. A fierce look would come into his eyes. "That Lully Mansi's strange. A witch. She shouldn't be raisin' little Emma out there in that cemetery."

"Those girls aren't living in the cemetery," Freeda Lott was rumored to correct her husband.

"Don't know what else you'd call it. The house sits not thirty feet from Ezra Mott's headstone."

And the conversations would continue as the girls walked slowly toward the big, old Victorian house they'd called home since they were born. They'd heard the comments. Apparently those who gossiped about the Mansi girls thought they were deaf.

But both Freeda and Lott had been right. The old town cemetery hadn't been used for fifty years. The property bordered the Mansi backyard. No one knew why a house had been built that close to a cemetery. Emma remembered hearing her mother tell that her great-grandfather, James Mansi, had set his heart on a piece of property where there was a small, abandoned house. Apparently no one knew why the original owners had left the house, perhaps because of the nearby cemetery. The lot was large and had majestic pines for shade that lent a sweet scent to the air. The location suited James, and he bought the lot in 1884 and moved his family into the abandoned house.

As the years passed, Great-Grandpa James continued to add to the original structure as funds permitted, turning the house into a funeral parlor. First, a second floor, then a third, a back porch, a wider front porch, until he'd created a strange mix. James kept changing his mind on architectural style and bought whatever materials cost least at the time. Soon the Mansi house fit right in with the growing cemetery's tilted, weathered headstones, run down and dotted with moss.

A short time after Emma and Lully were born to Ralph, James's oldest grandson, and his wife, Mary, they moved their family into the town fright. They cared for Ralph's parents until at age eighty-five they died within a few months of one another. Then their mother, Mary, got sick. In too short a time she was gone. Their father grieved. It was as if the light had gone out of his life. He brooded, hardly spoke. Ralph often forgot his girls existed. Within a year he gave up and disappeared, leaving Emma and Lully, then ages twelve and fifteen, to fend for themselves.

For months after their father left, Lully assured Emma that he'd come back. At first Emma had believed her. It wasn't until some time after Ralph disappeared that anyone in town thought to ask about him. The girls, fearful that someone might decide they couldn't take care of themselves and would notify authorities, fended off questions. "Dad was working out of town." "Dad was sick with the flu and couldn't get around." "Dad had gone fishing up in the mountains for a few days—we can take care of ourselves real well, thank you," they'd say. By then Lully was sixteen and the townspeople decided she could care for her sister well enough, so no one did anything about the two girls living by themselves in the big, old Victorian.

The Mansi sisters were happy enough to be left alone. They ate what they wanted when they had the money and went to bed at any hour. They cleaned house only when it was absolutely neces-sary—which wasn't often. Left to their own devices, they created their own worlds. Lully graduated high school and spent her days at home, drawing the jewelry designs she said she saw in her mind, until there were stacks of papers here and there about the house. Lully stayed by herself and Emma attended school, unwill-ing to share any information about her living arrangement. The rumors and talk about the girls grew. When anyone ventured to ask about her father, Emma would tell another lie and walk off.

Such was her life—until Sam. When Sam came into Emma's world, things changed. First the giddy happiness, then the awful heartbreak.

Emma's thoughts were interrupted when she saw Merle Mont-gomery coming out of his office as she topped the stairs to the second floor of the courthouse.

"Emma? Emma Mansi!" Merle reached for her hand. "It's been a long time."

"It has. How are you, Merle?"

"I was so sorry to hear about Lully—"

"Thank you," Emma inserted. She was on her last nerve now; if Merle was too sympathetic, she'd burst into tears and she didn't need that.

"I'm wondering if you—are you Lully's attorney?"

"Yes, as a matter of fact, I am. I was hoping you'd get here today. Ken said he'd contacted you."

"Someone from the sheriff's office did. I didn't get his name."

"Ken—Ken Gold. Sam's youngest brother. Sam was out on a case of suspected cattle theft all night—"

Emma's heart stopped at the mention of Sam. "Sam?"

"Sure. Sam Gold. He's the sheriff here now. About five years, I think. And Kenny is his chief deputy. Couldn't separate those two with a crowbar."

It was hard for Emma to imagine Sam's younger brother old enough to—well, she supposed he was only two or three years behind Sam. Emma cleared her throat. "I have to make some arrangements—"

"Sam will help you with that. There'll be an investigation, you know."

Emma had trouble following Merle. "Concerning what?"

"Lully's death—don't know that she died of natural causes. Found her sitting in the swing on the front porch—must have been there all night. It doesn't look like foul play, but you never know."

Foul play. This was turning into a nightmare.

"Well, now that you're here, would you mind if we took care of the reading of the will tomorrow morning?"

"Tomorrow?"

He glanced at his watch. "I'm due in court in a few minutes, a case that will probably spill over into tomorrow afternoon. But there should be a break in the morning, say, about nine. Will that work for you?"

Emma's mind was numb. Lully gone. An investigation. A will to be read. Too many things to think about. "Fine. Thank you. I'll see you here at nine."

"Good, good." He patted her shoulder. "I'm so sorry that Lully's gone. She was an interesting woman." He glanced at his watch again. "See you in the morning."

"Thank you," Emma repeated, watching him hurry away.

Merle had called Lully an "interesting woman." That was kind, considering all the things people had said about the Mansi girls over the years.

Well, there was only one of the "crazy Mansi girls" left, and as soon as possible Emma would shake the dust of Serenity off her shoes—for good this time.

EMMA shifted the rental car into Park and stared at the old house. The basic structure looked exactly as she remembered it: three stories, wraparound porches, a dilapidated garage on the right side at the back. But little else looked the same. The house had needed paint when she left, but now it looked like the Colorado wind had stripped every suggestion of color from the weathered boards. Everything was gray and leaning.

She tried the front door and found it unlocked. That surprised her a little. Lully had kept the doors locked because she had been the recipient of so many pranks over the years. The old cemetery that sat directly behind the house hadn't helped the situation, especially at Halloween. Kids thought of new pranks to try every year, from hauling a tombstone to their front porch to having full-blown spook parties in the cemetery at midnight.

The house was cold, echoing. Dust motes floated in the air as if the place had been empty for a long time, instead of one day. Emma shivered. The aromas of lilac, cinnamon, and other unidentifiable scents floated to her. Lully had been fond of incense and candles. Emma was surprised, after seeing the alarming condition of the house, that Lully hadn't accidentally burned down the place long ago.

"Well, here we are," she said.

Leaving her coat on the foyer table, Emma walked through the downstairs, noting the old furniture, the frayed drapes, the overall clutter that now drove Emma wild. Lully was still the worst house-keeper in history. "Stuff" was stacked on the floors, end tables, and sofa, ready to topple over onto the floor.

Returning to what was once a formal parlor, Emma perched on the edge of a worn Victorian couch and closed her eyes. This was worse than she expected. Memories rushed at her, overwhelming her with sadness.

Emma finally stirred and went upstairs to the second floor where her bedroom had been. She pushed opened the door to her parents' room; the interior looked like it hadn't been touched since her father had left some twenty years earlier. She firmly closed the door and walked on. The next room had been Lully's. The scent of her sister's perfume hung in the air, and clothes were looped over the back of chairs, the foot of the bed. Emma shut the door quickly. She couldn't face this now. The next room had been a guest room; Emma ignored it, going to the room that had been hers when she lived in the house.

Again, little had changed. A single bed with a threadbare chenille spread with a telltale burn hole in the middle (the result of her and Lully's one and only experience with cigarettes), the same awful sun-faded grape-colored drapes, the wooden-back chair and scarred dresser. The room smelled musty and unkempt; in other words, it smelled like home. Aware that she would have to sleep there tonight, Emma opened the window to let in fresh air and then went downstairs to find clean linens.

Emma woke early after a restless night. She ate a piece of toast and drank a cup of coffee, all that was available. Apparently Lully didn't keep much in the way of food handy, and certainly not boxed cereal. Emma didn't think she could stomach oatmeal, which had always been Lully's breakfast staple.

At eight forty-five she parked near the courthouse, wondering why Merle felt the will had to be read so soon. Yet she supposed the sooner legalities were taken care of, the sooner she could be on her way back to Seattle. The thought sustained her as she got out of the car and walked up the concrete sidewalk.

As Emma passed a group of people standing on the sidewalk outside the courthouse the conversation died. She felt their gazes follow her; she could feel their eyes burning into her back. That, it seemed, had not changed. Hadn't they expected her to come? Surely they had. She'd been gone a long time, but her sister had died.

Emma Mansi . . . Emma Mansi . . . Emma Mansi. She braced herself against the imagined voices.

Lully Mansi's sister. Don't you know about her?

The crazy girl's sister?

Thought she moved to Seattle or somewhere. Said she'd never come back. She had to—found that sister of hers dead in the porch swing early yesterday morning. Foul play, they think.

No! Here in Serenity?

It can happen, you know. We're not immune to trouble, and if anything strange was gonna happen, it would be to the Mansi woman.

You can guarantee there's gonna be trouble.

Well . . . just because Lully was a little weird doesn't mean Emma's—

Those Mansis were all alike. The acorn doesn't fall far from the tree.

Emma refused to acknowledge the whispers with even a flicker of an eyelash as she climbed the stairs. She reached the attorney's office and took a deep breath before going in. The door squeaked on its hinges when she opened it. No one was at the reception desk, but she heard voices coming from an inner office. She followed the sound and pushed open the door carefully.

"Emma." Merle Montgomery looked up and greeted her. "Come in, come in. I know this is all a little rushed, but there are decisions to be made."

Emma nodded. "I understand." She didn't, really.

The attorney's office hadn't changed a whit either, maybe a little more disorganized and cluttered.

"Come, come and sit down. Everyone is here and we're about to get things underway." Merle pointed to a chair near the back of the room.

It was then that Emma saw him. Sam Gold. Heat rose in her cheeks as he turned to look at her. Recognition mixed with surprise flickered briefly across his rugged features, as if her appearance had caught him off guard. But he had to know she was coming. She was Lully's only relative. Maybe she should have phoned—

No. You owe him nothing. Nothing. When he let his mother separate the two of you and didn't even try to see you again—stop it. That was fifteen years ago! You're doing exactly what you vowed not to. What if and should have are dangerous words. It doesn't matter now. Never did, apparently.

Sam saw the confusion on Emma's face, the flush that colored her cheeks. So, she was still angry with him for what happened. He shouldn't be surprised. He had hurt her—hurt her badly. Events had been out of his control, but she didn't know that, didn't know the whole story. Maybe now that she'd finally come back he could tell her what had happened.

She hadn't changed all that much. Still beautiful in an exotic way. Not as startlingly exotic looking as Lully perhaps, but enticing in her own way. He'd been captivated by her at seventeen, thought he'd get over her at eighteen, but now it was clear that he'd only boxed up what he felt about her, put a lid on it and shoved it to some dark corner of his mind in hopes that he could convince himself he could forget about Emma Mansi.

It hadn't happened.

And now she was back. Back in his life whether he wanted it or not. Her being back was sure to dredge up old hurts. He closed his eyes, wishing her return had been under different circumstances.

Emma sank into a chair and concentrated on breathing. The high altitude, eight thousand feet elevation in Serenity, was bothering her more than she'd thought it would. She looked out the window where wind was whipping the branches bare of leaves and ragged forks of lightning danced across the mountain range. A storm was brewing, and not just in this room.

A movement at her left made her turn. Her gaze met that of a young woman about her own age. A smile automatically curved Emma's lips and was met with a broad grin. Myline Yates. My, my. The ponytail, baby fat, and freckles were gone. Myline was a beautiful woman now. Trim, wearing a nice navy suit. Her slim fingers were tipped with long, bright red acrylic nails, and an impressive wedding band twinkled on the third finger of her left hand.

In junior high, Myline had been her closest friend. Closest friend? Her *only* friend. Pudgy, round-faced Myline had been as needy as Emma back then. They'd both come from what the town considered the "wrong side of the tracks," though there wasn't a train track in Serenity and the Mansi house sat in the middle of town. Both girls had been shy, quiet, reluctant to draw attention to themselves. All of which made them easy prey.

Two timid mice—Myline and Emma. Everyone called them the mouser twins. Cruel, hurtful barbs that Emma and Myline ignored. During lunch they sat in a corner of the school dining room, sharing a sandwich, watching their classmates laugh and pull pranks in which they were not included. Emma was never chosen for the gym volleyball team until the coach put her on a side; Myline would have fainted if she'd ever been appointed hall monitor.

Myline hadn't cared that Emma lived with her sister, one that everyone called "crazy" or "witch," just a spit away from a cemetery. And Emma didn't mind that Myline's cantankerous old grandfather was raising her. Old Man Yates's black disposition prevented his granddaughter from enlarging her social circle. Everyone felt it was better than Myline being raised by the state— the same opinion they'd had when the Mansi girls were struggling alone. "They seem to be doing okay, and at least they have each other," people said and left them alone. Emma and Myline had shared a close relationship, one that had sustained them both through those rough years. Yet before Emma left Serenity she and Myline had drifted apart, as so many relationships do.

Those times seemed distant now. In contrast to her terrible teenage years Emma realized that her preteen years had been happy. Those years when her parents had been alive had been her only taste of "normal" in her youth.

Clearing his throat, Merle sat down behind his large mahogany desk and shuffled papers. The office smelled of old books, ink, and paper mixed with lemon wax. Emma's gaze scanned the cramped space. What were so many people doing here? A half-dozen people were seated, some in the leather chairs that would have gone with the room, others sitting stiffly in straight-back wooden chairs. Lully had always kept to herself, like Ralph and Mary Mansi and their parents before them had. Lully had bothered no one and expected not to be bothered. But life had not obliged. Tears stung Emma's eyes when she recalled a portion of Lully's few but poignant letters:

"They accuse me of being a witch and a sorcerer, but I won't let it bother me. I refuse to let them drive me away. I won't let the busybodies and do-gooders destroy my life."

Then she would close with "You were the smart one, Emma. Maybe I should have known better, left town when you did. Maybe somewhere else I could find peace, be left to myself without cruel speculation and those 'looks.' Yet . . . Sam's good to me. Really good, Emma. Maybe you should have stayed."

Stayed? And do what? Watch Sam fall in love and marry someone else? She wasn't that brave. Emma had never realized how much the whispers and accusations had affected Lully. After all, she rationalized, they were Mansis. They'd lived with cruel innuendos and broad suppositions most of their lives. Mansis accepted what was given and turned a deaf ear to everything else.

Merle shuffled the stack of papers again, as if he was stalling, which made Emma wonder why he would be reluctant to get this meeting started.

"Good morning, everyone," he said.

Three or four voices returned his greeting.

"I appreciate your coming on such short notice. It was Lully's wish that all be taken care of with expediency."

The distinguished gray-haired gentleman slipped on a pair of wire-rimmed glasses, then opened the folder in front of him. "As you're aware, we are here this morning to read the last will and testament of Lully Mansi."

Emma closed her eyes briefly. *I will not cry. I will not cry. If you cry I'll pinch the snot out of you.*

She opened her eyes and the attorney's gaze caught hers.

"Lully's death came as a shock to us all." His eyes gentled. "She was in my office finalizing her will the week before the Lord took her home."

That statement surprised Emma. Had Lully somehow sensed she was going to die? Had God instilled in her the urgency to complete her business? Though she was often accused of witch-craft and sorcery, Lully hadn't believed in powers other than God. "There's only one power," she would tell Emma when they knelt to pray each night. "Only one, Emma. The Lord Jesus Christ. Don't ever be fooled into thinking otherwise."

Emma closed her eyes again as memories overcome her. How long had it been since she'd thought of those innocent, simple bedtime prayers and Lully's admonitions? When she'd left Serenity she'd closed the door on everything that had happened here, and she'd not prayed since.

Merle began to read: "'I, Lully Mansi, being of sound mind, do hereby bequeath . . .'"

Emma listened to Lully's bequests in a dreamlike trance. Nothing seemed real. The bequests were simple ones, things only Lully would think about. A sizable amount to the community church about a block away, which would cause a few lifted brows in town since Lully supposedly had never darkened its doors.

A token remembrance went to a few whom Lully had respected in her own way—Tom Nelson, the butcher; the paperboy who got a small commemoration. There was a small sum for Ray Sullins, who apparently helped Lully run a small jewelry business. The mysterious Ray wasn't in attendance today. Three hundred dollars went to the lady who helped Lully clean when the clutter became intolerable, which, Emma knew, for Lully had to be really bad. A smile touched Emma's lips when she thought about her sister's relaxed housekeeping standards. Unless it fell over or kept her from her work, Lully simply walked around the stacks of things she couldn't bring herself to throw out. The woman who helped clean was one Lully trusted to keep her own counsel and who would not feed gossip or superstition mills about the Mansi mansion.

Those receiving bequests were both surprised and pleased, a bit bewildered. When the smaller bequests were finished, those already named were allowed to leave the room.

Finally, only Emma and Sam were left.

Sam Gold, now the sheriff of Grandee County. Her almost-husband of fifteen years ago. He shifted in his chair and shot her an uneasy glance.

Clearing his throat again, Merle Montgomery peered over his glasses at the couple sitting on opposite ends of a row of chairs near the back. Emma twisted a white tissue in her hands, wanting desperately for this to be over.

"Emma, rest assured that Lully left enough money in her account at the bank to cover these bequests."

Emma nodded numbly.

"'Now, to my beloved sister, Emma. Don't grieve for me. Today I am with God. I leave the remainder of my worldly possessions to Emma with one provision.'"

Emma swallowed against the tight knot crowding the back of

her throat. She'd cried so much the past twenty-four hours she hadn't thought there were any tears left. Every time she vowed not to cry, she did, and she was on the verge of breaking down again.

One provision. Emma slid to the edge of her chair in apprehension. Merle had said there was one provision. Her pulse pounded in her temple. What provision had Lully made?

Merle dropped the hammer. "'I leave my house to Emma and Sam Gold.'"

Emma's jaw dropped. What?

Merle continued reading: "'I know this may seem like an odd request. I hope to outlive you both, Sam and Emma. Ha! But if I don't, I leave the house to you both to do with as you see fit. I hope you'll decide to keep it. It was once a happy house, contrary to common opinion. Our grandparents were happy there; our parents were once. Nothing would make me happier than for you two, together, to make it a house filled with love and laughter again.'"

Stunned, Emma sat holding her breath, the words sinking slowly into her mind. Lully had left the house to Sam? and to her? Her home was half his? What on earth had possessed Lully?

Resentment flooded Emma and her gaze darted to Sam, who looked like he'd just been hit by a speeding concrete truck. Had he known? Wouldn't he have known? For some reason, Lully had changed her opinion of Sam. He'd had more contact with her than Emma had had. Had he coerced Lully into this provision?

Emma ached to demand of Merle what had prompted Lully to do such a thing, but Sam beat her to it.

"Merle—"

The attorney held up one hand. "I know what you're going to say, Sam. Lully anticipated it. We discussed the stipulation at length that day she came to finalize her will. Spent over an hour on the ramifications of such a gift. But she was adamant. She wanted you and Emma to have the house. Said she'd understand if you wanted to sell it, but that you'd make her happiest if you kept it."

Keep it? Emma wanted to scream. Keep it? Together? Had Lully lost her mind? How could she keep a house that half belonged to Sam? What had Lully been thinking? Wasn't it enough that Sam had abandoned her like a hot coal when his mother and Lully had joined forces to stop their marriage, as if the love he'd so grandly professed to her hours earlier had blown away with the spring wind? Everyone in town had known by noon the following day what that younger "crazy Mansi girl" had done. She'd tried—"Can you even imagine that!" the gossips crowed—to trick the mayor's son into marriage. Poor Sam—why, he was thriving on testosterone and didn't know what he was doing. Thank goodness her "crazy sister" had shown good sense for once and stopped the two from getting married.

In other words, Sam was the golden boy and Emma the laugh of the town. She'd been hurt and humiliated, and Sam hadn't even cared. He'd avoided her from that day on, acted as if she didn't exist. And that had stung worse than the ridicule of schoolmates and judgmental parents.

Sam sent Emma a glance over his shoulder.

"One more thing," Merle said, peering over his glasses at Emma. "Lully said, 'Tell Emma she'll find her true legacy if she looks hard enough.'"

Emma tried to absorb her sister's final wishes and failed. What on earth had her sister done?

"Well." Merle closed the folder. "If there's nothing else, that does it. I have a copy of the will for each of you. See me later if there are any questions."

Emma sat, unable to move, and stared at the row of bookcases. Her eyes focused on a thick textbook of amendments. She heard the protesting squeak of Merle's chair when he stood.

"I have a few questions," she managed.

She looked up to see Sam, Stetson in hand, standing beside his chair. Now she could see the changes in him, the smile lines bracketing his mouth, the faint lines fanning from the corners of his eyes from squinting into the sun. Character. His face now had character.

"Yes?" Merle smiled pleasantly.

"Can the will be broken?"

The attorney shuffled papers, stalling for time.

"Emma," Sam began.

Emma raised her hand to halt whatever he was going to say. She focused on Merle. "Can it?"

"I wouldn't advise attempting it, Emma," Merle said. "It would be a long, drawn-out process, and you'd probably lose. Lully might have been . . . different . . . but she knew what she wanted. I'd have to say that in court." His gaze shifted from Sam to Emma. "I'd advise the two of you to decide together what to do with the house and try to be civil about it."

This wasn't what Emma wanted to hear.

"Emma," Sam began again.

She fired a warning look at him. "I don't want to talk to you. Not now."

He hesitated. "All right. There's no hurry. We can talk later."

With that, he settled the Stetson firmly on his head and strode from the room, leaving Emma glued to her chair, still fuming.

Oh, Lully. What have you done?

"So? How'd it go? Did you see Emma?" Ken glanced up when Sam slammed into the sheriff's office.

"Yeah," he said, tossing his hat onto the rack with an accuracy honed by years of practice. He marched into his office and over to his desk. He grabbed a file and opened it, hoping his brother would drop the subject.

"She still a skinny redhead?" Ken called from his own desk.

"Still redheaded," Sam murmured. "Still stubborn as a brick wall."

Ken laughed. "Then not much has changed."

Not much has changed. A lot had changed. Emma Mansi had grown up, had changed from a girl with stars in her eyes, eyes that had shone for him, to a beautiful woman full of bitterness, who wanted nothing to do with him.

"So, what did Merle want with you this morning?"

"He read Lully Mansi's will."

Ken's eyebrows lifted. "She had a will?"

"Um-hum," Sam stared at a report without seeing it.

"And?" Ken prompted.

Sam drew a deep breath, knowing his brother was not going to take the hint and leave him alone with his thoughts. "She left Emma half the house."

Ken got up and leaned against the door frame of Sam's office. "Half? How can you leave somebody half a house?"

"Apparently when you leave someone else the other half."

"And who has the other half of Lully's house?"

Sam finally looked up. "Me."

Ken pursed his lips. "Well now, that's an interesting turn of events. Doesn't the mayor want that property for a municipal parking lot? He's tried every way in the world to buy Lully out. He's going to be ecstatic that the house will be up for sale."

Oh, yeah. It's going to be interesting, Sam thought. "I'll probably have to work with Emma to get the property in shape if we hope to get anything out of it, because I don't intend to let Tom Crane take advantage of the situation and Lully's untimely death. Emma can't stand the sight of me, so how are we going to work together?"

Ken chuckled. "You don't know that."

Sam raised a brow. "Oh, but I do. If looks could kill, I'd be a dead man right now."

"Are you okay with that?"

Closing the file, Sam sank into his chair. "Dandy." He threw the file on his desk. "Just dandy."

Dusk settled over the Colorado Rockies. No matter how stirred up Emma felt, she could look to the mountains and peace would creep into the dark corners. No matter how many times she witnessed the glorious orange-and-gold spectacle, she knew there was no greater joy than seeing the bright hue of exquisite colors slowly dip and disappear behind serrated peaks.

In October, Colorado weather could be tricky. You either dealt with an early snow or with lingering warmth that made you think winter was going to pass by. Her first evening in the house, the Mansi Mansion, as people now civilly called it, had been cold. This second night promised no better. Already snow was deepening on the mountains. It wouldn't be long before it came to the foothills. But she'd be gone long before snow came to Serenity.

Emma sat on the porch, wrapped in an old jacket she'd found in a closet. She'd escaped Merle Montgomery's office before she'd totally dissolved into a fit of hysteria and resentment or tears. Both warred inside her. She'd come directly to the house, knowing no one would come here to bother her. People had actively avoided the house since she arrived. And that's what she wanted right now: to be left alone. Alone to think through what she was going to do next.

But a stupid casserole or a home-baked offering from a neighbor would have been politically correct.

Memories assailed her in spite of her unwillingness to go back in time. She'd left Serenity fifteen years ago. Left it and all it meant behind. On her seventeenth birthday she'd gotten on a bus and rode away. After changing busses several times, she'd ended up in Seattle, hoping Lully wouldn't follow and bring her back. She'd stayed at a women's shelter until she got a job at a local café. With help from the director of the shelter, she'd gotten her GED, then enrolled in college. Only after her eighteenth birthday had Emma written Lully, telling her she was fine and not to worry. But she wasn't coming back. Not ever.

To supplement her income while she went to school, Emma had begun to teach aerobics at a spa, working classes around her college hours. It had taken five years but she'd gotten her degree in horticulture. She loved growing things, the beauty of flowers, and the beauty she could create in the landscaping for a large office complex or in a private yard for people to enjoy. When she'd started working for The Cottage, Sue told Emma that she had "the touch." She smiled to herself now. Better to have "the touch" than be touched, which is what the townspeople of Serenity thought about the Mansi girls.

Emma knew the rambling old Victorian wasn't haunted. That was pure fantasy, the fabrication of people with a need to put a tag on everyone and everything that wasn't like them. The Mansi Mansion wasn't like other homes in Serenity.

For one, it sat next to a one-hundred-twenty-five-year-old cemetery. Supposedly the cemetery held the remains of slaves buried during the eighteen hundreds, most graves unidentified, and a few Civil War soldiers who had no family plots but were sent home to be buried. According to local legend, these men and women roamed the three-story house at night, rattling chains and banging doors. Emma had rarely heard a door close without a reason, unless you counted the drafts from frequent windstorms that sprang up in the spring, and certainly she had never heard chains rattling.

Lully had once thought she heard someone walking around in the attic. Huddled together, they had explored, flashlight in hand, eyes surely as round as saucers. It turned out to be rats. Lully had located two traps the next morning and baited them with cheese. Within twenty-four hours the "ghosts" had disappeared.

Until about a year ago.

Lully had insisted on sending an occasional letter to Emma, though Emma had written back only once or twice. They never talked by phone, though Emma had never had her phone number unlisted. She supposed something inside her knew that in case of an emergency someone in Serenity might need to reach her. Maybe.

In her letters, Lully told about starting a business with the jewelry she'd always designed. She'd also mentioned hearing strange sounds coming from the basement, but had passed it off by saying she guessed the dead folks were "acting up again." The private joke always brought a smile to Emma's face.

Guilt and sadness welled inside her. She was going to miss those letters. Though she'd stubbornly refused to reveal to Lully anything about her new life, telling herself she'd put her past and God in a box she'd never need to open again, Emma had always known Lully was there. God she wasn't so sure about. Now Lully was gone. And the knowledge hurt. Worse than she'd ever imagined.

Sighing, Emma watched the sun sink lower. "Are you up there Lully? Because if you are, I'm going to break your rotten neck for what you've done."

Tears pricked her eyes and she closed them. Then the sound of a car in the drive made her open them again. Someone was coming. Her mood lightened. Maybe a neighbor with that casserole? Someone, anyone who was compassionate enough to care . . .

Getting up to stand at the edge of the porch, Emma wrapped the jacket tighter, trying to make out who the visitor might be. Probably Merle coming to see if she needed anything. She didn't. She'd stopped at the market on the way back to the house, accepting condolences almost absently as she'd gone up and down the aisles gathering her few purchases. She'd bought enough to last a few days, if she stayed that long.

She looked out at the black-and-white car parked next to the house; the sheriff's insignia was clear on the side. Emma frowned, trying to ignore the way her heart rushed into her throat. After all these years you'd think—

Sam got out of the cruiser, adjusting his hat in what Emma knew was a habit, before starting toward the house. She couldn't help but take stock of the changes in him. As a teen he'd been painfully thin with a thatch of curly hair. The unruly locks were now tamed into a fashionable cut. A sullen mouth was now firm with determination. Slim, hunched shoulders had broadened into muscled bulk, and he had stretched to an impressive six-plus feet. Maturity looked good on Sam Gold. Really good.

Lully had once written that when Sam had returned to Serenity there wasn't a woman within fifty miles who wouldn't surrender her MasterCard to put her brand on him. His brother, Ken, she'd written, ran a close second.

It wasn't hard to see why. Sam Gold was one ruggedly handsome man. Emma would have surrendered everything at the tender age of fifteen to marry the boy who'd only had promise.

This was the fulfillment of that promise.

She refused to go there. His betrayal had cut too deeply. And that was a wound that would never heal—one she fiercely protected. She had realized not many years later that every man she'd ever been attracted to had been compared in some way to Sam, and she'd always found some reason to break off the relationship. She wouldn't be hurt like that again.

Sam's tall frame was a silhouette against the sunset as he approached the porch. He stopped at the bottom step. "Emma."

"Sam."

Her chin lifted a notch. Battle stance, she realized. The last time they'd spoken in private had been in the hallway in high school when he'd told her in no uncertain terms to get lost. Well, not in so many words, but the meaning had been clear. "Forget about me, Emma. Our families are going to fight this from now on."

It had taken her two years to save up enough money to do just that. She'd gotten lost, and put Sam and Serenity behind her. But here he stood, looking up at her.

So cotton-picking handsome.

The intensity in his gaze unnerved her. Sympathetic, but unwavering, unyielding.

"I'm sorry about Lully."

Emma swallowed against the thickening in her throat. "You didn't even know her."

"Yes, I did."

A thousand thoughts raced through her mind. Swallowing back tears, she focused on the sunset. "What happened to her?"

"We don't know yet."

Could her sister's death have been the result of foul play? The idea was ludicrous, yet hadn't her own relationship with Lully been strained? Was it possible that someone had carried a prank too far? The townspeople had held little tolerance for Lully's eccentricities. Instead of offering help, they'd judged her. Emma couldn't understand the degree of Lully's isolation. But that some-one in Serenity would purposely do something to harm Lully—that was beyond imagination.

Sam broke the silence, his gaze moving over the old house. "We're working on it. The autopsy results will be ready in a few days."

"Do you suspect foul play?"

There was no evidence that Emma had heard of. Lully had been sitting in the swing as if she'd gone to sleep. Nothing had seemed amiss. The paperboy, delivering his early route, had found her.

While Lully had lived a reclusive lifestyle, she was a woman of routine. From Lully's letters, Emma knew that her sister rose early in the morning to work in her flower garden with Gismo, her little dog, beside her. The dog itself had caused some specula-tion. Gismo was not a pretty dog. His one crossed eye and fur that went every which way gave him a face only a mother, or Lully, could love. Gismo would trot out among the headstones in the cemetery, pausing occasionally to "do business." Lully had said some folks didn't care much for the idea of Uncle Henry or Grandma Nelson getting a good watering every now and again by the golden-eyed sprinkler, but no one did much other than complain loudly enough for Lully to hear from the porch or her garden.

"I don't think the coroner will find anything. It looks like natu-ral causes."

Emma went back to the swing. "That's impossible. She was thirty-five. No one dies of natural causes at thirty-five."

A person could die at thirty-five in a car accident or plane crash. Not just sitting in a porch swing. Lully wasn't the sort to indulge in drugs or hard liquor. Or was she? Emma realized she didn't know. She didn't know her sister, not really, not anymore.

"I can't imagine . . . Lully has always been there. She raised me when the family fell apart."

"I know."

Lully had been her mainstay after their father left. Three years after Ralph left, Emma and bad boy Sam Gold had run off to get married and had been stopped. And now, it seemed, they were drawn together by the same woman who had helped tear them apart.

"I know this is difficult for you, Emma. As soon as the reports come back we'll know more. Meanwhile," Sam looked away, "you'll need to identify the body." His gaze softened when he looked back. "It's a formality. I know the will's been read, but . . ."

"Yes, well . . ." She stood, brushing lint from the front of her skirt. She simply would not let the sound of his voice affect her. He could still be the most handsome man she'd ever known, he could still make her heart beat faster just by looking at her, but things were different now. "Now?"

"If you feel up to it."

Did anyone ever feel up to identifying a deceased family member? "Okay."

"You're sure."

"I want to get it over with." She glanced at his cruiser. "Shall I follow you?"

"I'll take you."

"I have a car."

He took a deep breath. "I wrote you, Emma."

"I never got it, Sam."

His gaze locked with hers. "That doesn't mean I didn't write it."

Well, fine. He wrote a letter. Where was it? In the same place his loyalty was fifteen years ago?

As she brushed past him, a faint hint of aftershave and Irish Spring soap reached her. Masculine. So Sam-like. She shoved the barriers firmly in place and locked them. With fifteen years of practice it should have been easy, but it wasn't.

At least it sure wasn't tonight.

chapter

THREE

DARKNESS had settled over the mountains when Emma emerged from the morgue, her knees still shaky. The facility was small—one room in the courthouse basement. When the stainless-steel drawer had been opened, Emma had glanced briefly at Lully's strangely peaceful face and then looked away.

"Are you all right?" Sam steadied her elbow.

"She looks older."

"Don't we all."

He matched strides with her, his long legs outdistancing her more often than not. She didn't want him touching her yet felt powerless to ask him to stop. She'd thought she was well beyond Sam's having any power to affect her, but she was wrong. As they strode toward their parked vehicles she was acutely aware of the man she'd fallen in love with so long ago. The words she'd defiantly erased from her mind rushed back in such clarity:

I, Emma, take thee, Sam to love, honor, and cherish 'til death do us part.

I, Sam, take thee, Emma.. . .

They'd practiced their vows while they'd driven toward Santa Fe, so certain they would be married before sunrise . . .

Sam glanced at her sideways. "If I know you, you haven't eaten all day."

You don't know me! Emma wanted to shout. He didn't know her at all. If he had, he'd know that she wanted this to be over, wanted to be on her way back to Seattle. To sanity. To a life she'd made on her own, a good life, a satisfying life.

"I'm not hungry."

She rummaged in her purse for car keys. Where were they? Why was it keys always fell to the bottom of the purse? Checkbook, credit cards, empty gum wrappers. Those she could find. But keys? She dug deeper.

Sam plucked the bag out of her hands and extracted the keys, the ring balanced on the tip of his finger. "Brisco's still makes the best hamburger in town."

The lump in her throat grew until she thought she would choke. *I will not cry. I will not cry.* "No, thanks." She took the keys and turned toward her rental car.

"Emma."

The softness of his voice compelled her to turn. He was leaning against the cruiser, arms crossed, a patient look on his face. Had he married? Were there a wife and child—children, nearly grown children—waiting for him at home? It could have been Emma waiting. It *would* have been her if Lully and Mrs. Gold hadn't—

"You're underage, Emma. This is ridiculous. No justice of the peace would believe this doctored birth certificate," Lully had said.

Emma had tried to pull out of her sister's grasp. "No! Sam and I love each other."

Lully's mouth had firmed, and she yanked Emma out of the tiny motel room Sam had rented, shoving past Emma's soon-to-be husband and his glowering mother.

"You can't do this!" Sam had shouted. "I can take care of her—"

He had tried to block their way, but between Lully's determination and Mrs. Gold's angry insistence that he leave that moment, his attempt failed.

Lully had paused on the sidewalk, scorn marking her face as her gaze swept Sam's lanky frame, his youthful chin with a razor nick.

Her red hair stood nearly on end, dark eyes burning with anger, darting from Emma to Sam. Right at that moment she looked every bit the witch some said she was. "You're seventeen years old, Sam Gold," she'd hissed. "You barely know how to wipe your own nose, let alone Emma's. I'll see you dead before I let you near my sister—"

Sam's chin had firmed and he grasped at Emma. "How old are you, Lully?"

Wrestling Emma away from his grasp, Lully refused to confirm what they all were thinking. Only a year separated Sam and Lully.

"Sam!" Emma had screamed as Lully dragged her toward the beat-up pickup they'd used since Ralph had disappeared. Lully roughly thrust Emma inside and slammed the door. Turning again, she'd pointed an accusing finger at Sam. "You stay away from her! You hear? Stay away!"

Biting her upper lip, Emma paused with her key still in her hand looked up at Sam. He had stayed away. In fact, he'd hardly looked at her that following Monday and had carefully avoided her from then on. She'd cried, she'd prayed, and then she'd realized she had been every kind of fool. Sam's "love" no longer existed and what she felt didn't matter.

"What?" Emma queried.

"I'm sorry about Lully," Sam repeated. She snapped out of her daze. "I wanted to call you myself, but I thought the news should come from someone else."

Nodding, she took a deep breath. "I'm tired, Sam. I'm going . . . home."

"You're going to stay out there? at the house?"

She turned finally. "Where else would I stay?"

"There's a room vacant at the bed-and-breakfast in town. I could call Lois Jackson and—"

"That won't be necessary."

"Right. You'd die before you'd let me help you."

"You're right. I would."

Emma couldn't bear talking to one more person today. Besides, the old house was hers. Partly. The stories about ghosts and goblins haunting the halls didn't bother her, nor did the cemetery. None of the tales were true. It was simply an old house—an old house in need of repair. A house she now co-owned with Sam Gold. She closed her eyes, sucking in breath.

"Do you mind if I stay at the house?" Emma's tone held a hint more animosity than question.

"Stay wherever you like." He straightened, adjusting the brim of his hat so it hid his eyes. "There is one thing, though."

"Sam, I'm tired. It's been a long day, and tomorrow I have to make arrangements for . . . for Lully . . ."

Sam opened the back door of the cruiser and took out a carrier. He set the transporter on the hood of her car.

"What's that?"

A snuffling and soft *woof* came from inside. She peered in through the holes of the cage to see a pair of strange-colored gold eyes, one crossed, staring back at her.

"Gismo," Sam announced.

Touching one finger to the brim of his hat in polite salute, he strode around the cruiser and got in, leaving Emma staring at the cage with Lully's cherished pet barking to be released from his prison.

"Gismo," Emma breathed. What else could go wrong today?

Sam went to Brisco's for a hamburger, if for no other reason than because he didn't want to go home to the small house he owned at the edge of Serenity or to the sheriff's office.

He didn't want to answer any questions that Ken might have, because he didn't want to think about why Emma's coming back to Serenity bothered him. It shouldn't, not after fifteen years, but he knew it did and he knew why. There was no question in his mind: though he'd tried, he'd never gotten over Emma Mansi. He remembered that spirit and those sparkling brown eyes so well. What was the old saying? There's no fool like an old fool?

His hamburger tasted like sawdust, and he finally gave up and left half of it on the plate. He went home and, not for the first time, wondered what it would have been like to have married Emma, to be coming home to her vibrancy and warmth instead of to a cold empty house. To have a couple of kids with Emma's eyes.

"Get over it," he muttered, stripping off his uniform. "Past history now and there's no way she's going to revive it."

And neither was he. *Let sleeping dogs lie*, he thought, and realized the corny clichés sounded just like his mother.

Emma wandered through the old house, touching familiar objects. The house was drafty and a chilly, musty smell penetrated her nostrils. *Memories are a strange phenomenon*, she mused. Often the sweetest ones could instigate raw ones; painful ones could be the most gratifying. A chipped goldfish bowl won one warm July evening when the fair was in town. A fading picture, with a corner missing, of two young girls grinning into the camera, arms wrapped around each other's waist, wind-tossed hair held back with matching barrettes.

Lully almost never grinned, but that day, in the picture taken near Mommy's rose garden, she'd smiled. A rare thing caught forever in sepia tone. Maybe it had been Daddy saying, "Grin, Puddin' Stick." That's what he'd always called Lully. Puddin' Stick. Or sometimes, Popsicle Stick. Emma was Tootsie Pop. Mommy had been Angel Eyes before everything had changed.

Emma stood at Lully's dresser, the chaos around her, the mingled aromas of candles and incense surrounding her with reminiscences. Funny, Emma thought, staring at the picture, her thumb rubbing away the dust on Lully's face. She hadn't thought of those pet names in years. She'd put them with all the other memories in a tightly sealed box and pushed it into a dark corner of her mind. They weren't important, she'd told herself. She'd spent seventeen years in this house and fifteen on her own. In two years the balance would be even: half her life as a "crazy Mansi girl" and half as Emma Mansi.

Did shadows of abandonment follow from childhood to adulthood? Psychologists indicated a link, but Emma had worked hard to break it, to put the past behind her. She had rarely thought of cold Colorado nights, of the chaotic home life after her mother died, and then of the quiet desperate years when it had been just her and Lully.

Mom's dying, Dad's leaving. Sam's deserting her. Unfounded gossip and name-calling. She shook her head. No wonder she was a basket case.

A psychologist friend had explained that a *chaotic* childhood didn't necessarily mean "hectic" or "frenzied." It could simply mean "unstructured," which certainly described Emma's and Lully's lives. And feelings of abandonment were natural, considering Emma's past. But she'd thought she'd dealt with that, put it all behind her, until the phone call. Until those few words had again forged a link back to Serenity and what the town represented.

Emma picked up the small gold compact that was nestled among strings of beads on the dresser and examined the gift she'd sent Lully one Christmas when she felt guilty about not staying in touch. What had she been thinking? The gift wasn't Lully at all. What did one sister get another sister when they had nothing in common? when all connection between them had been severed? Were they family? Did birth certificates indicating they'd both been born to the same mother and father define a family? They should. Something should. Legal documents should have the power to make their holders loving, caring, compassionate, committed members of the same family. But it wasn't so.

A scent drifted to her that encouraged yet another recollection of their time together. Lully had had a closetful of powders and potions concocted from herbs. She had discovered aromatherapy the year before Emma left home. The house had reeked of scents that were sometimes not so pleasant, the rooms lit by smoldering pots and flickering wicks. Lully had been searching for something. Emma realized that now. Some deep, hidden meaning in life. For a while she'd gotten into meditating and tried to entice Emma to sit with eyes closed, hands folded, clearing her mind of all thought. Lully had once thought that if she could empty her mind of everything, then God could fill it. Emma couldn't do it, though she'd tried. She'd come home many an afternoon to find Lully standing on her head in a corner, eyes closed, thin body flattened against the wall, long red hair spilling onto the dark, oriental carpet that dominated the overheated living room.

Lully had started chanting; she'd found out that monks chanted, and she said it cleared her mind of clutter. Her reedlike voice floated in and through the dusty crystal chandelier, along the stained plaster ceiling, saturating the heavy crimson drapes and fading cabbage-rose wallpaper, straining to sift through the locked front windows to reach the outside world. Emma had wondered what was in that outside world that Lully avoided so ardently and why she sought God so desperately.

At some point Lully finally realized that God could not be found through her own devices. She threw away the books on meditation and chanting and spent her time in the Bible.

She didn't have friends. The few times she ventured to town had been only to go to the bank or to pick up extra groceries. After even the briefest venture into the outside world she'd scurry home as if chased by something or someone unseen. Chased by fears unnamed, by people who looked and leered behind their hands about the "crazy Mansi girl."

Emma sank onto the edge of Lully's unmade bed, holding the small compact in her hands, warming the cold metal. The Mansi girls were thought to be too strange to be invited to school dances and Friday evening football games, and they were too tired of dealing with the gossip to be brave enough to go on their own. While Lully feared going out, Emma had longed to be part of everything, to join in, to prove she wasn't weird. Until she was fifteen and Sam insisted she go with him. Sam, the lanky senior who'd pushed a tormentor against a locker one afternoon and ordered him to leave her alone.

"Let up on Emma," Sam had said. The words sang in her heart for two days afterward. The hecklers hadn't let up, of course, but when Sam was around they left Emma and Lully alone. The other girls had simply ignored them.

Then Sam started to be around more often. Sometimes standing outside the school beside the bicycle rack at three-thirty. Often, and quite coincidentally, Emma had marveled, he'd be somewhere in the immediate vicinity of her locker between classes. On rare occasions they would sit in the shade beneath a row of aspens near the football bleachers during lunch break and eat together.

Emma had cherished every moment with Sam. She didn't know why he was there, and she didn't want to examine the miracle too closely. He was a protector by nature, she told herself, and she was his beneficiary. He confessed much later that she was mistaken. She'd said she'd known he was there because he had nothing better to do and sharing a sandwich with one of the Mansi girls was a way to prove his machismo. He'd laughed. He wasn't afraid of Lully or of her very quiet sister, and his machismo was never in doubt.

Sam had invited her to a football game, then to a school dance. He'd told her to ignore everyone but him. And she had. Then he'd kissed her and she'd fallen totally and helplessly in love.

And then one snowy Saturday afternoon he had asked her to marry him. He convinced her to elope, because they were too young in the eyes of everyone but themselves. On that day she felt like a princess, a beautiful princess, with the world at her feet.

Gismo whined at her feet, breaking the spell of this bittersweet memory. Emma glanced down at the dog staring up at her, his crossed eye winking comically. The eye was the result of a birth injury, Lully had written the Christmas she'd gotten the pup. Gismo's mother had rejected him and made a deliberate attempt to kill it. The grocery boy had brought the injured pup to Lully on his delivery, saying no one else wanted him. Lully had taken the puppy, probably identifying with him in some way. The odd pair had bonded immediately. Until the will was read, Emma had thought the dog was the only friend Lully had.

Reaching down to rub his ears affectionately, Emma smiled. "We knew the real Lully, didn't we, Gismo? A tad odd. Much confused. But we loved her anyway." *Oh yes, we loved her,* Emma repeated to herself. Love mixed with guilt and regret.

Gismo missed Lully. That was clear. He searched for her in every room of the house, then trotted back to Emma to look up with a sad question in those strange gold eyes. Where's Lully? Where's my friend?

Wasn't that what life was about? Loving someone so much that when she was gone she left a void, a big hole, in your heart? That's how it had been with Mom. When she died the world stopped for a time, at least for the Mansi family.

Emma remembered how Lully would read the Bible aloud about how God was the comforter in times of sorrow. Emma would climb into bed and pull the sheet over her head and cry, trying to pray like Lully told her to. She'd asked God to take away the awful, terrible ache inside her, the pain that seemed to be eating her alive. The house was cold and empty, so silent when she and Lully came home from school. No good smells came from the kitchen. No chocolate cake with chocolate icing sitting on the glass cake stand on the counter. No chocolate chip cookies fresh from the oven. Only a musty-smelling house with the fire in the woodstove gone cold, unmade beds and macaroni and cheese still clumped on dishes piled in the sink waiting to be washed.

Sometimes she thought prayer helped; sometimes a little peace had come over Emma that allowed her to sleep, get her through the next day. But the emptiness always came back—swift, penetrating, blinding in intensity. God wasn't helping. He'd abandoned her as everyone else had.

Emma shoved the hurtful memories aside. Her stomach reminded her that she hadn't eaten all day. She didn't think she was hungry, hadn't been when Sam invited her for a hamburger.

She wouldn't have gone with him anyway. Gismo's nails clicked on the floor behind her when she went to the kitchen to see what she could find there to eat. She looked the other way when she passed Lully's rather sizable work area. Pieces of unfinished jewelry were scattered about the long worktable—lovely jewelry. Familiar-looking jewelry, as if she'd seen it somewhere else. But she couldn't place where.

The house was even colder than the night before. She chafed her arms with her hands to ward off the chill. The house had always been one of two things—miserably cold or insufferably stuffy. Lully didn't open windows. That might have been because after so many years they were warped, unable to be opened. Or it might have had something to do with Lully's desire to avoid anything to do with the outside world once she'd graduated high school. Emma wondered briefly if Lully had ever had any real desire to go somewhere else, do something else, be someone else. Had all the ambition been hers? Or had Lully simply been too afraid to leave the Mansi house? If so, what about that outside world was so frightening to her? Sure, there was the talk, the unkindness. Emma had hated it too. But Emma had been able to push herself out into the world and make a life for herself. Why hadn't Lully?

The house sat on a small rise so it got a nice cross breeze when the front and back doors were open, but even in summer Lully had been reluctant to open windows. Emma had managed to open her bedroom sash a couple of inches for better sleeping in July and August. Fortunately, Serenity had rare days of hot temperatures and they had survived. Lully complained of being cold all the time, though Emma couldn't imagine why. She would lie in bed at night, covers thrown aside, the sound of wind in the pines underlaid by Lully's chanting.

When Emma had rented an apartment in Seattle, she'd chosen one that, though small, had wide windows—windows that she kept open an inch even in winter. Rain didn't bother her. She loved to hear the patter of drops on the roof as she fell asleep at night. And ordinarily there wasn't enough snow to worry about. One of her first purchases had been an electric mattress pad. When her room grew cold, she'd simply nudge it up a notch higher and snuggle deeper into the covers while breathing deeply of the clear, crisp air coming in the window, and she'd thank God she wasn't in Colorado.

Emma opened the refrigerator and stared at the contents. A half-eaten carton of low-fat cottage cheese, a can of refrigerator crescent rolls—last year's expiration date. A container of refried beans with a layer of mold on top. A carton of soured milk behind the fresh one she'd bought earlier. A carton of I Can't Believe It's Not Butter—and Emma couldn't believe it either—in a squeeze bottle. A bottle of catsup, one of mustard, half a jar of mayonnaise, and a jar of red pimentos that had never been opened. Emma couldn't imagine what had possessed Lully to buy red pimentos. Pitching the old staples in the trash, she reconsidered the options.

Nothing appealing here. Emma closed the refrigerator and wished she had bought more groceries earlier. But she hadn't been hungry then. She surveyed the kitchen as if something should beckon to her. It was huge, reaching across the entire back of the house. Ugly, since it hadn't been updated since being built. Unsightly, dark-stained pine cabinets met a faded and worn, green block linoleum. A Kelvinator stove—top of the line when it was new—was the same one her grandmother had used. Beside it a sprung mousetrap had flipped on its back. There were no furry feet peeking out, so Emma breathed a sigh of relief. In the middle of the room was an old wooden table with six chairs that evidenced the wear of fifty years of use.

Six chairs. The Mansi family had never had two extra guests at one time in their entire lives. A minister had visited once shortly after Mom died. He didn't stay long, obviously uncomfortable with the situation. He left several pamphlets on salvation and grief after inquiring if it was all right to pray with the family. When Dad didn't say it wasn't, Emma wagged her head and he prayed briefly and left. She'd picked up the pamphlets entitled *How to Deal with Loss* and *Turning to God in Times of Trouble*. Emma read them under the covers that night with a flashlight, hoping there would be something there to help ease her pain. Dad had ignored the whole event. He sat in his chair and stared at the wall, drinking a beer.

The refrigerator was the only new thing in the room. The side-by-side had an ice maker and buttons that offered either crushed or cubed ice and cold filtered water. Emma hadn't known Lully had made the purchase but figured the old one had finally given out.

She turned to the pantry that was to the left of the cabinet. The shelves had once held all kinds of goods canned from the garden's fresh produce. Now there were fewer than a dozen jars lining the shelf. She picked up a can of tomato soup she'd bought and a box of crackers with one tube of crackers unopened. Probably stale, she thought, but better than nothing. She'd forgotten to buy crackers—and Sam had forgotten to give her Gismo's food. Wasn't that just great? A crunch under her foot caused her to look down. A crushed roach.

Yikes.

She turned when she heard a knock at the back door.

Still thinking about Sam's thoughtlessness—here she was, all alone, and now she had to make a trip to the grocery store—she opened the door.

Sam handed her a sack of dog food and turned around and left without saying a word.

She shut the door. *Great. Just great.*

She found a hand can opener in a drawer and dumped the soup into a pan with milk to heat, after she'd washed and wiped the pan first. After dumping dog food in a bowl, she sat down to eat. After dinner, Emma decided she might as well go to bed. The sheets she'd found in the linen closet smelled faintly of lavender. She'd also found a stack of threadbare blankets and had taken them all.

Her room was as cold as a meat locker, but at least the musty smell was almost gone. Wind whistled outside, coming in around the warped window. The sheets were icy when she got into bed, and she held her breath a few moments before she could move. She absolutely hated cold sheets and longed for her electrically warmed bed back in Seattle.

Sleep evaded her. Finally she got out of bed and yanked the heavy drapes open. Weak moonlight sifted in through the dirty pane. Directly in view was the tombstone of Ezra Mott. The moon slid behind a cloud, momentarily throwing the stone into shadowy light. Emma shivered, wrapping her arms tightly around her middle as she sat huddled in front of the window. In the darkness, the familiar cemetery turned sinister, the darkening of the moon a premonition of things to come.

Emma shook herself, tossing off the idea of premonitions. She'd forgotten how she could see Ezra Mott's headstone from her window. She could almost touch the cold granite.

Her grandmother, Celia Williams, had planted flowers in porch boxes and in patches in the large yard. Grandpa Frank, a carpenter, had spruced up the inside when they'd moved in. Still, once a funeral home always a funeral home.

When Emma's parents had moved into the house, all traces of the funeral home had been removed, but the superstitions and tales had remained in the minds of the townspeople. The kids liked to think the house was haunted, and the Mansi girls bore the brunt of the stupidity. Lully's unruly red hair, pale skin, and slanted green cat eyes had made her the butt of jokes. A redheaded Morticia—like in the television show *The Addams Family*.

The moon came out again, and Emma could read the inscription on Ezra's tombstone, though she could almost recite it by memory.

Ezra Mott
Born March 8, 1839
Died March 23, 1864
Beloved son of Mattie and Mason Mott, devoted husband, loving father. Asleep in Christ.

When she was little Emma had wondered how long someone could sleep? Once she'd figured up how long it had been since 1864. Ezra had been asleep for . . . well, a very long time. Over a hundred and twelve years! Maybe time was different in heaven, she'd told herself, or maybe people were just more tired. She'd never decided.

She used to listen on warm summer evenings, when children gathered beneath overhanging limbs of the cedars beyond the cemetery's rusting iron gate to swap stories. They told of how Ezra prowled the graveyard on dark nights looking for young children to snatch away. Now, no one had actually seen this mysterious, brave soldier who reportedly perished in a fight with a "dirty, rotten Union polecat." For all they knew Ezra could have been a deserter—but then Emma preferred to think he was a hero.

Many a night she would sit at her bedroom window staring at the tombstone, imagining a handsome, powerful young Mott sitting astride a sturdy mount, bayonet drawn, charging the enemy while loving parents, devoted wife, and adoring children cowered in fear and dismay.

A sad smile touched Emma's mouth when she remembered that even then her image of the dashing young cavalryman had taken on Sam Gold's features. The skinny kid, the oldest son of the town's mayor, always told the scariest stories about Mott and his fellow soldiers. Once, when Emma had felt her skin chill at one of his exaggerated stories, she'd jumped up and shouted out what she could remember of a Bible verse that Lully had read aloud the night before: "Fear is not of God. Fear comes from the devil."

Instead of comforting, the mention of the devil had made the children's eyes grow larger.

"Go home," Sam had told Emma before he turned his back on her and continued his tale.

That brash young man who had irritated his mother, the mayor, by causing all kinds of mischief in his early teen years was a far cry from the man she'd encountered today. Experience had matured him, and the chin that had held the barest hint of a cleft was now well defined, strong, and determined.

Emma's cheeks warmed. As a preteen she'd spent hours fantasizing about Sam Gold. And when he'd become her protector years later, she'd held hope that he'd always had feelings and fantasies about her. In those moments before sleep came, did he think of her? When the world wasn't looking and the town wasn't talking about the "nutty Mansi girl" and his parents didn't know of his feelings, did he think of her?

No, she reminded herself. He hadn't. His feelings for her had been, at best, infatuation. Lully had told Emma she was a foolish romantic and she needed to grow up. Emma had thought that funny since Lully lived in the fantasy that their father was going to come home any day. Still, it was clear that her love for Sam had been a foolish dream on her part. He rode no charging steed, swung no sharp bayonet in her defense. There had been no passion there. Only his quiet submission that had cut her more deeply than a bayonet ever could. He'd simply done as his mother had wished and walked away from Emma.

Now he said he'd written a letter. Should she believe him? If there were such a letter, would it have made a difference? Yes, it would have—a big difference, if he had explained his actions. Maybe he just affirmed that it was over; that would have been worse.

But what if there had been a letter and he'd told her he loved her and somehow they would find a way to be together? The possibility tore at her heart.

Had he thought of her since? Doubts flooded back. But she'd thought of him, especially in those first days. She'd prayed for a sense of peace, knowledge that all would be made right, with the same desperation she'd prayed after Mom had died. She'd sat on the front porch for hours, her gaze fixed on the rutted lane, ignoring Lully's shouts to come inside, hoping for the sound of his pickup. Any kind of sign that Sam was coming for her, his true love—rushing to proclaim his undying devotion, eager to assert his fidelity, for how else would a true hero have handled such a travesty? Someone like Ezra Mott would never have allowed such an outrageous act.

But had Sam come? No. Had he longed for her? No. Men like Sam Gold didn't long for much. Emma knew that from experience, with Sam and since. But still, had he thought of her? In those moments when he least expected it, did her image pop into his mind? Had he thought of the shy girl who had been nearly shaking with fear when she'd slipped out of the house and climbed into his pickup for their flight to a justice of the peace that cold spring night?

Unfortunately the justice of the peace had been out of town. A service station attendant had told them that when Sam asked for directions to his house. The same service station attendant who informed Lully and Sam's mother where he told the young couple they could find a room for the night.

Oh, it had seemed so romantic, Sam holding her hand while driving to the motel.

"It will be all right," he'd said. "We'll just sleep. I'll sleep in a chair. Tomorrow we'll leave and by noon we'll be married."

But by noon Emma was back home crying in her room, and Sam was nowhere to be found. She guessed the ole devil had a good laugh at their expense that night. And it seemed he had been laughing at her ever since, because she'd never found anyone she'd felt the same about again.

Emma crawled back between the cold sheets and closed her eyes tightly.

"You might not have thought of me in fifteen years, Sam Gold," she whispered. She wiggled her toes, inching them lower beneath the blankets. "But I'll bet you're thinking of me tonight."

chapter
FOUR

EMMA stared at the woodstove, a cup of coffee in hand, debating whether to attempt to start a fire. She had forgotten the dying art, and it seemed an intimidating task, but the house was too cold to ignore the stove any longer. Contemplating the iron monster, she bit her upper lip, trying to remember how to begin. Building the fire had been Lully's responsibility, so Emma hadn't bothered to pay attention to the mechanics of it, and she was fairly certain there were some.

She jumped when the phone rang. A glance at her watch told her it was not quite 7:00 A.M. She picked up the phone.

"Make it through the night without clanking chains and images in the hallway?"

She might have known Sam would call. It had nothing to do with her personally; it was his job now. Still, the sound of his voice made her want to soften hers and ask . . . what? *How are you? What are you doing? Where have you been for the last fifteen years?*

"What time do you go to work?" Emma yawned.

"Before you get up."

"Well, smell you." Early morning was not her thing. Her brain didn't function until nine o'clock.

She sensed a grin in his voice before his tone sobered. "Are you going to the funeral home this morning?" he asked.

"Yes." What a rotten way to start a day.

"Need some moral support—"

"No," she interrupted. "Not from you."

"I was offering Ken."

"Oh."

There was an obvious hesitation on the other end of the line. She knew she was being unfair, but the bitterness she thought she'd long misplaced came back to haunt her.

"Well, it's here if you change your mind." He hung up.

She hung up. *You weren't there for me fifteen years ago, so why would I need you now?*

Neither was Ken.

Leaving the fire for later, she went upstairs and turned on the small gas heater in the bathroom. By nine-thirty she was bathed and dressed and standing in Mr. Willow's strange-smelling office in the funeral home. What was that odor? Flowers? Death? Sorrow?

"I'm so sorry for your loss," Mr. Willow said, indicating that she take the chair opposite the desk.

"Thank you."

He sat across from her, his demeanor clearly offering comfort. She didn't need sympathy. She needed to get this done quickly.

"Have you thought what you'd like in the way of a casket? We have some lovely—"

"That won't be necessary." She drew a deep breath and nearly choked on the scent of lilies. "Lully wanted to be cremated. I plan to have a small, graveside service." Was that her own voice that sounded so strident and cold?

There was no point in having a funeral. Few people would come. Sam probably, out of some misplaced sense of duty, and maybe Myline, for the same reason. "We all return to dust anyway," Lully had said once. "It's the Lord's plan."

"Of course," Mr. Willow said. "There are forms and the choice of a resting place."

Emma was drained by the time the paperwork was completed.

Mr. Willow said that he would call when Emma could claim the remains. Emma wasn't sure when all remnants of Lully, except for a pitiful handful of ashes, would be erased from the earth. She was glad she didn't know. She couldn't have stood to think about it.

Emma walked to the car with a sense of dread and relief. She wanted to hide from curious eyes, but she couldn't. Instead, she lifted her chin and walked faster, unaware of how close she was to tears. A brisk wind had sprung up and she pulled her coat closer. She studied the sky, catching her breath, knowing that it was bound to get colder, and she shivered. She would not cry. She would not.

Emma's prediction proved accurate. By the time graveside services were conducted, Emma had chosen Momma's grave in the old cemetery in back of the house as the place to sprinkle Lully's remains. A small group of mourners—more than Emma would have imagined would be interested—came. Sam positioned himself thirty feet behind Emma, far enough, she knew, not to be intrusive, but close enough to make his presence known.

The urn Emma had chosen was encased in a gray metal box. A spray of gardenias and roses lay across the top. The scene seemed dreamlike; Emma was going to awaken any moment and give Lully that long overdue phone call. Lully was supposed to be alive, eager to forgive her. Instead, the ashes of her too-young-to-die sister now rested in a small gray metal box on an incredibly cold, overcast day.

A pastor, one Emma had never met, stood under the bare branches of a spreading oak and spoke of Lully and of how no one could ever understand why someone so young could be taken. Trust in God's will. Faith in eternity. Assurances punctuated by the snapping of the overhead canvas. Emma wondered if the pastor had even met Lully. Was he new to Serenity? Had he heard the stories about the Mansi girls? The woman he was extolling as a "beloved member of the community" and "a lovely and upstanding young woman with many gifts" didn't sound like her sister. No. He quite obviously hadn't heard the lies and hateful remarks, the taunts that had plagued Lully all her life.

Funny how lies had a way of gaining validation when repeated often enough. She hadn't understood that until years later.

And the mean-spirited teenagers who had thrown rocks through the front window, had rung the doorbell then disappeared. Where were they today? Thinking up more mischief or enjoying warm homes with loving families? Emma wondered.

Once, she and Lully had gone to the door to discover a cross on the porch. The cross itself was beautiful. A twelve-inch creation made of cut glass that sparkled in the porch light. Emma had been struck immediately by its delicate craftsmanship and eagerly picked it up, but Lully had snatched it away in anger and flung it off the porch as if it were venomous. Though she'd heard it shatter, Emma had tried to rescue the cross, but Lully had dragged her back inside the house.

With tears streaming down her cheeks, Emma had whirled on her sister. "Why did you do that? Someone brought us a present!"

Lully's eyes had flashed bitter resentment. "It wasn't a present, Emma!"

"It was too! It was too beautiful to be anything else!" She faced her sister defiantly. "God will be mad at you, Lully. Really mad!"

"That cross didn't mean what you think, Emma."

Defeat had slowly replaced anger in her sister's face. Lully drew a protesting Emma into her arms and held her.

"What do you mean, it doesn't mean what I think?" Emma snuffled.

"Whoever put that cross on the porch didn't mean it as a symbol of grace and salvation like the cross on which Jesus died. They meant it . . . they meant it in a mean way."

Emma figured out that the idea of putting something beautiful on their porch was meant as a kind of talisman to drive away a curse. That was cruel and mean. Emma had wiped her nose and face, thinking about what Lully said. The cross was bad. The pretty glass cross was meant to hurt, not bring happiness. "It's the witch thing, isn't it?" she said, her tone flat.

"I'm afraid so," Lully said. "It's the witch thing."

Then Lully had held Emma at arm's length to search her face. "You know the stories aren't true, don't you? You know I'm not a witch or a sorcerer or any of those things ignorant people have said, don't you?"

Emma had nodded little by little.

Lully had combed her fingers through Emma's tangled hair. "I'm sorry you have to hear those ugly things. I'm sorry Momma is dead and Daddy has gone away. I'm sorry I'm sixteen and I don't know how to be a mother to you. I try. I promise to try harder, Emma. I'm going to do my best. We're all we have—each other—and we have to believe in ourselves because . . . because nobody else does," she'd ended in a whisper.

That had been at Christmas, and it was one of the best Christmases she and Lully ever had. Lully had baked her first turkey, a small one that was a bit overdone, and they'd made stuffing . . . though it turned out dry and had too much sage. But they'd set the dining-room table with the best china and crystal goblets, the real silverware, the red-linen napkins Emma hated to iron. Emma broke the gravy boat when they were washing the dishes and cried because it had been Momma's. Lully dried her tears and told her it didn't matter; it was only a dish. Momma would be in their hearts forever.

"I don't know what forever is," Emma bawled.

"More time than we can imagine. Everlasting," Lully had whispered, "Tootsie Pop."

Emma's attention returned to the minister's soft words. She hadn't thought about that Christmas for years. Thinking of it now brought a knot to her throat. How Lully had tried to make their lives better. She'd read the Bible aloud every night. "Blessed are the poor in spirit, for theirs is the kingdom of heaven." Lully had found such comfort in Scripture. Emma had listened because Lully insisted.

Touching a shredded tissue to her eyes, Emma listened to the remainder of the brief service. Lully was gone. Emma knew that, understood that. And she wanted so hard to believe that Lully was in a better place. A place where there were no accusations, no cutting words, no hateful gossip, and no judgmental people. No more pain. No more tears. And the only cross there was the one that represented grace and mercy.

"Let us pray," the minister said.

Those huddled against the wind bowed their heads. The minister prayed for Lully's soul and petitioned the Lord to forgive sins. Then it was over.

The preacher's ears were red from the cold, his fingers like ice when they took her hand. She felt a hand cup her right elbow, and she was only vaguely aware that Sam was leading her away from the site. Two bouquets, her gardenia spray and a bouquet of carnations from Sam and his brother, Ken, marked Emma's remains.

Someone pressed a plant into her hands. "Honey, I want you to have this," a gray-haired woman said. "It'll just die out here."

"Thank you," Emma managed, taking the plant.

"That's Elizabeth Suitor," Sam murmured near her ear. "She owns the bookstore, Elizabeth's Corner. Lully ordered books from her."

Emma nodded, not trusting her voice at the moment. She stumbled on the uneven ground, but Sam's grip kept her from falling. She'd forgotten to pack dress shoes, so she was wearing a pair of Lully's, which were a half size too small and pinched her toes.

"The coroner's report came back."

"And?" Emma swallowed, bracing herself.

"Lully's heart was weak. Apparently it was congenital, and she had known for a long time that her life would be cut short."

A sob caught in Emma's throat. Heart? Did the disease run in the family? Did she need to be examined for the same gene?

Sam read her thoughts. "Doc Radisson said to stop by his office before you leave, and he'll run some tests."

"I have my own physician, thank you." She'd had a yearly physical six months earlier and everything was normal.

When they reached her car, Sam opened the door for her.

"Thank you." She couldn't look at him.

She slid behind the wheel, set the plant on the passenger seat, and fumbled for the ignition. She could have walked the short distance to the house but Lully's shoes were killing her, and she didn't want to traipse through the cemetery, knowing all eyes would be on her. The engine caught and she flipped the heater on high. Sam continued to hold the door, but she refused to meet his gaze. Her emotions weren't exactly granite, and she'd be either crazy or just plain sadistic to open herself to further distress by looking at him. She'd lost her only family, and she hadn't yet come to terms with that.

Blood is thicker than water, Toostsie Pop. We may not be the normal family, but we're all each other has.

Emma looked back at Lully's grave. Mr. Willow had thought she was not thinking clearly when she'd requested burial on her mother's grave. He argued that no one had used the old cemetery in fifty years, but she insisted. Lully would have liked that. She'd never strayed far from the house in her lifetime; she wouldn't want to be in the new cemetery on the other side of town.

Bye, Puddin' Stick.

"I'll stop by the house tonight, make sure you have everything you need."

Emma blinked; Sam's voice barely penetrated her bruised senses. "I'd rather you didn't. It's been a long day."

The silence stretched between them. Strained, filled with unspoken accusations, old resentments yet unvoiced. Yet his manner indicated that he was sympathetic to the fact that she'd just laid her sister to rest. "Then tomorrow night. We need to talk."

She looked up in surprise. "What about?"

Sam stared over the top of the car, toward the house, then back at Emma. "About the house."

"What about it?" She didn't want to talk to him. About anything.

"We have to make some decisions—do we list the house or give the town first dibs?"

"Sell? Who said anything about selling?"

Sam looked at her in amazement. "That's what we'll do, isn't it?"

"I don't know. I haven't had time to think about it."

"You haven't shown your face around here in fifteen years, and you're thinking about keeping the house?"

"Did I say I was going to keep it?"

He took a deep breath and expelled it slowly. "What exactly *are* you saying, Emma?"

Sam wore his sheriff's uniform: cocoa brown shirt and khaki slacks with a sheepskin-lined, all-weather coat. A wide belt carrying a cell phone and a gun snapped in a leather holster circled his waist. Everything about him spoke of authority.

"I'm saying—" She didn't know what she was saying. Her head hurt, and if she didn't get these shoes off, she was going to scream.

"Okay," Sam conceded. "You think about it and I'll call you later."

"Fine."

"Fine."

He stared at her as if he wanted to say more, then seemed to abandon the effort. He released a sigh. "You're sure there's nothing I can do to help?" he asked.

"Thank you, but no."

He turned to walk away and she called him back. "Look. I haven't had time to think about the house—give me a little space. Okay?"

He frowned. "You would actually consider keeping it?"

She hated the old monstrosity and what it represented in many ways, but still, it was her childhood home and she wasn't necessarily ready to let it go. It was all that was left of her family, of Lully, and she wasn't about to auction it to the highest bidder. Not yet—not until she had time to think.

It wasn't as if the house meant anything to anyone except her. It never had—not then, not now. Sam had no right to have a say in what happened, no matter what Lully had put in her will.

She shrugged. "It might make an ideal tearoom." Where did that come from?

She glanced up to see an incredulous look on Sam's face—a look that only strengthened her stubborn refusal to consider selling the house.

"A tearoom?"

"Certainly. They've been very successful when opened in a Victorian atmosphere. Some renovation—cosmetic things like paint, pale walls I think, lace curtains, small tables with floral table-cloths." She described a tearoom she'd gone to in Seattle, hoping Sam would think she'd thought this plan through. "Bud vases with fresh flowers. Delicate china, French pastries, and maybe some sandwiches on the menu."

"You think Mrs. Masters and Molly Montgomery are going to sip tea and eat cucumber sandwiches among hundred-year-old tombstones?" He stared at her. "Somehow it doesn't strike me as the right . . . ambience."

She hated it when he was right, but she wasn't going to give him the satisfaction of admitting it. Besides, she couldn't let go. Not yet. It would be as if she'd abandoned Lully and every member of her now-gone family who had lived in the house and called it home.

"Turning it into a tearoom is better than selling it. Who knows what the new owner would do with it?"

"I'll tell you what they'll do with it. The mayor wants it for a municipal parking lot."

"A what?"

"Parking lot—the town needs one badly, Emma. The old house is a prime location. We can get a good price out of it if you'll use your common sense."

"I don't think so," she snapped back.

"Don't use that tone with me," he said very softly. "Whether I want it or not, Lully left me half of the house. I have a say in what happens to it."

"You're not selling my house to bulldoze down for a municipal parking lot!"

His jaw firmed. "We will discuss this at a better time. The idea is new to both of us—"

"I am not selling the house."

"If you're not going to be here, how do you intend to protect your investment?"

There was that look in his eyes that said he was firm on the subject. Maybe a tearoom wasn't the answer, but there had to be one. She wasn't going to sell the house, on principle alone. Give up the only thing left of her family for a parking lot?

"Be sensible, Emma."

The softly spoken words carried more weight than if he had shouted them.

She kept silent for fear she'd say too much.

"You've been running on nerves for more than seventy-two hours. You need to stop and think about things. And we need to talk this through. The house is falling down and it makes no sense to keep it. Besides, I can use the money."

She snorted. "For what?"

"A Ferrari. What else?"

She snorted again.

"Okay, if you really want to know, Mom's in a nursing home and her money's about to run out. I have the choice of paying twenty-five hundred a month or moving her to a facility three hundred miles away, where she'll get zippo care. Neither Ken nor I will be able to visit her except a few times a year. Ken doesn't have the money, and a sheriff's pay sure can't take the hit. This may be an answer to prayer. Who would have ever thought Lully would have left me half a house?"

"Yeah. Who'd ever think."

"Look, I know this is hard on you. We don't have to talk about this now. Rest up, and I'll call you."

She wouldn't look at him. She drew a deep breath.

His mother. A letter I never saw. What next? A sick uncle? A deranged aunt?

He shifted to his opposite foot. "I'm not kidding."

She could hardly debate a matter this serious, but she'd dealt with all she could today.

"The will can't be changed. We have to decide, reasonably, what to do about it." He straightened then. "I'll be by the house in a few days. Think about what you want to do."

Sam stepped back, and Emma caught the door handle and slammed the door. He was barely able to escape being hit by it. She popped the car into gear and spun away, leaving the way she had fifteen years earlier—without looking back.

Sam watched the car speed away from the cemetery and turn toward the house. She might not realize it, but Emma was hiding in that house just as Lully had. Not for the same reasons, because Lully had a reclusive nature. But Emma was hiding just the same, and he was the reason. She was still bitter over what had happened between them so long ago. Well, he had his own bad feelings about that time. Feelings that he wanted to resolve, one way or another, whether she stayed or left again for good. He'd never gotten her out of his system, but one way or the other it was time he settled it with himself.

Storming into the house, Emma snatched up the phone and called Sue, who told Emma to take all the time she needed. She then called Janice.

"I didn't do well with the job interview," Janice said. "I know they're not going to hire me."

"What makes you think you didn't do well?"

Janice had been looking forward to the job interview with nervous anticipation. There was a secretarial opening in an automobile parts store.

"It's not exactly life and death," she'd told Emma. But Emma knew she desperately wanted what she called a "real job." She'd taken accounting and English classes, hoping for at least an office job where she could advance. This was her first interview, and Emma could empathize with Janice's fears.

"The guy just kept looking at me as if he couldn't believe I was in there wanting a job. It was like I had *mistake* printed across my forehead."

"Jan, even if you don't get this job, it doesn't mean you didn't interview well—"

"I'm a jailbird, Emma. Let's face it."

Emma heard the defeat in her friend's voice and felt great sympathy for her. She wished she could be there with her, felt she needed to be there to help Janice over this hump. "First, stop thinking like that. People make mistakes," Emma said.

"Well, I make big lulus."

"Remember, attitude is everything. You walk into a place with an attitude of 'I can do this job,' and you'll do all right. Now, what do you think you could have done better?"

"I fidgeted. Couldn't keep my hands still. He had to notice."

"Did you hold something? Like a pen?"

"No, I forgot."

"No matter," Emma said. "Even if this job doesn't work out, another will. Count it as good practice. You learned something today."

"Yeah," she managed to laugh a little, "not to forget my pencil."

"What's next on your list?"

"I've got an interview set up for tomorrow."

"Hey, that's great! What's the job?"

"Receptionist at a small company. They make plastic screws or something like that."

"Okay, now you know what you've got to do. Walk in there like you're Ivana Trump, hold your pen, don't fidget, and thank them for the opportunity when you leave."

Janice's sigh came to Emma over the line. "Okay. I can do this, I can do this, I can do this," she repeated.

"Yes, you can; yes, you can; yes, you can." Emma grinned. "Call me after the interview, okay?"

"Okay." A pregnant pause and then, "Em, I don't know what I'd do without you—"

"You'd do fine. Just believe in yourself. I'll talk to you tomorrow."

"Have you seen Sam yet?"

The question caught Emma off guard. Why had she told Janice about Sam? In a weak moment one evening she had admitted her own weaknesses with men, and naturally Sam Gold's name had surfaced. "I've seen him."

"And?"

"Nothing, Janice. That's all over. I have to run—honest. I'll talk to you tomorrow." *Emma, that was an outright lie. Over? Ha. In a pig's eye.*

Emma hung up and made herself a sandwich and ate it while thinking about the tearoom idea. Where had that come from? It was as if someone had whispered the suggestion in her ear and she'd blurted it out. Sam thought it was a ridiculous idea, but was it?

She spent the remainder of the day bundled in two sweaters she'd found hanging on hooks in the hall closet, contemplating what could be done with all the stuff Lully couldn't bring herself to part with over the years. Magazines. Stacks of them. Books that Emma had no interest in and wondered why Lully had. Novels, history, medical and psychology books. Books on religion and philosophy. Books on art and design, and minerals and gems. Emma couldn't comprehend how her sister could have lived in such chaos. A junk dealer would have a field day in the house.

There were also stacks of files holding the jewelry sketches that Lully must have spent hours on. They were all there, in no particular order. Lully's computer sat in one of the empty bedrooms on a rickety table that held more file folders filled with designs. Obviously she used the computer software for her designs, but what else might be on file there? Emma turned on the computer but couldn't get any further than that. No password she tried would allow her entrance. Finally she turned it off in disgust.

"Gismo, if you could only talk."

But the dog could only wag his tail.

She let the dog out to do his business and turned her thoughts elsewhere.

Emma attacked the house over the next two days. She started with the front room. She sorted piles of junk and packed some of Lully's personal effects.

Weary from the seemingly impossible task, she headed for the rose garden on the third day. She raked beds and pruned bushes, thinking about Momma and how pretty the garden had been when she was alive. The plants could be beautiful again with proper care. She stood back, picturing the trellises overflowing with dashing pink climbing roses offset by dark rose zinnias. She shook the disturbing image away. It came back—the perfect surrounding for a teahouse.

Don't go there. You're going back to Seattle and your former carefree, Sam-free life. There were roses and zinnias aplenty in Washington. Besides, it had been three days since Mr. Sam Gold had said he would be by. He'd failed to show up yet.

She heard the phone ring. Setting her tools aside, she ran to answer it.

Uncannily, it was Sam. "Emma, I'd hoped to come over tonight, but I'm not going to make it. There's been a bad wreck out on 550 at the junction. But I haven't changed my mind. We still have to talk."

"Sam—"

"Gotta go. Let's talk tomorrow." The dial tone droned in her ear. Slamming down the receiver, Emma could have screamed in frustration. Leave it to Sam to have her tied in knots over a confrontation, then not show up. She wanted to kick something and she did. She kicked the leg of the computer table and then had to catch it before it fell. Her kick had loosened a leg. She lifted a corner of the table and used one foot to maneuver the leg back in place. Then she braced it with a stack of books and prayed it wouldn't collapse totally, taking the computer with it. Hadn't Lully ever repaired anything?

"Gismo, Sheriff Sam Gold is . . . is . . . I don't know what he is, but he's met his match in me."

She returned to the kitchen and tackled the dishes. By the time she'd won that battle she was exhausted. When she fell into bed she dropped into an instant, sound sleep.

So sound that she didn't hear someone trying to jimmy a basement window open or the muffled groan of frustration when the attempt failed.

FINGERS of muted light gradually spread across dull lino-leum, filtering through sun-faded curtains hanging at the window over the sink. Emma sipped a glass of orange juice, watching the weak ray creep across the kitchen floor.

She hated late-autumn mornings, when it was dark when she awoke and dark before she left for work. It had snowed during the night; fluffy white patches nestled in cedar branches and in puffy skiffs along porch railings. Emma shivered, pulling her coat collar closer around her neck. The house was freezing. When she had rolled out of bed the floor felt like ice. She had made a mad dash for the bathroom, only to do a jig there on a threadbare rug in front of the old claw-foot tub. No more delay facing the task. She had to build a fire in the stove using whatever knowledge she had retained.

Burying one hand in the tangle of her thick, russet-colored hair, Emma stared at the dirty vinyl floor. The house was a mess. Dust lay everywhere. Floating air particles coated everything and made her sneeze. The kitchen floor was worn through in places and should have been replaced years before. The hardwood floors should at least be cleaned, waxed, and buffed, if not stripped and refinished.

If she were to keep the house she would have to practically

remodel the whole thing—house, floors, drywall, plumbing fixtures—the list was endless, and would the effort really produce anything different? Maybe a house in better condition, but who wanted an old house next to a deserted cemetery?

Emma's weary gaze swept the room. Lully had wanted the house to remain untouched—or was it only because of Lully's laziness and lack of initiative? Maybe both. Now that Lully was gone, no one would know for certain. Emma's eyes paused on the boom box that sat on top of the refrigerator. She didn't need to switch on the cassette inside to know what it would be: Lully's weird music.

She turned on the radio and found a news broadcast on KIQX. She rested her head on the back of the straight-backed chair, contemplating the stained ceiling. What would a roof for this thing cost? Emma didn't want to entertain the question. A lot more than she had, that was certain.

Her gaze moved from the stained ceiling to the yellowed walls. When had the room had a coat of fresh paint? Never in her memory. And this was her legacy. Hers and Sam's. Maybe the house *should* be bulldozed.

Had Lully lost her mind? Maybe the years of isolation had somehow damaged her thought processes.

Emma noted the flaws in the kitchen, but deep inside memories stirred. Not all were bad. There had been happy times in this house too. Her gaze shifted to the dirty window. Light snow was falling on the withered rose bed. Momma would have had a fit if she'd known how Lully had let weeds overtake the bed. When had Lully lost her spunk? When she got sick, perhaps. Emma recalled that Lully had written about how she loved to garden. So perhaps her illness explained why Lully had let everything get so run down. Maybe she just didn't have the energy anymore to deal with everything. At the same time, Emma recalled that Lully was never an overachiever. She could stare at work for weeks and pretend it didn't exist. Perhaps Lully never even noticed the house was falling down around her head.

Yet Lully had made her choices and stuck with them, while

Emma still didn't know exactly what she wanted from life. She'd sought counseling a year after she settled in Seattle. It hadn't been easy, talking about her parents, about why she had run away from Serenity. She felt like a fool. It had been so hard to talk about Sam and about how she felt abandoned by everyone close to her when he turned away. But she had continued the weekly sessions because she was determined to make a new life for herself, and that meant facing harsh realities. She'd faced the past—most of it. Seeing Sam again, however, had set her back ten years. She owned her own business, was doing work she was trained for and enjoyed. She'd built a good life for herself—one she was proud of and felt she was succeeding in—until the phone call informing her of Lully's death.

Lully had been the one who buried her head in the sand and pretended that if she didn't physically see it, it wasn't there. But Emma knew different. It—whatever "it" was—always lurked in the shadows, hiding in that mental closet where people hid things they wanted to forget but ready to pounce at the slightest invitation.

Emma's heart ached and tears stung her eyes. Lully's world had not been based in reality. Lully had left the house to both her and Sam, thinking it a grand gesture, no doubt. But Lully had no idea what a quagmire she'd create.

Sam, Emma knew, couldn't understand her ties to the house. If she didn't stay and make sure he didn't sell it for a parking lot . . . she couldn't let that happen.

But what about Sam's mother? Was what Sam said true? He may have a lot of other faults, but Emma had never known him to lie. Sam needed the money from the sale of the house for his mother. That nagged at Emma's conscience.

Perhaps there was some way to keep the house and help Sam's mother. Maybe she could stay until she convinced Sam not to sell the house. And, in that time she could have the house checked out to see whether it was basically sound. But then what? Was the idea of a tearoom viable?

Emma chewed her lip, sorting through the facts. She could have all the time off she wanted. If Sue had to bow out because she wanted more family time, she could hire someone. Emma hated to take more time from her business, but Lully's house was her business now.

Why did Sam object so strenuously to a tearoom? The town didn't have one; it would be a sound venture, a business that in the long run would pay out far more than an outright sale. Her mother's rose garden could be salvaged, other flowering bushes and perennials planted. A line of tall flowering bushes would hide the cemetery if necessary. She could hire someone she trusted to run the tearoom. She could keep in touch by phone. It could be done. It would take some planning, but it could be done. Maybe Janice . . .

Emma decided right then and there to move forward with pursuing the idea of a tearoom. She phoned the bank to check what accounts, if any, were in Lully's name.

Darrel Masters, president of the bank, came on the line. "Emma, good to hear from you. My sympathy for the loss of your sister."

"Thank you, Mr. Masters. I'm trying to settle Lully's affairs, and I wondered if she had any accounts there."

"Well, yes, she did. She kept that account your father set up. She did change some things—"

"What kinds of things?"

"You know Lully had an Internet business—"

"She did?"

"Jewelry. She designed jewelry, you know, and then sold it on the Internet. Had accounts set up through MasterCard and Visa with the sales amounts directly deposited into her account. She came in once a week on Friday noon, just like clockwork, and drew out the exact amount that had been deposited. Last week the amount was $1858.64. I'd leave that account open because more transactions are sure to come in—"

"She drew out all the money each week?"

"Every Friday. I tried to convince her to keep what she didn't need in a money market account so it would draw interest, but she refused. Said she didn't trust banks, which is rather strange since she used the account all these years. Anyway, I was concerned about her keeping money at the house—"

"She kept her money at the house?"

"Well, I'm assuming she did. She was a frugal woman, you know."

Except for the books, computer, and software, Lully certainly hadn't spent much on herself and none at all on the house.

"Is that an average total for a week?"

"Oh no—sometimes the sum was much higher. I imagine orders will slow dramatically now unless you plan to continue with the business."

Not likely with a greenhouse and tearoom to consider. That was one decision, at least, that was clear-cut. "No, I won't be continuing the business, but I'm going to have to figure out a way to close it out." *But I have to get into the records first.* "Well, thank you for the information."

"If I can do anything to help, please give me a call or come in. I'd be happy to accommodate you."

"Thanks, Mr. Masters, I'll do that."

Emma hung up slowly. Why had Lully taken all of her money out of the bank? And what had she done with it? Suddenly the addendum to Lully's bequest came back to her: *Tell Emma she will find her true legacy if she looks hard enough.*

True legacy. Now what was that supposed to mean? What did Lully mean by "if she looks hard enough"? Look where and for what? Emma was standing in the middle of her legacy, an old house that was about to fall down from neglect. Emma carried her empty glass to the sink, rinsed it out, and laid it in the plastic drainer. *How could Lully exist without a dishwasher?* Emma rubbed her cold hands together. *And a decent heating system.* Restless, Emma paced into the chilly parlor. The huge, black relic of a stove squatting on a brick hearth challenged her. She shook her head.

The weather was getting colder every day and she had to keep warm, but how was she going to heat that monstrosity?

Emma peered behind the stove and found a wood box stacked with split wood. In one end were stuffed newspapers, magazines, and some kindling. *Okay. Might as well try it,* she decided. *It's either that or freeze.*

Wadding up old newspaper, Emma pulled open the protesting door at the front of the stove. A cloud of cold ashes puffed out into her face, nearly choking her. She coughed, glaring at the stove, then knelt and shoved a wad of paper inside. Adding several pieces of kindling, she studied the mound with satisfaction, then grimaced when she noticed the smear of greasy black soot down her forearm. Wiping at it, she managed to smear the soot on both hands as well and stopped herself from wiping her palms down the sides of her slacks.

"Okay, matches," she murmured, peering around the stove. She found a box of wooden matches balanced on the edge of the wood box. "Not a good place," she said, deciding the bookshelf to the right of the stove was probably better.

Emma closed the matchbox and drew a deep breath. Now came the test. Squatting on her heels, she struck a match and held it to the corner of a piece of newspaper, hoping it would flame enough for the wood to catch fire.

Hadn't Lully realized the virtues of a furnace and automatic thermostat? Hot: rotate down. Cold: twist up. So simple. Surely putting a unit and ductwork at least on the main floor wouldn't have been too difficult. There was certainly plenty of room in the basement.

The corner of the newspaper turned black and the flame fizzled out.

"Okay, not successful. Try again."

Gismo padded into the parlor to investigate; after seeing what Emma was doing, he immediately retreated.

"No faith, mutt," Emma muttered.

She struck a second match. Again the paper sizzled, then fizzled out.

She looked up, wondering what would be the next step.

"Ah-ha!" She spied a can of charcoal lighter fluid behind the wood box. Apparently Lully had encountered the same stubborn lighting problem.

Emma grabbed the can and flipped the lid open, wincing at the strong odor that wafted out. Squirting a couple of hefty squeezes over the paper and kindling, she hesitated a moment as she read the label. This stuff was highly flammable. That was good—to a point. At least something would catch fire. Probably the whole house.

Once again she struck a match and flung it into the belly of the stove. Nothing. She leaned closer. *What's wrong with this stupid thing?* Finally one end of the newspaper turned brown, like the outside coating of a marshmallow exposed to extreme heat. Then it turned black. Suddenly, the fire exploded in a burst of red-hot flame.

Emma rocked back on her heels, then sprawled on the floor, the stench of singed hair burning her nose. Frantically, she patted her scorched eyebrows and hair around her face.

Coming to her senses, she quickly slammed the stove door and ran to the bedroom, where she peered anxiously into the wavy mirror over the vanity. Even in the murky glass she could easily see her blackened face framed by singed hair.

Emma closed her eyes in defeat. *Lully, I can't do this! What on earth were you thinking? This is no treasure! It's purgatory!*

"How does it feel to be part owner of the old Mansi Mansion?"

Sam Gold turned a page of the report he was reading before answering his brother. "You plan to get a lot of mileage out of this, don't you?"

Ken Gold leaned against the door frame of Sam's office with a mischievous grin on his face. Tall and muscular, Ken was a physical match for his older brother and had broken about as many hearts over the years.

"You a little surprised by Lully's will?"

"Surprised isn't quite the word," Sam admitted, leaning back in his chair. "Lully and I'd kind of come to a truce over the years and I kept an eye on the place, chased off that pack of young hoodlums who kept harassing her—"

"And half the town."

"Yeah. But I never expected her to do something like this." Lully had always been eccentric and unpredictable. She'd always had her own reasons for doing things.

"I was surprised it was so easy to find Emma," Ken offered.

"She went straight to Seattle from here," Sam said. "Sent Lully that card after she turned eighteen to let her know she was okay. She never moved again."

"Humph. A nester."

A nester. Sam's insides turned over when he thought of Emma. "Guess so." He leaned back and knit his fingers behind his head. "You never knew what Lully was going to do, but you could always predict Emma's reactions."

"Except for the time she ran away."

"Except for that," Sam amended.

"I didn't think Lully ever heard from Emma."

"She didn't often. But Lully told me she kept sending Emma notes and Emma wrote every few years."

"If you knew where she was—" Ken began.

"Leaving was her choice."

"But you're glad she's back."

"Mind your own business, baby brother." Sam reached for his hat. "I'm going out for some decent coffee."

He left the office and strode across the street and into the café. Coffee was on his mind, but he needed fresh air and a change of subject more. And, if he'd admit it, time to sort through feelings he thought he'd dealt with years ago. Right now they were a tangle of contradictions. Obviously Emma wasn't happy to be back in Serenity or to see him—so logically, he should let her go. But logic had nothing to do with his feelings for her—and those were back in full force.

At seventeen he'd surrendered his intense feelings for Emma in what he thought was a selfless act. Broke, underage, without a future at that point, he had been forced to bend to the decisions of others.

Now he knew that Lully had been right to oppose the marriage. He had a lot of growing up to do, and so had Emma. Lully had known that Emma needed security—security he couldn't provide then. Now he could, but it didn't matter. Emma had built a new life and it had nothing to do with him.

Fifteen years ago the only thing he could have offered Emma was the starry-eyed hormonal blitz of a seventeen-year-old boy. That wasn't good enough for Emma. Now he knew that. Even then he'd wanted more for Emma than he could provide. But he'd wanted her so much he ached. When Lully and his mother thwarted their plans to marry, he'd been furious. Though his job prospects were few at age seventeen and no one else thought they would make it, he knew he and Emma would have. They would have grown up together, had kids. It would have been hard. There would have been rough times, but the passing years had only served to convince Sam that there was only one woman, one other soul so perfect, so in tune with his soul that she couldn't be replaced.

For Sam, that woman was Emma Mansi.

When Emma had turned seventeen and disappeared, it hurt him. For years he hadn't been able to find her. Lully wouldn't help; she contended she didn't know Emma's whereabouts, but deep down he had known differently. Lully was protecting Emma, and at the time he couldn't say that he blamed her. His head knew it was for the best, but his heart twisted at every thought of her. Eventually he'd joined the service and left Serenity.

The years had given him a better perspective on life, on everything but what he'd done to Emma. Some part of him had still hoped Emma would one day return to Serenity or he wouldn't have come back himself. So he'd come back after his father died and after a while settled into the job of sheriff. He pushed Emma out of his thoughts; at least he tried. He'd hoped to marry, start a family. But that never happened. Every time he thought he'd found the right woman, something got in the way. Now he knew it was Emma. None of the women he'd been serious about had been Emma.

When Lully died and Emma was forced back to Serenity, faith stirred. Maybe, just maybe, God was finally answering his prayers. He'd hoped the years had softened the edge of the abandonment he knew Emma felt, hoped she would feel different toward him. But that was clearly not the case. The cold condemnation in her eyes when she looked at him confirmed his conviction. She still resented him, and pigs would fly before she forgave him.

Ken was hanging up the phone when Sam walked back into the office thirty minutes later. "Kids have been vandalizing the cemetery again."

"Who called it in?" Sam tossed his hat toward the hatrack and grinned when it hit dead-on and hung there.

"Edna Pierson had been to visit her husband's grave early and found the headstone overturned."

Small towns seemed to have a problem with teenage boys raring to make some kind of commotion. Not always real trouble, though often it bordered on serious, but enough to keep the townspeople stirred up. Things like overturned tombstones.

Ken shook his head. "What is the attraction in turning over tombstones?"

Sam smiled. "Didn't we ever do something like that?"

"Privy tipping isn't in the same category," Ken argued.

Sam grinned. He and his brother had been inseparable since they were toddlers and still enjoyed a special kind of adult closeness. Sam's old office chair squeaked in protest when he settled into it.

Ken followed Sam into his office. "It's a shame we can't catch the culprits. We both know who's responsible."

"Yeah, but we've got to catch them at it or we don't have a case."

They both knew the Coleman boys were responsible, and a

couple of others were suspect. But Don and Brice Coleman could be held responsible for more than cemetery vandalism. They'd been suspected of putting sugar in gas tanks, of stealing porch furniture, breaking gazing balls and windows at the school, and stealing hubcaps. For two years these teenage nuisances had driven people to the end of their ropes, but nothing could be proven. Once they'd learned to drive, they'd collected a surprising number of speeding tickets.

Their father, Jack Coleman, had walked out a few years back, and the mother couldn't control her three boys. She quit trying when Sam and Ken hauled the boys home at least once a week. It wasn't right, and Sam was about to lose patience with the situation.

"I'll call someone to reset the stone."

Ken nodded. "I told Edna we'd take care of it." He sat down in the chair by Sam's desk, leaned back, propped one foot against the corner of the desk, and winced at the protesting squeak. "What are you going to do with the house?"

Sam shook his head. "I don't know. This could be a godsend, Ken. You know, with my part of the money we could take care of Mom."

Sam didn't want the house. It was about to fall down. The town did need a new parking lot. "I think Emma's going to fight me on this—she's mentioned a tearoom."

"You're kidding."

"Nope, she thinks the town needs some class."

"I'd settle for a decent parking spot." Ken grinned. "You got a problem, buddy."

"What's new when it comes to Emma?"

"Or the Mansi girls in general."

When Sam had been elected sheriff five years ago, he had crossed paths with Lully on a professional basis more than he wanted. There was always some kind of nuisance call to the "witch's house." Lully would call the office four or five times in any given week and report trouble. There had been rocks thrown through the front window, odd noises coming from the basement, black cats bound in tow sacks put on the porch. The complaints were varied and endless; with these kinds of nuisances happening on a regular basis, it was understandable that she would be a recluse.

But the idea that Lully Mansi was a witch was ridiculous. He'd always suspected that someone had been startled by a wild-eyed, chanting Lully who didn't want children playing in the old cemetery, and that's how the rumors started.

"What are you going to do?" Ken asked. "The town does need the parking lot, and the mayor is chomping at the bit to get his hands on that property. You could make a sizable chunk if you wanted to hold out long enough."

"That's not a bad idea. Keep the mayor chomping and give Emma time to cool on this tearoom business."

Ken glanced at the files on Sam's desk. "Can you hold the mayor off that long?"

"Can you keep a tiger from fresh meat?" Sam shrugged. "I'll do my best, but I won't push Emma into something she doesn't want, money or no money. If she gets her head set on a tearoom, then—"

"Then what?" Ken asked

"I'll walk that road when I come to it. Meanwhile I'll try to talk some sense into her. The town will be better off if the cemetery is relocated to the new plot. It would take both properties to make a decent-size parking lot."

If Emma stayed in Serenity with this bitterness between them, it would bode trouble for him. He couldn't see her every day and know that one day she'd find someone, marry, have a family. He'd have to leave—

"Oooh, a haunted parking lot." Ken grinned. "Old Ezra Mott spooking our cars?"

Sam scowled at him. "Those stories are ridiculous. Besides, Ezra would be moved with the rest of the gravestones to the new lot."

"That's spooky."

"I'm going to talk to Emma soon—maybe tonight. Yeah, tonight. I've put it off long enough," Sam decided.

"Now that should be interesting," Ken commented dryly.

Sam stared into his coffee cup. "Not looking forward to it."

Emma could be headstrong, and he had a feeling she was going to dig in her heels about selling. She could dig in all she wanted, but the only smart thing to do was sell the house.

Ken chuckled.

"What's so funny?" Sam demanded.

"Still got it bad for her, haven't you?"

"Get out of here. What makes you think so?"

"You've been staring into that cup for fifteen minutes. Never thought cold coffee was that interesting."

Ignoring his brother, Sam set the cup on top of the file cabinet and sat down at his desk. Sometimes Ken knew him too well.

"Admit it. You still have those same ole feelings for Emma Mansi."

Sam gave him a dark look and got up again. Sometimes working with family wasn't as great as it seemed to be. The two had been hired as deputies together under the old administration. As soon as the old sheriff had retired and Sam had been elected sheriff, he'd named Ken his chief deputy. He could trust Kenny like no one else, and he wanted him by his side in the tough situations. They might disagree upon occasion, but they had always been close. They'd played football together and gotten into a few scrapes with the local authorities together, nothing serious. Ken had sat silently with him when their mother, who ruled her household and the town with an iron hand, had threatened to send him to military school if he saw Emma Mansi again. And it was his brother who had listened to him rail on at how unfair it was when Emma ran away from Serenity before he could explain to her about the threat.

Settling his Stetson on his head, Sam said quietly, "Someone's been stealing cattle from the Harrison place. I'll be up there this afternoon if you need me."

Ken grinned. "Coward."

Giving him another dark look, Sam left the office, knowing Ken was right. He was running.

THE FOYER clock chimed seven as Emma made one last check of her hair and lipstick in the mirror before answering Sam's knock. She'd managed to trim her singed hair with a pair of dull scissors she'd found, but the stench of scorched locks was still in her nose. Nervous stomach butterflies made her feel nauseated, but she kept reminding herself she wasn't fifteen anymore.

A rush of frigid air assaulted her when she opened the door. Sam hunched inside an all-weather coat, the sheepskin collar turned up around his ears. Miniature snowflakes danced around him in the cold air.

She motioned him inside.

For a moment, Sam almost wished he hadn't come. Seeing Emma in this house brought back a rush of memories. She didn't look like the shy fifteen year old who had taught him what loving someone was all about. The wide-eyed innocent gaze had been replaced with a cold direct stare of mistrust. The silent accusation hurt. To think that she didn't trust him anymore, couldn't trust him, made him—what? Angry? A little, but he was responsible for the reaction. Should he confront her or ignore the look? What if he reached out and drew her to him, held her for a moment . . . ?

Sam entered the foyer, removing the Stetson and shaking the snow from it. He met Emma's distant look. "Looks like winter's come especially early this year. But it's warm enough in here," he said.

Heat radiating from the woodstove in the parlor was more than doing its job of warming the downstairs. In fact, the parlor was hot as blue blazes in spite of everything Emma had tried to regulate the heat. If she opened the vents wide, heat poured out in waves, engulfing the downstairs rooms in desertlike heat. But if she closed the vents, the stove sat there almost quivering with the need to expel the heat, which scared her. A north wind howled and freezing air wafted across the floor from the cracks under the door and around the windows. So she elected to have the stove vents wide open and opened every window an inch. It was a strange way to regulate the heat, but it worked.

"Can I take your coat?"

Sam shrugged out of the heavy parka, and Emma hung it in the small closet in the hall. She led him into the parlor. He frowned, his gaze going immediately to the open window, where the cold wind was flapping the heavy drapes.

Emma smiled lamely. "I haven't quite gotten the hang of operating the stove." She cleared her throat and motioned toward the worn sofa. "Please, sit down. Can I get you anything to drink?"

"No. Thanks."

He sat down, rigid as a poker. She hoped they could settle the issue of the house quickly; the tension in the room could be cut with a knife. Bickering like children wouldn't get them anywhere.

Taking a wooden straight-backed chair opposite him, she tried to appear at ease but failed. When the conversation lagged, she cleared her throat. "Have you thought any more about the possibility of establishing a tearoom here?"

"I have."

This was good. She was excited about an idea that had at first seemed illogical, and he now seemed willing to consider the idea.

"Great," Emma said. "So have I. We'll need to paint, hang new draperies, maybe something in a pretty shell pink and mint spring green. I'm sure I can find matching tablecloths and china—"

"No tearoom, Emma."

She thought she hadn't heard him correctly, and then her eyes narrowed. How dare he make that kind of statement without discussing it? "Why not?"

"Because a pink-and-green tearoom in this town would be about as smart as building a glass house at the end of the Purgatory ski run." His gaze met hers directly. "We sell the house and split the profits."

Emma lifted an eyebrow. "Tearoom."

"Parking lot. If we play it right, Emma, the town will give us ninety thousand for this place. That's top price, and we won't get that anywhere else."

Reality seeped into her thoughts. Sam was right—as he always was, which annoyed her. Why did she continue to fight the one man who offered a logically sound solution to her dilemma—keep the house and face childhood memories or return to Seattle? Now he had upped the stakes when he told her about his mother. She had witnessed Edwina Gold getting out of Sam's car Sunday. She was an old, feeble woman. Emma might not care for the curmudgeon, but she couldn't stand the thought of Sam's mother not receiving the best of care in her waning years.

Yet Emma couldn't accept his terms. The odd thing was, at first she wasn't willing to sell simply because she needed to spite him. The dinosaur of a house had been her home, Lully's home, but admittedly it was a contractor's nightmare. Serenity was filled with memories she wanted to leave behind, but in the past twenty-four hours her feelings had begun to change. Maybe it was the memories; maybe it was the growing awareness that she couldn't blame everything on her childhood. Whatever, she honestly thought the tearoom might be a sound investment and Serenity a place for Janice to make a new start.

Sam's gaze went to the stove again as he loosened his tie. "Isn't it hot in here?" Sweat popped out on his forehead. "What are you burning in there? Plutonium?"

Emma got up and opened the window wider. "I'm having trouble regulating the heat."

"It's not that hard. The vents are—"

"I know where the vents are. I lived here, remember? Seattle residences have central heat and air. You don't have to go to this much trouble to keep warm."

She yanked the window even higher. Due to the stove eating voracious amounts of wood, she was almost out and had no idea where to buy more. Apparently Lully had wood fairies.

Sam rolled up the cuffs of his shirtsleeves. "Look, I didn't come here to argue. We have a legitimate difference of opinion." He leaned back on the sofa, pitching a hard throw pillow aside for more comfort. "Convince me your plan is better."

Emma collected her thoughts. "For one thing, it is the only thing left of my family."

Not in her wildest moments could she think of moving back to Serenity. Her life was in Seattle, in her work at The Cottage, but she could fly back and forth monthly. If nothing else, giving Janice a new start would make the decision worthwhile. Dare she trust Sam with her thoughts?

His features softened. "I can appreciate that."

"I don't want to seem selfish and uncaring. Your mother—well, if you were telling me the truth about her—"

"I have never lied to you, Emma. Now or in the past."

Sighing, she sat back. Biting her lower lip, she chose her next words carefully. "Can I offer a compromise?"

"I'm listening."

"I'll agree to have a realtor look at the house and give a fair market value. That will give us some idea where to start if—and I stress *if*—we feel selling is the best option. If I turn the house into a tearoom, your share of the money should more than adequately take care of your mother."

"And if it doesn't turn enough profit?"

"I've been successful with my business in Seattle." Yet the idea did concern her. Would she be stretching herself too thin with two businesses? What if she held out and didn't sell, the tearoom flopped, and Sam's mother— She sighed. "We'll pray that it will be successful."

She turned to the stove, considering its complications. It had to be ninety-plus in the room if it was a single degree. She pushed at the vent slots and jammed them completely closed. When she peered into the glass-fronted door, she saw the flames die down. She decided to push the vent open partway, but it stuck.

She jumped when Sam's large hand closed over hers. For a moment she concentrated on the warmth of it, the calloused palm against her skin. Her heart hammered so loudly he could surely hear it.

Shoving the vent a quarter way open, he released her hand and she felt bereft. His closeness unnerved her. Together like this felt so strangely familiar and so good. The years peeled away and suddenly she was fourteen again and deliciously, hopelessly in love with Sam Gold.

"Leaving the vent one quarter open allows air to feed the flames. Completely closed chokes off the air supply and the flames die down." His breath was warm against her cheek. "You always make things more difficult than they have to be, Emma."

The undertone in his voice was more pronounced than the gentle admonishment.

Emma wandered into the bookstore the next morning. Elizabeth Suitor, the elderly proprietor, looked up when the bell over the door tinkled. Emma stood for a moment, perusing the sunny interior. The scent of candles mingled with the aroma of fresh coffee; comfortable chairs and settees in muted prints formed conversational clusters before the two front windows.

Emma slowly pulled off her gloves and let her woolen scarf fall off.

"Welcome to Elizabeth's Corner, Miss Mansi."

Emma was surprised when the clerk called her by name, but then she supposed everyone in town knew she was back. "Please call me Emma. And thank you for the plant you gave me; it's thriving."

"I didn't know Lully that well, but she always stopped to look in the windows when I had them decorated for holidays. And she'd sometimes bring Gismo in for a treat. But generally she ordered books by phone, and Ray picked them up for her."

"Ray? The man who worked for her?"

"He's a good soul, rather shy. You didn't notice him at the funeral?"

"No." But then Emma's mind had been preoccupied.

"Lully liked to read about anything. Seems everything caught her interest. Are you looking for something in particular?"

Emma scanned the shelves of best-sellers. "I enjoy reading mysteries."

Elizabeth smiled. "Oh yes. A good mystery is hard to put down. Right over here."

Elizabeth led the way to the back of the store to a large rack of novels. "Please let me know if I can help."

"Thank you."

Elizabeth returned to the register while Emma continued to browse. After fifteen minutes or so Emma returned with two titles. Setting the books on the counter, she opened her purse and brought out a red checkbook.

"Twenty-one-fifty-four," Elizabeth said.

Emma started to write a check, then changed her mind, handing Elizabeth her MasterCard.

"Will you be staying in town long?" Elizabeth asked as they waited for the charge to go through.

"A while," Emma said, clearing her throat.

Elizabeth shut the register. "Goodness, all this work—been trying to find someone to come in a couple days a week, but nobody seems interested."

"Oh?" Emma handed Elizabeth her credit card.

"Say. You wouldn't be interested in part-time work, would you?"

"No, I have a business in Seattle." She smiled.

"Oh. Well, I thought you might be staying around a few weeks what with settling the house and all. I was thinking of a few hours a day—not much. Just enough to fill time and help me out a bit."

The "filling time" part caught Emma's interest. Apparently she wasn't going to return to Seattle soon, not if she had to go through the process of pretending to consider putting the house on the market. Sam had said the city would pay ninety thousand. The Realtor would probably come in with a much lower offer. Once the dust settled, Emma would hold out for two hundred thousand and watch the bidders faint and die away. She didn't like deceiving Sam, but using this ploy was the only way she was going to get the tearoom. And she would make the business a success so Sam wouldn't have to worry about his mother's care. Personally, she thought she'd overcome a touchy situation with this brilliant plan.

Sam might think differently.

"Well, actually, it has been a little quiet at the mansion."

Elizabeth smiled. "Having nothing to do driving you up the wall?"

Emma returned the gesture. "I'm not used to having a lot of time on my hands, and there's only so much I can stand to do at the house at this time." She winced at the thought of all the clutter and boxes. Then there was Lully's business . . . it all felt overwhelming to deal with by herself.

"I can offer a few hours a week. As you can see, it's a very small store and we don't sell everything. No magazines, and the only paperbacks are the ones on the best-seller list. Mostly hardbacks, old and new, and some collectors' volumes."

Emma nodded, her gaze traveling the cozy interior of the store. "You've made this a lovely place."

"Would you be flexible on the hours you could work?"

"Absolutely."

"Because I open at nine and close at six, unless someone comes in at the last minute. Then I stay open as long as needed." Elizabeth smiled. "I'm alone and have no one to consider except myself, so the hours are never a problem for me."

"Me neither," Emma said. "I have no one but myself to look after. And Gismo."

"Ah, yes. Little Gismo. Intuitive little soul. Well, then," Elizabeth said, ripping off the receipt after Emma's purchase had cleared with the credit-card company, "why don't you come by on Monday and I'll put you to work a few hours. It might be only dusting, watering the plants, unpacking a few new books for the best-seller section."

Emma signed the credit-card receipt. "That's fine. I work with plants in Seattle. I'm a horticulturist."

"How nice. We might think about how to decorate for Christmas, maybe a little earlier than I usually do. What do you think about having a nice live green display in the front window?"

Emma studied the space. "That could be done and be very lovely."

Elizabeth handed Emma the shopping bag with the name Elizabeth's Corner in black script printed on a slant. "Around ten then?"

"Ten will be fine. Thank you."

"Down, Gismo. Don't be so greedy," Emma scolded as she scraped the Alpo can clean while trying to avoid the dog's lapping tongue.

The little dog gobbled the meaty chunks as if he hadn't eaten in days, and then scooted the bowl around in a circle, licking it clean.

Though she'd been appalled at first to have responsibility for the dog, Emma found she kind of enjoyed having Gismo greet her whenever she returned to the house. She'd never been as fond of animals as Lully was. When they were young, every stray dog or cat that ended up at the Mansi house turned into Lully's newest pet. Emma was almost surprised that Gismo had been Lully's only companion.

Emma dumped the empty dog-food can in the trash. What had Lully done with her money? It seemed she'd had a sizable income from the jewelry she sold, though Emma couldn't determine the amount, since she couldn't get into the computer files and couldn't find a ledger of any kind. New jewelry orders arrived in the mail each day, but without more information Emma didn't attempt to fill orders. Jewelry supplies came in, and she set the boxes on Lully's workbench as if life went on, which for Lully didn't. As youngsters, they'd learned to stretch a dollar, so it was likely that even with buying a computer and all the books that were stacked around and the colorful clothes, Lully had not spent everything she made. Lully must have had a lot of money, but the bequests in the will had been small.

Other than the house, there was nothing of value.

Gismo trotted to the trash and nosed around. Emma nudged him away with her foot. "Go play."

Gismo looked up, wagging his tail as if to say, "I was just checking." He missed Lully, she knew. At night he would go through the house, peeking into corners, peering into rooms. Once she'd found him in the middle of Lully's bed, his chin on his paws, looking so pitiful she almost cried. She'd picked him up and held him, fighting her own tears. How could an animal be expected to understand that his "person" was gone, when Emma didn't understand it herself?

The morning stretched before her. There were things to do: clean out closets and drawers, pack Lully's personal things away, choose what things should go to a local charity. But she didn't want to do those things. Not today.

When the church bell tolled, Emma glanced at the clock. That was a familiar sound, one that brought a rush of memories. They'd never gone to Sunday school or church. "We can worship the Lord right here," Lully would say when Emma asked why they couldn't go to services. Then she'd pull out the old Bible that had been their mother's, and Lully would read Scripture and talk about its meaning until they heard the noon bell.

It wasn't until she was a teenager that Emma learned that Lully would have loved to join her neighbors, dressed in their Sunday best, greeting one another in front of the church before going in to sit together, pray together, sing together. But Lully couldn't bear the stares, the silent questions, and the gossip. So she stayed home and tried to instill God's teachings into a questioning younger sister. Emma wasn't sure her sister's attempts had been successful. She'd didn't know who God was anymore. He certainly wasn't the kind of "personal" God that Lully had written about in her letters in recent years. God didn't talk to her, as he seemed to do to Lully. Emma drew a long, deep breath of decision. Well, maybe it was time to see if he talked to others in Serenity.

The church bell finished tolling as she left the kitchen and went upstairs. A few minutes later she was downstairs again, wearing the only suit she'd brought, the dark blue one that she'd worn to Lully's service.

"You watch the house," she told Gismo, then locked the front door behind her.

It was a cool morning. The heater in the car felt good as she drove to the church that sat at the end of Aspen Street. She could imagine that a church had sat there since the town was accidentally founded. A bright sun shone on the picturesque setting. Like many old towns, a Gothic-style courthouse sat in the middle of the town square. Aspen Street ran in one direction, with the church at one end. Noble Street ran in the other direction, toward the newer residential section of town. In the older section, smaller Victorian-style houses dotted the curbs, some built at the end of World War II when veterans were returning home to build lives for themselves and establish families. Centered on the square were the shops—The Bread Shop, Willis's Grocery, Elizabeth's Corner, and Brisco's Café. Lott's Restaurant was newer and located at the opposite end of Noble Street. Ford's Insurance Agency, now owned by a third-generation Ford, was on one corner, Howard's Pharmacy that Bruce Gold had owned, on the other. The name had never made sense to Emma, but she supposed a man named Howard had owned the establishment before Sam's father bought it. Miller's Dry Cleaning was next door to Howard's, and Rockies Realty. A Piggly Wiggly grocery was a block off the square, new to Emma. She'd overheard someone say it had been there ten years.

Then there was Floralee Harris's Cut & Curl, where Floralee's daughter worked as a manicurist and answered the phone. Emma smiled, remembering the time Floralee had fried her hair with one of her "sale" permanents. Emma's hair had looked like an electrified Brillo pad. She had cried for hours until Lully had taken pity on her. She'd cut Emma's hair in a boyish style that Emma wasn't sure was an improvement, especially when the kids at school stopped in midstep and gaped at the drastic change. She absently ran her hand through her thick, shining locks. She hadn't had a permanent since.

Emma parked beside the church and, drawing a deep breath for courage, got out, walked up the steps, and slipped into a back pew. At the front, an older man waved a hand in the air, directing a hymn: "'Joyful, joyful . . .'"

She picked up a hymnal and joined in. Two couples in the back pews turned to look and blinked when she began to sing. Apparently a new voice drew attention.

When the hymn ended, Emma sat down, aware that news of her return was quietly spreading. Why had she come this morning? Maybe to feel a little closer to Lully, though as far as she knew, her sister hadn't stepped foot inside the church. Still, there was something here that drew her. Not curiosity, yet she felt a need to understand what people found in church. Lully had searched for God yet never looked here. It was the central location people generally went to seek him, wasn't it? Why was that? A wood-and-stucco building with four walls and a choir loft? Was this the only place God existed? Somehow Emma felt he lived in one's heart.

Emma soon became aware of a man sitting at the end of the pew studying her. He discreetly sneaked periodic looks her way as they stood to sing again and when they sat to listen to announcements. She didn't recognize him, but then, she wouldn't. There were few familiar faces, for which she could only be grateful. Serenity was fortunate, it seemed, in that several new families had moved in. They chose to work in Durango but live in a small-town atmosphere like Serenity.

The minister was the same man who had performed Lully's service. His message was simple and tied to Scripture, so Emma prepared to listen and perhaps gain something. His words had comforted her at the cemetery, and something deep inside her needed comforting today.

This morning the message went straight to her heart. Selecting a text from 1 Corinthians 13, the pastor reminded the congregation that of all the commands God had given, love was the key to real peace and contentment. There had been little love in Emma's life; yet as she let the words linger in her mind she realized that perhaps she had pushed love aside far too many times. How many opportunities to love had God placed in her path the past few years that she had conveniently sidestepped to continue in self-pity? She didn't want to think of herself as self-pitying—she wasn't shallow or lacking in compassion. She had friends like Janice and Sue whom she loved, yet a troubling part of her wanted to blame someone for the last fifteen years. Love could suffocate in a hostile environment.

The minister greeted people as they left at the end of the service. When Emma would have sneaked past, he reached out to her. "I'm so glad to see you here on this glorious Lord's Day."

"Thank you," Emma managed, taking the hand he offered. She felt foolish, not knowing what she'd expected to gain from attending a church service. She felt out of place and hated it.

Stepping out into the bright sunlight, she shaded her eyes and caught a glimpse of Sam escorting his mother to a brown sedan. Edwina Gold had aged. She handed Sam her cane and slowly eased into the front passenger seat. Sam closed the door and turned, catching sight of Emma. He hesitated briefly before striding around the car and getting in on the driver's side. She watched the car disappear down Spruce Avenue.

"Miss Mansi?"

Emma jumped nervously and saw the smallish man who had been staring at her in church. Thin, with a receding hairline and wire-rimmed glasses, he was dressed in a brown tweed suit and white tennis shoes. He held out a pale hand, the kind unaccustomed to physical labor.

"I'm Ray Sullins."

Curious, Emma finally took his hand.

"I knew your sister. I was her . . . friend."

"I'm happy to meet one of her friends."

He hung his head. "I loved Lully." His childlike demeanor made Emma realize that he was shy and a bit slow.

His eyes teared and Emma suddenly felt uncomfortable with his obviously deep grief. She hesitated and then reached out to touch his arm. "Thank you. I . . . loved her too. I'm sorry for your loss."

Lully had never mentioned Ray, which made Emma wonder if they'd truly been friends. Perhaps Ray only imagined the friendship, since she'd never known her sister to have a close relationship with anyone. If he and Lully had been friends, why hadn't Lully mentioned him? In fact, Emma couldn't remember a single person Lully had written about.

Ray sniffled, then dragged a handkerchief from his pocket to dab at his eyes. "I–I used to go to the house and sit with her. We'd sit in the porch swing and talk. Lully was a good talker and a good listener."

"I'm sure she enjoyed your company."

He nodded, tears rolling down his cheeks. "We had a good time. Sometimes we'd take cheese and crackers out there and have a picnic. I like picnics."

"I do too," Emma said, feeling her throat grow tight.

"I like that old house."

"You know she left the house to me and . . . and the sheriff."

He brightened. "Are you gonna keep it? That's Lully's house. Lully loved that house."

"I–I don't know." She looked away. "I may have to sell it."

"Sell it?" His face fell, bewilderment seeping into his eyes. He didn't seem to understand. She didn't, either.

"I live in Seattle. Sam, Sam Gold, thinks we should sell it."

He shook his head. "Oh, Lully wouldn't like that."

"She knew I lived in Seattle. I work there."

"In a greenhouse. You grow plants."

Emma was surprised by his knowledge. "Yes. I grow plants."

"Your momma used to grow flowers in the yard. Roses. Lully couldn't grow flowers like your momma, but she always said, 'Ray, those roses will bloom again.'" His eyes shimmered with grief. "I believe her. Lully always told me the truth."

This Ray person knew a lot more about Lully and their family than Emma would ever have suspected. The thought made Emma a little curious.

"If there's anything I can do—any way I can help . . ." Ray offered.

"Thank you. I appreciate that."

He fished in his pocket and pulled out a marble, a shiny red-and-black agate, and gave it to Emma.

Emma took the gift, feeling a little foolish. "Thank you."

"You're welcome."

Emma suddenly realized they were blocking the flow of people coming out of the church.

"I've got to go now. It's nice to meet one of Lully's friends."

"She was a good friend," he said. He shuffled off slowly down the walk.

Emma went to the car, wondering about the strange little man. He was surely older than Lully—perhaps by as much as ten years. He appeared simple, where Lully always had a thirst for knowledge. Emma tried to picture the two together and decided maybe their friendship wasn't as odd as she'd first thought. They were both "different." Opposites in many ways, yet alike in others. Perhaps Lully had found a soul mate in Ray Sullins. Maybe Ray had brought a measure of love, a sense of happiness to Lully's last days. Emma hoped that was so.

That afternoon Emma thought about tackling the dining room when Sam called. "I talked with Ned Piece today."

Emma nudged Gismo out of the trash with the toe of her tennis shoe. "Who's Ned Piece?"

"Rockies Realty. He can take a look at the house tomorrow morning if you're available."

"All right—before ten o'clock."

Dead silence followed her remark. Then Sam chuckled. She shut her eyes against the warm memories that threatened her resolve to forget about Sam Gold other than in terms of an unwilling real-estate partner. She could hear a fax machine reeling off a transmission in the background; he was calling from the sheriff's office.

"Do you self-destruct at ten o'clock?" Sam asked with another chuckle.

"No. I took a part-time job."

"You what?"

"Took a part-time job at the bookstore."

"At Elizabeth's Corner?"

"How many bookstores are there in Serenity?"

"I thought you would be eager to leave as soon as possible."

Was that a hopeful tone she heard in his voice? *Just your imagination, Emma.* "I'm staying only until I can get the house cleared out and Lully's estate settled." She thought about the jewelry orders and the new shipment of supplies that just came in. What on earth was she to do about Lully's jewelry business?

"What about your job in Seattle?"

"That's the nice thing about being your own boss." Emma hefted herself onto the kitchen counter and stared down at Gismo, who seemed to question why she was sitting on the counter.

"Elizabeth doesn't have enough business to keep her busy. She likes it that way. Why would she hire you?"

"I do have some qualifications," she reminded, irritated by the question.

"For growing flowers," he returned.

Emma bit her tongue. Sarcasm wouldn't get her anywhere, and

she was starting to look forward to their chats. "It's only through Christmas. It helps Elizabeth during the busy season and gives me something to do for a couple hours a day."

There was another moment of silence. "Mom asked about you this morning."

Well, that was the last thing she expected to hear. The change of subject threw her. She curled the phone cord around her finger. "How is Edwina?"

"Broke her hip last year. It's slowed her down."

Edwina Gold had always been an active woman. As mayor of Serenity she'd been something to deal with, pushing plans through city council with a strong will, practically dragging the city offices into the twentieth century by herself. The woman had never particularly liked the Mansi family because they didn't fit the mayor's profile of families who should live in Serenity. And she'd definitely not liked Emma after she and Sam had tried to elope. The mayor had plans for her sons and Emma Mansi didn't fit into them, certainly not as a daughter-in-law.

"I'm sorry to hear that," Emma said politely. "That must be difficult for her."

"It is." There was a pause. "Emma?"

She held her breath. The soft slide of his baritone caused a familiar ache in her heart. "Yes?"

"I really don't want to fight you on this house. I'm willing to do whatever it takes for us both to make a sound business decision."

"Me too," she admitted. "But you know how I feel."

"I do know how you feel, and I respect it. I only want the best for both of us. Okay?"

Why did he have to be so nice? It was much less complicated when he blocked her every move. And now she was feeling guilty about Ned Piece looking at the house. . . . But it hadn't been appraised, ever, and they needed a base to start from if the worst happened and the new parking lot won out over the tearoom.

"Okay—I want the same." Vulnerability had crept into her voice. She hoped he hadn't detected it.

"By the way, you're not having any trouble with pranksters, are you? This time of year they gave Lully a lot more trouble. Ken and I will be patrolling the area on Halloween night more than usual, but the kids are resourceful. They find a way to make trouble, especially in that old cemetery."

"I'll be fine. I'd heard Kenny was your deputy."

"Yes, he is."

"Working with family must be nice. Any little nieces or nephews running around?"

It was the first personal question she'd asked, and she was sorry now that she had. The less she knew about Sam's personal life the easier it would be.

"Ken isn't married."

The logical question would be for her to ask *his* marital state— Emma hadn't heard and Lully never mentioned if he'd married or not. But a phone ringing in the background saved her the embarrassment.

"I've got to go," he said. "I'll bring Ned over about nine in the morning—oh, by the way, I'm not married, either, in case that was what you were leading up to."

She hung up. *Ohhhhh.*

"Gismo, you're looking at an idiot. Why did I ask Sam Gold that kind of question?" *Any nieces and nephews running around?* She might as well have asked, "Any ring on your third finger, left hand?" Naturally she had looked, but some men didn't wear wedding bands.

She'd been about as subtle as a baseball-size hailstone.

Sam dropped the receiver back in its cradle and stared at the phone, oblivious to the sounds of office equipment around him or the answering machine clicking on for the call he'd ignored. Emma had asked if Ken had children, if he had a family? *No, Emma. I don't have a family. You were supposed to be my family.*

He drew a deep breath of resignation. He'd seen Emma at

church this morning, but he hadn't spoken to her there. His mother wasn't feeling well and wanted to get back to the nursing home.

What would it have been like to sit beside Emma in church, to share that experience with her? Church and God had been important to him since he'd started going to chapel while in the marines. The surroundings were crude, but it hadn't made a difference. He'd learned there what a true relationship with God was and had never lost the security of it.

He had to smile sometimes when he remembered how he prayed to find Emma after she left Serenity, and then prayed for peace when it was clear she wasn't coming back. Then he prayed she would remain safe and maybe one day she'd return.

Now she had . . . and he wasn't sure it was the answer he wanted. *What, God? What is it you're trying to do here? Is there something I'm supposed to learn from this?*

If there was, he wasn't getting it.

THE WIND came up late that evening as Emma was getting ready for bed. The howl through the eaves of the old house brought back memories of cowering under the covers with Lully for comfort when she was little. Shivering, Emma stood at the bedroom window, arms crossed over her stomach. Ezra's headstone shone in the moonlight. She wondered how she had ever considered this a normal setting. The house creaked with age. Lightning flashed in the distance and a low rumble shook the rafters. A full-blown fall storm was brewing over the mountains and would soon sweep down upon the sleeping town.

She pulled the drapes closed and sat on the side of the bed. Gismo settled on the rug next to the bed, his cockeyed gold eyes peering up at her. She bent and scratched behind his ears, then decided she wasn't ready to go to sleep yet. Instead, she went back downstairs for a Coke and some popcorn. She'd watch a *Cheers* rerun on the old television.

Just as she flipped on the kitchen light, a huge thunderclap shook the house. Cringing, she found a package of Jiffy Pop and turned on a stove burner. The rattle of popping corn would drown out the storm. A few minutes later she'd just turned off the burner when she heard it.

In the basement. Glass breaking.

Her heart shot into her throat. She held the Jiffy Pop package suspended in air. Listening. The refrigerator kicked on. Emma stood very still, ear tuned for other sounds. Had Gismo somehow gotten into the basement? She didn't think so. She'd never opened the door.

Emma turned slowly. The basement door was firmly closed. Rats? Could it be? She shuddered. There had been rodents in the basement once, and she and Lully had set traps. That was it. Rats.

Another sound, less distinct. Muffled, as if someone . . . something . . . was moving down there.

Kids. It had to be kids. Sam had warned her that this close to Halloween kids would be playing pranks, trying to scare her. She could call him— No. She wouldn't call him. He wouldn't be at the office anyway. It was Sunday. He didn't work Sundays. He was probably with someone. She found that thought strangely disturbing.

She heard the sound again. This time it sounded distinctly like footsteps, as if someone was down there walking around.

A clap of thunder boomed, seeming to come right inside the house, and she jumped. Her glass of Coke went flying, smashing against the floor, splattering onto her robe. Rain spattered against the window like needles. Forgetting her fear, Emma grabbed a cloth and mopped at the sticky liquid. Her slippers were Coke-soaked.

Then she heard the sound again. *Bang! Bang!*

That sound she identified as an open window slamming in the wind. All the basement windows were closed. Had been for years. But someone had gotten in, and now whoever it was was gone but had left the window open. The sound of her glass breaking must have scared him off. Well, that was good, she decided.

Emma located a flashlight in a drawer and switched it on, amazed that the batteries were strong. Gathering her nerve, she eased the basement door open. A cold breeze came up the stairs, making her wet feet even colder. She had to close that window and check things out. The logical thing to do would be to call Sam and ask him to investigate. But she wouldn't do that. She could take care of this herself. After all, it was probably kids and they'd gotten scared when they found she was still awake.

The window banged in the wind again, and Emma found herself praying, *Dear God, please let it be the window and not somebody down there trying to scare me.*

Funny, she hadn't talked to God in years. Would he even recognize her name now? *Hi, I'm Emma. Remember me? I used to pray . . . I'm one of your lost sheep.* Lully had used the lost sheep picture hanging in the living room as one of her Sunday lessons, telling Emma that when a sheep was lost, Jesus brought it back to the fold. Emma hadn't known what a fold was, but she'd guessed it had something to do with the robe Jesus wore. She had been so naïve. Lully had tried to instill some knowledge of God in her, but Emma guessed it hadn't taken very well.

Why would Jesus know her? Emma wondered. It wasn't logical. He certainly had more worthy subjects to address. This particular sheep had never really been in the fold in the first place. Not like the sheep in the picture. Back then Emma had wanted so badly to be one of the sheep in the picture. Maybe not the one Jesus held, but perhaps one of those behind him. Jesus looked kind and gentle. His hands, she imagined, were strong as he cradled the sheep so gently, as if that one meant more than any of the others.

Lightning flashed again and Emma jumped. Thunder rolled as she started down the stairs. She would not call Sam. This was her house. She'd lived in it for years. Why should she be afraid? She'd already made it plain she didn't need help. Closing a basement window wasn't exactly a crisis. And a thunderstorm didn't warrant a 911 call. Still, the thought of having a six-foot-plus pillar of muscle standing between her and whatever was down there in the basement appealed to her. After all, her great-grandparents had embalmed people down there—

No. I won't call him.

Emma eased down the staircase, sending light into all corners as she descended. A musty smell filtered up and the stairs creaked ominously. When was the last time Lully had gone into the basement? Were the stairs safe?

Bang!

This is ridiculous, Emma decided and went down another step. Holding tight to the wooden handrail, she inched her way down the nine stairs, her sodden slippers making a squishing sound. Finally she stepped onto solid ground. She stood still, allowing her eyes to adjust to the darkness. The flashlight was unable to penetrate the dark corners.

There it was again. The hair on the nape of her neck stood up. *Bang!* She jumped and nearly dropped the flashlight. Focusing the beam on the window, she saw immediately that it was indeed the window banging open. The latch hung almost off the frame.

Several boxes were stacked beneath the window, blocking her intent to reach it and somehow lean something against it to keep it closed. She laid the flashlight on the nearest carton and shoved a smaller one aside. The boxes were heavy, and she had to move them by using the calves of her legs to leverage them into an opposite corner to clear a path to the window.

Rain was pouring in, soaking the boxes. Maneuvering herself toward the window, she bumped into another box, causing the flashlight to roll off and fall to the floor behind the boxes.

Grumbling beneath her breath, she climbed on top of one of the containers, trying to reach the flashlight that was still beaming. She lost a slipper somewhere between two boxes but decided to find it after retrieving the flashlight. The storm raged outside, sending periodic flashes of lightning through the cobweb-covered rafters. The flashes were too brief for her to get a good look at where the flashlight lay. Cold air burst into the basement with every swing of the broken window, creeping into her bones. Images of rats played through Emma's mind.

Reaching with a grunt, she fumbled between the boxes in search of the flashlight. Jammed between the boxes, the cylinder was an inch from her fingers. She flexed her fingers, almost willing her arm to stretch enough to reach the light. She had to get it! She didn't want to climb those stairs in the dark, barefoot—well, half barefoot.

Straining . . . straining . . . the tips of her fingers brushed the metal, but she managed only to dislodge it so that it tipped and rolled farther toward the wall.

Shoving herself upright, Emma buried her face in her hands. *Keep cool, Emma. It's a basement. A place where you and Lully used to play on rainy days.* She didn't remember all these boxes being here, but maybe they had been. She'd have to go through them, probably throw out a ton of junk.

A scurrying sound sent a ripple of fear over her skin.

I have to do this, she told herself. *The window is broken; someone could get in—again. Rain will soak these boxes, ruining whatever is inside them. The window has to be wedged closed . . . tonight.* She drew a deep breath. *But I can't get to the window without help*, she finally had to admit. *I can call a repairman tomorrow, first thing.* But the thought of sleeping all night with the window wide open was not one she wanted to contemplate.

"Okay," she whispered, gathering more nerve. "Think. Reason this out. If you can't get to the window, it's unlikely anyone would, could, get in over the boxes without making some racket. So, you'll listen more carefully."

She eased off the box, trying to get her bearing in the lightning flashes. She could still see a sliver of the flashlight's beam. Now, the steps were to the left . . . a few yards away. No problem. *You can do this, Emma Mansi. You're in your own house, after all.*

Putting her slippered foot on the floor, she slid off the box and hopped a couple of feet, hardly touching the toes of her bare foot to the floor. Standing there, she plotted her course. Four hops to the left and that should bring her to the railing.

One hop.

Two, three hops. Thunder rolled and lightning flashed. The window whipped back and forth. *Bang!* Something skittered across her foot. She froze, swallowing hard, praying it was her imagination. She was cold. Goose bumps rose on her skin. *Maybe a mouse,* she told herself, hoping it was just a mouse. She could handle mice. It was rats she couldn't abide, but she hadn't actually seen any rats.

She was ready to take another hop when something definitely crawled across her foot and started up her ankle. This was not imagination!

Screaming, she kicked out, trying to dislodge it. Something else was crawling up her leg! Then on her bare foot! Crawly things, clinging to her feet and legs, crawling under her housecoat!

Stamping her feet, she stumbled toward the stairs. Dancing to dislodge whatever was crawling on her, she batted at her hair where she felt something moving. Plop! Something landed on the step in front of her. She screamed again, leaped over the step and scrambled awkwardly up the stairs, batting at her hair, shaking her feet, cracking both shins on the painted wood in her hasty flight. She burst through the door and slammed it, flicking the lock. Her sudden entrance into the kitchen made Gismo jump and bark.

Hysteria clawed at her throat as Emma leaned against the door trying to breathe. What was that! Rats? No. She'd heard not a squeak. There would have been squeaking. Finally able to breathe, she opened her eyes. Dare she get another flashlight and look? Anything could have come in through the window . . . but what was that crawling all over her? Sam. She had to call Sam!

No. She needed to handle this herself. She wasn't a child. She was a grown woman, a responsible woman. She didn't need anyone to hold her hand.

She drew a deep breath. Maybe it was just her imagination. After all, it was a stinky basement with cobwebs. She expected to find creepy things down there. The mind could play cruel tricks.

Emma sank onto a kitchen chair and ran her fingers into her hair to make sure there wasn't anything there. How many times had Lully experienced this kind of fear? How many times had she sat up all night because something scared her, because she was afraid someone was either in the huge old house or would get into the house?

This time she knew what the noise had been. Wind blowing through a broken window. That was all. The wind causing a draft to blow across her feet . . . and her hair. That was all.

Taking another deep breath, Emma opened a drawer and got a second flashlight. With some determination, she unlocked the basement door again, easing it open . . . just in case. Holding her robe close so the hem wrapped around her knees, she stepped down one step. Then another. She flashed the beam one step in front of her . . . nothing.

Imagination, Emma. It's just your imagination. She went down another step, then another. Six, seven steps. *Be careful, Emma. The steps aren't too secure.* Eight steps. She paused, running the beam of the flashlight across the concrete floor.

The floor was dark. And moving! Her heart stopped.

"No!" The word clawed from her throat.

Spiders! Huge, black spiders. Crawling over each other, swarming at the bottom of the steps. At least . . . fifty? More. Furry legs lifting, seeking, probing the stair to get a foothold. Her skin crawled and she searched her hair again to make certain there wasn't one still lurking there. She recalled the feel of their furry bodies on her feet, crawling up her legs, beneath her robe—

She spun and bolted back up the stairs, slammed the door, and shot the lock firmly in place. She closed her eyes, struggling to catch a breath, her heart pounding, her skin prickling with fear.

Maybe she wasn't so adult after all.

Sam was early. He and Ned drove up at eight forty-five the next morning. Emma watched him stride from the patrol car toward the house. She studied his immaculate appearance. Was there someone who picked up his dry cleaning, who called to remind him the alarm had gone off twenty minutes earlier? There was no Mrs. Gold, and maybe there wasn't even a "special woman" in Sam's life, though she couldn't imagine it. But he did seem to work a lot of hours. Perhaps no one would put up with him being at the sheriff's office nights and occasional weekends. At least he'd not admitted there was anyone in his life. But then, why would he tell her if there was?

Buttoning the last button on her ivory blouse, Emma finished dressing on her way to answer Sam's knock. She glanced at the grandfather clock on her way down the hall. She hadn't had coffee yet . . . and she needed some after the night she'd spent curled up on the couch, making sure her feet didn't touch the floor.

"Get back, Gismo," she admonished.

The dog stayed at her heels, growling. Emma turned the dead bolt and pulled the sticky door open with a pop. Sam and another man, who wore a blue blazer with the name Rockies Realty stitched on the pocket, were giving the unkempt yard a good once-over. The other man turned and flashed a wide smile.

When Sam turned, Emma's breath caught. He was so good-looking; Sam Gold had become a lady-killer. When had that happened? At seventeen he'd been cute, with curling hair a bit too long to be fashionable. But cute had evolved into rugged, masculine looks that could turn any woman's head.

Memory tugged at her.

Give me a kiss, Emma girl.

Stop it, Sam. Someone will see us.

So? Let them. I want everyone to know that Sam Gold loves Emma Mansi.

Really? You . . . you love me?

Really. Always, Emma. For always.

Always hadn't lasted as long as she'd hoped. One school year. At fourteen she had reached out to Sam as her lifeline. He was the one person she could count on. The one person who loved her, really loved her. Momma had loved her, of course, but she'd died. Dad had loved her enough to stay for a while, but he'd left without a backward glance. No one even knew what happened to him. Lully had been in her own world. So Sam had been her anchor, the thing that held her together for a while.

Perhaps she had become too emotionally dependent on him.

But at the time she desperately needed someone to lean on. Everywhere she looked there were families—brothers and sisters, moms and dads—all part of a unit. They shopped together, went to movies together, attended school functions together. But she had walked snowy sidewalks at night, alone, looking into store windows at the holiday decorations, looking in the windows of houses where people lived together, catching a glimpse of what families should be. Maybe she'd see moms and dads eating dinner together or watching television. At Christmas they'd be stringing lights outside or decorating the Christmas tree in the front window of the house. Sometimes she'd see a mother washing dishes in the kitchen with a daughter drying, or the father in the living room reading his paper.

Envy. That's all she could call it. She had been envious of those people and resentful that her life could never be that way. She'd tried not to feel resentment. She told herself she was lucky to have Lully. She wouldn't have wanted to go to a foster home where she wouldn't really belong. With Sam she'd found new hope. With him her dreams could come true. But then, it was all gone. Gone a long time ago.

"You're early." She pushed open the screen.

"Sorry, but Ned had the time right now. Is there a problem?" Ned Piece smiled at her. "Rockies Realty at your service."

Emma smiled. "Thank you—come in. There's no problem," she said to Sam. No problem except she had this crazy urge to ask him to put his arms around her and hold her. No problem except a basement full of spiders.

"Ned Piece, Emma Mansi."

Ned stepped inside and extended his hand at the same time. "Miss Mansi, my deepest sympathy."

"Thank you." She avoided Sam's gaze. "Shall we go into the kitchen? There's a table we can work at, and I've made a fresh pot of coffee."

The two men trailed her toward the back of the house.

"Fine old house," Ned commented, his gaze scanning the

yellowed walls and fourteen-foot ceilings. "Used to be a funeral parlor, didn't it?"

"My great-grandparents ran a funeral home from this house. My grandparents lived here, then my parents."

"Can't find that kind of workmanship anymore," he said, nodding at the wide woodwork, the carved roses at the corners of each door frame. The Realtor pulled out a chair and sat down at the table, opening his briefcase to extract a file of forms. "You probably don't know much about the time it was a funeral home."

"Only the stories I heard from my grandmother, who died when I was about eight or nine." She didn't plan to elaborate.

"Yes, well, it's still a fine old house."

Sam opened a cabinet door. "Coffee, Ned?"

"Yes, thanks. Black."

Emma watched Sam pour three cups. In one he added two teaspoons of sugar and added the right amount of cream. He set that cup in front of Emma, catching and holding her gaze for a long moment. Her mouth went dry. He grinned as if he could read her mind. She felt her face flush and pulled her gaze from his. Sam set a cup of black coffee in front of Ned, keeping the third for himself as he sat at the end of the table, adjacent to Emma.

"What do you think the place is worth, Ned?"

Emma shot Sam a dark look, remembering why he was here. They hadn't discussed price. She didn't even want to think about the details of selling, though last night's experience should have made her reconsider. What Ned might think the house was worth might be vastly different from her opinion.

"Needs some work," he commented, his gaze sweeping the kitchen.

"Some," she agreed. *A little extermination here and there.*

"You might think about that. Anything you can do will help." Ned's pen poised over the long form. "How many rooms?"

"Fifteen."

Ned let out a low whistle. "Baths?"

"Two."

"There's a bunch of porches, aren't there? I think I remember—" Ned squirmed in his chair, peering out the window through the back door pane to get a better look at the service porch. A frown knitted his heavy brows. "This where they used to wheel 'em out?"

"That's the service porch. There's a sunporch off the parlor."

"Oh." He seemed to digest the information. "Sunporch, huh. What's it called now?"

Emma glanced at Sam, who was concentrating on his coffee cup. "Sunporch."

"Okay. Fifteen rooms, two baths, sunporch." He checked spaces on the form. "What else?"

"Basement. Attic."

"Garage?"

"Detached. Triple. Room enough for two hearses or a horse-drawn carriage. Maybe a caisson or two," she said, unable to keep the sarcasm out of her voice.

Sam gave her a cool look. "Oversized garage, Ned. Full-sized car and a pickup fit easily, plus space for a riding lawn mower and a workbench."

"Good, good," Ned murmured, writing the information on the form. "I'll do some measuring." He took a tape measure and scratch pad out of his briefcase. "Be back in a jif."

Ned left, starting to work in the large dining room. Emma could hear him pull out the metal tape and flop it on the wood floor. He wrote down measurements, both length and width, then went on to the next room, nearly stumbling over a barking Gismo, who apparently wasn't happy to have a stranger in his house. Sam refreshed his coffee and sat back down.

"I'll be glad when this is over," Emma murmured, resting her elbows on the table. She shoved her fingers into her hair and rested her forehead on her palms.

Just having the house appraised was going to be harder than she'd thought. For her, Lully was still here. Lully's clothes hung in the closets; some were strewn here and there in her room. Her candles and incense were still on the shelves. Gismo was here, looking for Lully every night and every morning. What would Emma do about Gismo? She couldn't take him back to Seattle. Her apartment building didn't allow pets, and she couldn't afford higher rent. Besides, he'd never lived anywhere else . . . not since he was a puppy. It wouldn't be fair to take him away from familiar surroundings. He'd have an even harder time adjusting.

Sam sipped his coffee. Early morning sunshine dotted the old worn linoleum. Emma had scrubbed it on her hands and knees the day before, but the pattern was so worn and faded it still looked dirty. She wondered if Sam noticed, then wondered why she cared.

"You look awful. Didn't you sleep well last night?"

Sleep? She hadn't slept at all. Every time she closed her eyes she saw spiders crawling up her legs.

"Thanks," she muttered.

A slow, mischievous grin spread across his face. "I didn't mean you didn't look good, just tired." He sobered, his gaze touching her face. "You look great, Emma."

He sat forward, setting his cup on the table, then reached out to brush his knuckles along her cheek line. Granite against silk. She liked the feel. "This has been hard for you." His voice was soft, brushing against her senses. "Lully. The house. All these changes."

Changes. Yes. Changes in her. In him. Everything was changing, and that frightened her. Change meant loss, and she couldn't stand any more losses.

"Why didn't you sleep?" he asked gently.

She shuddered and then met his gaze, wishing he were still touching her. Wishing there were no questions, no doubts, that he would just hold her, tell her everything was going to be all right. But it wasn't ever going to be all right. "I had a bad night."

"Why? Did the storm bother you? You never liked them."

He remembered. "That was it . . . at first."

He frowned. "Did something happen? I told you to call me—"

"No . . . yes . . ." She drew a deep breath. "Spiders."

The softness in his eyes changed. "Spiders?"

"In the basement."

Concern darkened his craggy features. "What kind of spiders?"

"Big ones. Hairy ones." She rubbed her arms, trying to soothe the goose bumps.

"What were you doing in the basement last night?"

She drew a deep breath and picked up her coffee cup to warm her fingers. "I thought I heard something. Glass breaking. When I went to investigate I found the storm had blown open the basement window. The latch is broken. The window was banging against the wall, and one pane had shattered. There's a ton of boxes down there in front of the window. The rain was coming in. So I tried to close the window. Shoved some boxes aside and started crawling over the rest to reach the flapping window." She set the cup down. "Of course, I set the flashlight down, and in the course of moving the boxes, I knocked it off and it fell behind the carton. Then it was so dark I couldn't see my hand in front of my face, except for lightning flashes—"

Irritation flashed across his features. "Why didn't you call me?"

Emma shook her head. "I thought it . . . it wasn't necessary. I thought I'd come back upstairs. But when I stepped back onto the floor, I felt something. I thought I'd imagined it. Then I could feel it . . . crawling—" she shivered—"furry things. They were crawling up my legs." She closed her eyes. "I screamed and ran. I didn't know what it was until I managed to get upstairs and convince myself to go look."

"You went back!"

Emma knew that sounded stupid. She hated movies where after a close escape from a crazed man the heroine always went back.

"Only partway down the stairs. I wanted to see if it was real or my imagination. It was real. Spiders. A lot of them. More than fifty, Sam. And I couldn't see them all. Big, huge ones, furry, with those tiny black eyes. The kind you see crossing the highway."

He looked astounded. "Tarantulas?"

"Maybe. Big anyway. I shut the door and stuffed a towel beneath it. I called an exterminator first thing this morning and left a message. Said this was an emergency." She glanced up, hearing Ned moving about in the bedrooms. "Maybe we shouldn't let him go down there until the exterminator gets here."

Sam went to the cellar door.

"No!" Emma hissed. "Don't open that!" She could still feel the furry little legs on her ankles, the airy scurry across her feet.

"I want to see what's down there."

"Do you think I'm lying?" She sprang out of the chair and grabbed his arm. "Spiders are there. Lots of them. They're there. Believe me."

"I believe you," he said, glancing toward the front of the house. He reached for her hand.

His touch was like electricity on her skin, but his soft voice was strong, protective, comforting. Her gaze left his mouth and moved to where his hand clasped hers, before she looked up again..

"I believe you, sweetheart. But I want to take a look at the situation to see what we're dealing with. Tarantulas are not . . . usually . . . in a house, and certainly not in those numbers. It's probably an infestation of those garden spiders, the kind with the gold zigzag on the back. Lully never sprayed for anything. Think you can keep Ned busy upstairs while I take a look?"

"Don't go down there," Emma pleaded, clinging to his hand.

"Em, we can't list the house with fifty spiders in the basement. It will lower the value. Trust me," he said. He squeezed her hand comfortingly. "Now, get a fresh cup of coffee, get a grip, and go upstairs and help Ned measure. Point out assets of the house. Keep him up there until I can see what's going on. Okay?"

He tipped her chin up with his hand and searched her face. Emma memorized every laugh line, every tiny crease fanning out from the corners of his eyes. This was the face that she would see in her dreams. This was Sam.

"Okay?" he whispered.

"I don't want to sell the house." Tears stung her eyes. "I know it's in bad shape; it has spiders, bad memories, but . . ." Oh, there were a million *but*s and he knew them all by now.

Sam released a long breath of resignation. "Emma."

"Please, Sam." She knew she was begging, but she couldn't sell, not this quickly, even if they got an offer they couldn't refuse.

Sam paused, his features drawn. The bleak look on his face assured her he didn't like what he was about to say. "We keep the house on one condition."

Her pulse leaped. "What? Anything."

There was the slightest hesitation. "That you move back here and run the business."

"Anything but that."

"Then no deal. It's not feasible to keep it, Emma. I can't look after it—I don't want to look after it. It causes me enough head-aches trying to keep the kids clear of it."

Hope abandoned her. "That's not fair. I have a job, a life, in Seattle."

"One of us would have to oversee the business. You won't. I can't. It won't work, Emma." His gaze searched her stricken face. "So, what are you going to do? It's up to you."

It was always up to her. There was no one to help her, no one to give her advice. Just ultimatums. She couldn't sell the house, but she couldn't stay here either. She wasn't going to mention Janice until a last alternative. Sam seemed to sense that she wasn't up to a fight or a decision.

"Keep Ned out of the basement for fifteen minutes. That should give me enough time to look around."

"Okay."

Sam kicked the towel away from the bottom of the door and opened it. Emma held her breath, half expecting a hoard of furry things to fall out onto the floor. But nothing happened. Fortu-nately it was light enough down there now that he wouldn't need the single bulb that hung in the center of the room with a pull string. Sam stepped onto the stairway and closed the door.

Emma filled a glass with cool water and drank, then headed

toward the steps leading upstairs, wondering how she was going to keep Ned away from the basement.

Suddenly the basement door burst open and Sam rocketed out, slamming it behind him.

The commotion brought Ned to the stair landing. "Everything all right down there?" he called down.

"It's okay," Emma managed. "Just the wind."

"Spiders," Sam hissed, grabbing Emma's shoulders.

"You saw them?"

"Get out of the house. Get Ned out without letting him know why. I'm calling Pete Lansky to get him over here now." He shoved her toward the front door.

She stumbled over the clean house slippers she'd put on. "What do I say to Ned?"

"Think of something." He turned her to face him, his expression grim. "I don't know how they got down there, but there's a lot of them. Don't come back into this house until Pete gets here."

"Don't worry," she managed, her gaze going toward the second floor where Ned surely was about finished measuring.

"Get rid of Ned, and . . . and go somewhere. Take the dog."

Sam strode out the front door, and she could hear gravel spurt from beneath the squad car's tires as he sped down the lane. Emma shoved the towel back beneath the basement door, shivering. Exactly how did he expect her to get Ned out of the house before Sam returned with the exterminator?

Elizabeth Suitor's eyes widened when she saw Emma practically dragging Ned Piece into the store by one arm, talking a mile a minute.

"Have you read the latest Patterson?"

"Not really." Ned tried to pull from Emma's grasp. "I don't read much, honest." His gaze darted toward the door as if looking for a way of escape. "I really just want to list your house."

Elizabeth left her teacup. "You're a bit early," she commented to Emma.

"Morning, Elizabeth. I brought Ned." Emma smiled gamely, still holding to the man's arm.

"Yes, I see you did. What can I do for you, Ned?"

"Nothing. Nothing." His gaze darted around the shop. "I was measuring Emma's house. She and Sam are listing it. All of a sudden, Sam leaves, tearing off in the squad car, lights flashing, and Emma decides I need to get an early start on Christmas shopping. Books, she said." Ned gave Elizabeth one of those I-don't-have-any-idea-what's-going-on kind of looks.

Emma shrugged off her coat and hung it on a coatrack. "Coffee, Ned?"

"No, thanks. I need to finish that measuring and get back to the office—"

"Nonsense," Emma said.

Elizabeth decided to help Emma with whatever was going on. At the least it must be interesting. She'd never seen Ned so flustered. "Might as well drink a cup, Ned. Since you're here."

Emma dragged the realtor to a shelf. "Do you like Grisham? Robin Cook?"

"No, no," Ned mumbled, taking the cup Elizabeth handed him. "My wife's the reader in the family. I read the sports page and comic strips in the newspaper. That's all."

Paying no attention to Ned's protests, Emma guided him up and down each of the aisles, pointing out books on a wide variety of subjects, chatting with him as if he'd chosen to come in. Not satisfied with that, Emma introduced Ned to the candle section of the shop, handing him a vanilla-scented candle.

Ned sneezed. He pulled a handkerchief from his back pocket and blew his nose. "Allergies," he mumbled around the snow-white cloth. "Can I appraise the house now—possibly list it today?"

"Sorry about those allergies. Terrible time of year for . . . molds." She maneuvered him toward the candy section and the colorful jack-o'-lantern suckers standing among fake tombstones, which were inscribed with REST IN PEACE and DYING TO GET HERE.

Ned shook his head. "Wife's on a diet."

By the time Emma let Ned go, with a promise to let him finish measuring at some unnamed future date, Ned had bought, among other books, a devotional by Charles Stanley on people relationships.

An unmarked van pulled up and parked in front of the Mansi house. Sam's cruiser pulled in behind. Doors slammed. Equipment rolled out of the back of the van and men rushed up the cracked sidewalk. Sam and Pete Lansky disappeared inside the house, slamming the warped door behind them.

Pete peered down the basement stairs, shaking his head. Furry blackish brown spiders made their way back and forth across the floor, attempting to climb the stacks of boxes or find a foothold on the bottom step.

"Those aren't from around here," Pete observed.

"Didn't think so," Sam returned. "How did they get here?"

Pete unrolled a coil of tubing. "Beats me. Seems to me they'd have to be put here."

Sam's lips pursed. "Someone would have had to purposely put them here?"

"Can't think of any other way they'd be here and in such a large number. Ray keeps a few for pets over at the nursing home, but Lully wouldn't have let him bring them there. Never seen anything like this."

"This is the kind of stuff horror movies are made of," Sam observed.

Pete's gaze swept the basement, observing the number of corners and angles. "I'm gonna have to fog the whole area. Might have to do it twice to get them all."

Sam nodded, adjusting his Stetson. "This is one for the books."

Pete nodded. "Tell Emma we'd better keep this to ourselves.

Halloween being close and all, the kids would have a heyday with this."

Sam nodded in agreement. Halloween at the Mansi house was always a headache. This would make it a catastrophe, and Emma didn't need that.

"I'll get on this," Pete said.

"I appreciate it."

Sam left the house and got in the squad car, sitting there for a minute before starting it. *Put there.* Pete's observation rang in his ears as he drove down the lane. In town he saw Ned Piece hurrying down the sidewalk toward his office as if hounds were on his heels, an Elizabeth's Corner bag flopping against his leg. Sam had to smile, wondering what Emma had said to him.

Emma and Elizabeth looked up from where they were sitting on a settee at the front of the shop when Sam stepped in.

"I saw Ned running for his life. What did you say to him?"

Emma grinned and Elizabeth laughed out loud.

"Sam, you should have seen it," Elizabeth said. "Emma dragged that man in here and wouldn't let him go. He said he didn't need a key chain or a framed edition of the Lord's Prayer written with tiny seashells from the Sea of Galilee, but Emma wouldn't listen to him. He kept saying, 'I just want to list your house,' over and over like some kind of litany. Honey," Elizabeth said to Emma, "it's only a spider—every old house has them."

"Not like these, Elizabeth. *Spiders.*" Emma emphasized the plural.

Sam frowned. "But he bought something. I saw the bag."

"A book on relationships," Emma said. "I think he may have thought he needed one on dealing with a crazed woman—"

"And a Patterson novel and a book by Anne Graham Lotz for his wife," Elizabeth added.

Emma chuckled. "And a CD by a group he'd never heard of."

Sam chuckled. "I'll talk to him later. Tell him we're not ready to list the house, that it could stand work." He winked at Emma.

"Yes," Emma agreed, glad for the reprieve. "It needs a little work."

Sam straightened the brim of his hat. "Besides, maybe we should have thought about the repairs earlier."

"Thanks," Emma said softly, her gaze meeting his. "For everything."

He smiled. "You're welcome. We have to stay out of the house until late afternoon. Any problem with that?"

"No," Emma smiled. "I'll keep Elizabeth company." With all those spiders, she wasn't anxious to go back into the house anyway.

chapter
EIGHT

WHEN EMMA finally got around to going home it was already dark. She'd helped Elizabeth unpack new stock, then accompanied the store owner to Brisco's for a bite to eat after the store closed. Sam's cruiser was parked in front of the house when she arrived.

She found him in the basement sweeping up spiders. Shuddering, she stood on the top step and watched him methodically whisk mounds of dead furry stuff into a dustpan. Dozens of the creepy crawlers still littered the concrete floor, tiny feet poking straight up in the air.

"You didn't have to do this," she called. "I can sweep up my own spiders."

He paused, extending her the broom.

She backtracked. "But if you insist." She grinned lamely. "Thank you. I've been dreading the chore all afternoon."

"Just thank you? No, 'Oh my, Sam, I love you! I was dreading the thought of coming down here with all those scary things running around. I will eternally and forever be your slave—'"

"Don't get carried away. I appreciate it, okay?"

He shrugged and winked at her. "Okay. But I get a cup of coffee later."

"Fair enough." Her heart sang. "Maybe I'll throw in a Halloween cookie."

"Maybe you'll throw in a sandwich, too. I haven't eaten."

She smiled. "Maybe. Like Elizabeth says: 'It's only spiders.'" Gratitude swept Emma. Sam didn't have to sweep up the spiders. As cool as she'd been to him lately, he had every right to make her do the unpleasant chore.

"I'll be investigating the incident," Sam told her. "It's only a prank, but I'm not laughing."

"Neither am I."

Emma whirled through the basement door and went into the kitchen to rummage around for a box of cookie dough. "After all," she explained to no one in particular, "it's the least I can do."

"No doubt about it." The glazier slid the new glass pane into place the next morning and held it with his knee while he puttied it in place. "Kids and Halloween are a real headache in this town." Wiping his putty knife on his jeans, he jotted a number in a small spiral notebook. Emma peered over his shoulder, trying to read the entry.

"Fifty-two," he said.

"Fifty-two?"

"Fifty-two times I've replaced this particular pane."

Emma stepped back. "Vandalism must go on here constantly." She kicked a missed dead spider under a box before the glazier spotted it.

"Slows a little toward fall. Kids go back to school, and that keeps them busy for a month or two. Then Halloween rolls around and they're back to their old tricks." Dwayne Potter wiped his hands on a putty-stained cloth. "Lully took most of the pranks in stride, other than the broken window. Rarely got upset until the afternoon Randy Baggers dug up a grave."

He shook his head, his gaze distant with the memory. "It was a hot mid-August. Rained just enough to make the sidewalks steam;

the town hadn't seen a good soaker in months. Gardens and lawns fried in the ninety-plus temperatures. School started the first week of September and the kids needed a last fling. Milt Stars, editor of the *Serenity Local*, posted a warning on the front page that Sunday morning: 'Authorities Warn Cemetery Vandalism Must Stop.'

"Well, that reprimand should have been a little stronger and should have included this house, but it didn't. From what I heard, Lully came out of the house about sunup, carrying a small garden tray with a trowel and hand rake. Her dog was with her. They started down the steps and that dog—" Dwayne pointed at Gismo, who cocked his head to one side as if to say, "Who, me?"—"that dog froze in his tracks, his hair standin' straight up. He commenced to growlin' and Lully, well, Lully was cautious. She peered over the porch rail and right there—" he pointed at the floor—"right there in her eternal slumber was the body of Luella Ludwig, former Serenity librarian until her death fifty-three years earlier. Bones mostly, but her pink hat and gloves were still in pretty good shape.

"Well," he continued, "folks heard Lully's screams two blocks away. Somebody called Sam right off. He came on the run. Folks said Lully was nearly prostrate, her tray of gardening stuff scattered across the lawn. Sam called a town meeting and promised that the culprit would be caught and dealt with severely. 'This whole thing has gotten out of hand,' he said."

The glazier resettled his baseball cap on his balding head and went on. "It wasn't a week before Sam arrested that Crouch boy and two of his friends. The boys spent six months in a juvenile detention center, and when they got back home, they had to mow the cemetery for the next three summers straight. Yessir, Saturday afternoons, rain or shine, them boys did odd jobs for Lully and for Percy Ludwig, Luella's husband. Percy, you know, was too old to get around by then."

Dwayne started putting his tools back in his box. "Didn't stop the pranks, though." The glazier straightened, dragging a handkerchief out of his back pocket. "Mercy. You got her plenty warm in here."

Emma shrugged. She'd opened every window in the house a crack and still the heat was insufferable. "I haven't gotten the hang of that old woodstove yet."

Dwayne wiped his hands. "That should do 'er."

Emma paid for the repair and walked him out to his truck. It was nine-thirty when he rattled off down the street, so she got her coat and walked to the bookstore. Hard maples sported their colors of blazing reds and gold. Multicolored oaks lined the sun-drenched street. Halloween was right around the corner. She dreaded the holiday with all its additional pranks.

Emma drew in crisp mountain air. It was one of those mornings when she felt radiantly alive. Had Lully and Sam experienced the same euphoria? She knew her sister loved to work outside in the early morning. Surely the glorious air influenced her habit. And Sam must have loved his town because he'd chosen to live here when he could have gone anywhere else on earth.

As she entered the bookstore, she spotted Elizabeth crouched on the floor behind a stack of new novels, sorting titles. The shop owner peered over tortoiseshell rims when the bell over the door jingled.

"Emma!" Grunting, Elizabeth got to her feet, right hand pressed to the small of her back. "Glad you're here. These old knees feel like rusty doorknobs against this wood floor."

Emma stripped out of her coat and hung it on a peg in the back room. Returning to the front of the store, she smiled and took a stack of books from Elizabeth's hands. Glancing at the authors' name, she shelved the titles, setting aside the paperback best-sellers for the front rack.

"Everything settle down over at your place?" Elizabeth asked.

"Everything's fine. Sam even stopped by and swept up the dead spiders."

Elizabeth winked at her. "Mighty nice of the sheriff, don't you think? Most folks don't get that kind of personalized treatment."

Emma grinned but didn't answer.

Elizabeth poured a cup of coffee and shook a dab of flavored creamer into the steaming brew. "I imagine you'll be relieved to get rid of that old place." Elizabeth sat down at her desk and leafed through a Christmas catalog.

Emma stopped shelving books for a moment. "It's funny. I thought so, too. I used to think I hated that place, resented Lully. I couldn't wait to leave Serenity and get on my own. And I did. I thought everything would be fine when I left, but it wasn't. Not exactly." She studied the stack of books. "I was away, but I took a lot of it with me. That was scary. Not everything was as simple as I thought it would be. I still haven't found everything I was looking for."

Elizabeth sipped her coffee. "Nobody ever does."

"Don't they? Maybe not. We think, if only I had this or that. If I could lose twenty pounds or change my hair color or grow a prettier perennial. Or if my eyes were green or brown instead of blue, and if my forehead was narrow instead of wide—"

Emma paused. "I thought if I could leave Serenity and forget my childhood, then everything would be wonderful. Life doesn't work that way, does it? We're always us, no matter where we are or what the circumstances are." She picked up a Marry Higgins Clark novel. "Maybe that's not so bad."

"I've never thought so. Life at its worst is still good when you think about it. All the blessings we're given mixed in with the bother." Elizabeth smiled at Emma over the rim of her cup. "Maybe God intends for us to be content with who we are. You think? In my sixty-seven years I have yet to find a better way." She turned a page in the catalog and studied it. "Sam was by earlier."

"Oh?"

Emma's pulse took a leap at the mention of the sheriff. Nothing wrong with that, she told herself. Sam Gold is a fine-looking man, eligible, responsible. The list sounded like a singles advertisement. And he was that. A walking billboard for the perfect eligible bachelor, and probably every uncommitted woman in Serenity was willing to answer the ad.

"Seems you weren't the only one to experience some mischief the other night," Elizabeth continued. "Someone threw a sack of burning manure on the Oateses' front porch. Frank Oates is ready to strangle whoever did it. Ruined his best house slippers stamping out the fire. This morning Fred Tillman reported the air gone out of all four tires on his new tractor. Several tombstones had the usual graffiti on them. Things like, 'Baby it's cold in here' and 'I've been in better places.' Same old stuff."

"I thought Sam said they had a man patrolling the cemetery."

"They do, but those kids are resourceful, believe you me. It always happens around this time of year. Maybe they'll get it out of their system before Halloween."

The bell over the door tinkled, and Elizabeth got up to greet the customer. The two women visited a few minutes. After the customer left with her purchases, Elizabeth returned to her desk. "You're really going to sell the house?"

"That's what Sam wants."

Elizabeth picked up her coffee cup. "What does Emma want?"

What Emma wanted had never been a consideration until lately. Now she wasn't sure how to answer that question. "I think I would like to convert the house into a Victorian tearoom."

Now the words were out there, hanging in the air.

"A tearoom?" Elizabeth's head cocked to one side. "What a lovely thought. Serenity doesn't have one, of course. We ladies sometimes go to one in Durango when we're there. Why, I think that's a wonderful idea. Are you serious?"

Emma set the last stack of books on a shelf. "I thought about a tearoom in the house, with a botanical garden out back; maybe replant my mother's rose garden. I love plants. Did you know I'm a horticulturist? That's what I do in Seattle."

"Oh, that's right, you did mention that to me before," Elizabeth said. "This old memory isn't what it used to be. Can't keep details in my head anymore."

Emma grinned. "I own a small business that has a combined nursery and gift shop. We not only sell plants but contract to put plants in malls and office buildings and maintain them on a weekly basis, and we also provide landscaping service and care."

She hoped all her "babies" were thriving in Seattle. Her poinsettias ought to be ready to begin blooming, just in time for the Christmas holiday season.

Elizabeth stood and took Emma by the shoulders. "This is your dream, isn't it? Then follow it."

"But it's so . . . impractical. A tearoom and a botanical garden? We're talking about a lot of money. Money that I don't have."

"You have no savings?"

"Some," Emma admitted. "But I'm not a gambler. That money is the only thing that stands between poverty and me. I won't gamble my retirement on a project that most people would agree is frivolous."

"What about Lully's estate?"

"I don't know—I can't get into her computer files. I've tried and tried—do you know a hacker that could help me?"

"No, sure don't. Sorry, hon. I'm computer illiterate. Have you talked with Sam about this?"

"Sam doesn't want a tearoom; he thinks the town needs a new parking lot more. The Mansi house gives him a headache. And so do I if the truth were known," she admitted.

"I doubt that," Elizabeth said, gently squeezing Emma's shoulders before releasing them. "I wish I could help, but this shop barely earns me a living. The rent is astronomical, the roof leaks, the owner won't do any repairs, but I stay because the location is good and I love books." She paused. "A tearoom, with specialty teas, cookies, and gift items. Plants and flowers. Now that isn't so frivolous. The women here would love it."

Emma shook her head. "No, it's impossible."

"Well, maybe. But still, it would be nice."

"Don't say anything to anyone about this," Emma said. "It's a foolish thought on my part. At first I concocted it out of thin air so Sam would give me time to think about selling the house. But now I love the idea." She sighed.

"I won't say anything. We all have dreams."

"I suppose," Emma admitted, though few of hers had come true.

Half an hour later Emma lugged a box of decorations to the front of the store. Choosing cutout turkeys, pumpkins, cornstalks, and Pilgrims, she began affixing them to the front window with Scotch tape. Elizabeth had already chosen appropriate books to display on the tricornered shelf, and they were stacked to one side, ready to arrange. Emma was perched on a stepladder that had seen better days when the front door opened, bringing in a gust of crisp air.

Sam took two strides into the shop before turning to see Emma. As he turned, Emma's precarious perch teetered. He steadied the ladder and looked up at her. "Whoa. Be careful there."

"Thanks." Emma drew a shaky breath. Her emotions had nothing to do with the near accident. Nothing at all. "Are you looking for a book?" She asked as she descended the ladder. She wondered when he had time to read. He seemed to be on the job all the time.

"No. We've got an offer on the house."

Emma set the stepladder aside. "How? It hasn't even been listed yet."

Sam smiled in that exasperatingly knowing way he had when he knew she was irritated with him, not with the issue at hand. "Word of mouth. You forget the town and county are small—everyone knows the house is going to be for sale."

She shoved a turkey aside. "How come Ned came to you first?"

"Because he was going out of town to show property all afternoon and dropped the contract by the office. Is that okay? Or shall I take it back and tell him to talk to you?"

She was being unreasonable, she knew, but she didn't like feeling out of the loop. "No, let me see it."

Sam handed over the pink sheet. Emma frowned at the figure. "Well, this is stupid."

"That's what I thought."

The offer was ten thousand dollars short of Emma's expectation. And the idea of the tearoom and garden still dominated her thoughts. What if she had the money to pull it off? She'd have to give Sam money for his mother. He did own half the house. Would a bank loan the needed amount, using as collateral the house, The Cottage, and her experience? Would she need to prove there was a market for such a project? So much to think about.

Then there was Sam. Sam. Always Sam. What difference did any of it make? His name was on the deed legally, and if he didn't want to cooperate, there was nothing she could do but buy him out. And she didn't have enough money to compete with what the town would offer for a municipal parking lot.

"Emma?"

"No." She slowly tore up the contract.

A frown formed on his face. "We could have talked about it."

"It's too little money—the offer falls way short of what we can get if we make a few improvements. Agreed?"

Sam stared at her, his brown eyes assessing. "The idea is to sell and forget about improvements. Most likely whoever buys it wants it for the location or the property and will bulldoze the house down. It needs too much work." He shifted stances. "It's going to be this way with every contract we get, isn't it?"

"Not the right one."

"Right." He set his hat back on his head.

She swallowed and released the bomb. "Bring me two hundred thousand and we've got a sale." She smiled.

He just looked at her as if she were nuts.

"Too high?" she queried innocently.

"You think?" He laughed, but she knew he wasn't amused. "Why not a million?"

"Okay."

"You're playing me for a fool." His gaze hardened.

Offended, Emma's chin raised a notch. Sam met her visual challenge. "Exactly what were you thinking?" she countered.

"Ninety thousand, exactly what the city's offered."

"Too little—we could get more from an private buyer if we made the necessary renovations."

"And where do we get that kind of money?"

"From the bank. People do it all the time. It's called a home-improvement loan."

"You have to have a 'home' to work with. We have a pile of lumber and nails that isn't worth striking a match to. It's the land that's valuable, not the house."

"To you, maybe." She crossed her arms. "Not to me."

He looked like he'd gladly strangle her at this point. "Those are fourteen-foot ceilings, Emma. You'll need a scaffold to paint the room, and then there're new baseboards, new floors—"

"New roof," she admitted, then shut up when she realized she was defeating her purpose.

"Then there's the cost of labor."

"We could do a lot of it ourselves. I'm pretty good with a paint-brush and ladder."

"Finding someone dependable enough to show up—"

"Don't people in this town need work?"

"Apparently not. Ask anyone whose tried to have anything done lately. The cost to do the work, even by ourselves, won't be offset by the extra dollars we might—and I repeat, *might*—get."

Perhaps he was right, Emma allowed, but she wasn't about to let him know that. The repairs would give the house a better sales value, but more importantly it would give her time, and time was all she needed to make him see the light.

"Do you know what the zoning laws are for that property?" Sam asked.

"No." She hadn't thought to investigate. "Why?"

"Someone asked the other day."

"Who? Were they interested in buying the house?" Who in Serenity wanted the eyesore? And why?

"No, it was idle conversation about the property, and it occurred to me that since it sits in the middle of town, it might be zoned as something other than residential," he said.

"Or it could be grandfathered as a possible retail business prop-erty," Emma added.

The shop door opened and Ray Sullins came in. Picking up a weekly newspaper, he turned to Sam and Emma, grinning. "Hello."

"Hello." Emma nodded.

"How you doing, Ray?" Sam reached out and shook the smaller man's hand.

"Fine." Ray took a piece of red yarn out of his pocket and gave it to Sam. "I thought it was pretty, and you might need it sometime."

"Thanks, Ray." Sam stuck the yarn in his pocket.

"Have you sold Lully's house?"

Emma resented Ray's familiarity a little, but swallowed it. He had, after all, apparently spent some time there with Lully.

"No," she said. "It will take a while." Suddenly Emma thought of something. "Ray, do you happen to know the password to Lully's computer files?"

Ray nodded. "It's a secret."

"You can tell me," Emma urged. She had to get into those files!

"Can't," Ray said. "I promised." He smiled and his face relaxed. "The house will sell," he agreed. "But Lully won't like it."

"Ray, listen. It's very, very important that you tell me how to get into Lully's files. I can't settle the estate or do anything until I know her financial situation."

"Uh-uh," he argued. "That's Lully's business."

"But Lully's gone now, Ray. Please, you have to help me. Weren't you helping Lully? Are you part of the jewelry business?" Lully could have given him part of the business—who knows what she did?

A sly look came over his face, and he covered his mouth with his hand and giggled. "That's a secret."

"Why, hello, Ray. Haven't seen you in a while," Elizabeth greeted as she came from the back of the store. "Is there something I can help you with?"

"I wanted to look at comic books."

"Go right ahead—make yourself at home. I'll be in the back if you need me."

No wonder Elizabeth can't make a profit, Emma thought. She let Ray read the merchandise without buying it. How many others did the same?

Ray drifted over to the comic section and crouched down, apparently settling in for a while.

Elizabeth shook her head when she passed Emma. "A really nice fellow, but different," she said in a low voice. "Well, I'm going to be sorting through those paperback books we need to return if you need me."

"Okay," Emma shoved the box of cutouts aside. "Sam?" she asked softly.

Sam turned from the rack of mysteries he was spinning.

"Exactly what was Ray and Lully's relationship?"

Sam glanced toward the comic section, lowering his voice. "I don't know exactly. Many times I'd stop by to check on Lully during the day I would find them sitting on the front porch or working on that long table with some of the jewelry they made."

"Then he did work on the jewelry with her?"

Sam nodded. "I'd see them around town sometimes, at the bank, the grocery, other places. He picked up her mail a lot, took delivery of supplies for the jewelry."

Emma frowned. "I didn't know that."

"Ray is our Forrest Gump. Barely made it through school. Wouldn't have without a lot of help. He lives at the nursing home and washes dishes and sweeps and waxes the floors to pay for part of his keep. The state picks up the other half. He has the heart of a saint, and he's never been a problem."

"Just a bit of a character."

"No, not a character. The whole town looks after him."

Emma's cheeks pinked. What possessed her to make such an awful remark? "I know that sounded judgmental, and I didn't mean it that way." She paused. "I guess I'm surprised to learn that my sister had a close relationship with anyone, much less a man."

Sam spun the rack a final time before abandoning his search.

"I don't know how close they were, but anytime I stopped by and found them together, they blushed like teenagers caught kissing behind the barn."

Emma's jaw dropped. "You don't mean—"

Sam held up his hand. "I don't mean anything. I'm saying that your sister could blush as red as her hair. It was 'charming,' I believe you women say."

"Charming," Emma repeated, glancing back to look at Ray. The little man giggled to himself as he turned the pages of a comic book. It was difficult to think of her sister as Sam described her. Even more difficult to think of Lully and Ray . . . kissing.

"Ray's actually pretty good with computers. He helped Lully install software and explained the program to her—though how he knew how, nobody knows. She was always running over to the nursing home to ask him questions."

Emma was dumbfounded. "Life is like a box of chocolates," she murmured. Ray was the key to Lully's secrets and he wasn't willing to reveal them.

"Isn't it? There was the usual speculation about the relationship. The gossips said it was more than I think it was."

"What do you think it was?"

"Two lonely people who found each other. I think Lully and Ray enjoyed spending time together as well as working together. Nothing wrong in that."

"Two very different people finding something in common?"

"That's about the size of it." He winked. "I have to go. I'll be in Izzard County this afternoon. If anything comes up, call the office and Ken will get a message to me."

"Comes up?"

"If you need me." He brushed passed her and she felt goose bumps pop out.

The bell tinkled when Sam shut the door behind him. Emma watched him stride down the street toward his office. If she needed him. Well, now. He was about fifteen years too late with that offer, wasn't he?

She picked through pumpkin cutouts and, affixing cellophane tape, climbed back on the stepladder. How was she going to get Ray to reveal Lully's password? Even if he did, Emma knew nothing about jewelry or Lully's business, so she couldn't really do much. She would post a notice that the mail-order business would no longer be viable.

By the time Emma finished decorating the window the headache that had threatened all morning had moved to the base of her skull. It was six o'clock when she glanced at her watch. The afternoon had flown past.

"Time to close up," Elizabeth called from the back room.

"Sure thing."

Elizabeth clicked off overhead lights, tucked the money from the register drawer into her purse, and plucked her coat off the coatrack. "Sam is sure a hunk, isn't he?"

Emma shrugged into her coat, biting back a grin. A hunk. *Right, Elizabeth—a real hunk.* "I suppose so."

"You must have thought so when you were younger."

Elizabeth was smiling when Emma looked up. "So, you know all about that. Deliver me from small-town talk."

Elizabeth shrugged. "Someone mentioned it. I don't mean to bring up unpleasant memories."

"Nothing to it. We were young, full of foolish dreams, and his mother and my sister had a better grasp on life."

"I see. Well, I'll see you tomorrow."

"I'll start thinking about a Christmas display. The holidays will be here before we know it."

"Great. Good night."

Emma was glad when she could graciously leave. She didn't want to relive those turbulent teenage years. She'd dealt with too many memories already. Yet it took everything in her not to think about her past.

She pulled her collar up to her ears. A brisk wind made it seem even colder than the temperature indicated. If it weren't so cold and the wrong time of year, she would indulge her urge to plant a rosebush on Lully and Mom's grave site. Silly thought, but it made her feel good.

The sight of Brisco's Café invited her to abandon her thought of a tuna-salad sandwich for dinner. Cooking for one was too much trouble. Unfortunately, when she stepped inside, the first thing she saw was Sam sitting at a table with a group of men who were obviously friends. He must have finished his business in Izzard County earlier than he expected. Their laughter rang out and she was again captured by how handsome Sam Gold had turned out to be.

"Take a seat anywhere," the waitress sang out, drawing Sam's attention to Emma. He nodded and went on with his conversation.

"Thanks." Emma chose the only empty table available, which was, regrettably, immediately adjacent to Sam's group.

Tossing her coat and scarf into the empty booth bench, Emma occupied herself with the menu, though it would hardly hold her attention. The offerings were simple fare, though good. No fancy salads or appetizers here.

"What'll it be?" Penny asked, perching beside Emma's table.

"Hamburger, no fries, and a dinner salad."

"That's it?"

"Decaf coffee," Emma added. "Cream and sugar."

"Coming right up, sweetie."

Penny poured Emma's coffee before whirling around to pour refills at a half dozen other tables. Emma pulled a novel from her purse and opened it, ignoring the burst of laughter from Sam's table, which wasn't the only conversation she could hear in the crowded café.

"Know if there's been a decision on the old Mansi place yet?" Emma turned slightly to see Mayor Crane and the banker, Darrel Masters, sitting three tables away. She turned and lowered her head to stare at her novel again.

"Nope, not yet," another replied. "Seems the Mansi girl is holding out. Wants a tearoom."

Male laughter floated to Emma.

"That'll be a cold day in hades. The town needs the house and the cemetery, and they're willing to pay for it."

Emma noticed that Sam was unaware of the conversation, engrossed in his own.

"She'll have to sell; otherwise the house is going to fall down one of these days," another voice said. "Then we could get it for a song. I heard talk of some interest in time-shares or a condo complex. It would bring some money into town." Several voices agreed, but the mayor held out. "We need parking. Forget about time-shares."

Emma peeked out of the corner of her eye at the mayor and the banker.

"A lot of people are interested in that land for various reasons," the banker said. "Lully wouldn't hear of selling, but maybe her sister will be smarter—"

"Shush," someone said. "Emma's sitting three tables away."

Emma buried her attention in the book and forced the voices out of her mind. Was this why Sam wanted to sell the place? Did he have some interest in a time-share or a condo venture? Anger rose inside her. How could he consider such a thing? How dare he! Parking lot indeed.

"Here you go," Penny said, setting the hamburger and salad on the table in front of Emma.

Emma concentrated on eating, forcing Sam and her resentment out of her mind. Sam and his buddies got up within a few minutes. Emma refused to look up from her meal, though her appetite had waned.

Time-share property. How dare he!

"Emma."

Sam. She didn't want to talk to him. Not now. "Sam," she said, hardly looking at him.

"Headed home?"

She picked up her coffee cup and drank. "Mmm-hmm."

He was leaning on the table but she refused to look up at him. "Had a busy day at the bookstore?"

"Mmm-hmm."

"You're not going to talk to me?"

"I'm eating."

"Okay." His knuckles rapped lightly on the table. "Pout then."

She did look up at that. "I don't pout." She had every reason to pout—he had lied to her. Parking lot. Right. And she'd believed him.

He leaned close. She could see the extraordinary hue of his sienna brown eyes. "Yes," he said softly, almost in a whisper, "you do. But on you, it's . . . appealing."

When she would have sputtered, he laughed and walked away, glancing back at her before opening the door and disappearing into the darkness.

Penny walked over to refill her cup. "You two got it bad for each other, haven't you?"

"Don't be silly." Emma rearranged her fork and spoon. "Sam Gold is a jerk."

"You're the only single lady in town that gives him a hard time." Grinning, Penny topped off the liquid and turned to serve another customer.

The temperature had dropped even more when Emma started walking toward home, but the weather was definitely not affecting the temperature in the house. The stove was going full force, and the downstairs was hot as an oven when Emma stepped inside the foyer. She left the front door open to let in fresh air and cool down the living room. Gismo trotted in from the kitchen, panting.

"Sorry, Gismo. One of these days I'll get the hang of this thing."

She patted the dog's head and tossed her coat across the back of the couch. She let him out to do his business. When he scratched on the door, she let the little dog in and fed him. She freshened his water before returning to the living room and the long evening ahead of her. Deciding that continuing to read her book was about as entertaining as anything else available, Emma left the front door ajar and curled up on the couch. Licking his whiskers, Gismo came to join her.

As she idly stroked the little dog's head, Emma's attention was drawn to the picture that had hung on the far wall ever since she could remember. The familiar print of Jesus cradling the lost sheep. Hurt swept through her as she studied the picture. It was a feeling she recognized, a feeling she'd lived with most of her young life.

The town may be called Serenity, but it had hardly lived up to its name as far as she was concerned. She'd never felt serene here. The picture only highlighted that. She felt like that lost sheep.

Lost.

And there was no one to come after her. Or to protect her.

NINE

YAWNING. Emma dragged toward the kitchen Friday morning, half awake. Nightmares had wakened her twice. Once she got up and shook out the sheets and blankets to make sure no spiders had found their way into her bed; then she totally remade the bed at three o'clock in the morning. And at five-thirty.

Her slippers flapped against the cold floor as she pushed through the swinging door. She mechanically spooned coffee into the filter basket, then lifted the stainless-steel percolator and turned on the water faucet.

Oink.

Hmmm? A sound slowly began to penetrate her murky brain.

Oink.

Oink. Oink.

Not believing what she heard, Emma turned slowly while still holding the pot under the stream of cold water. Her eyes widened. Two gigantic sows were poking their heads out of the pantry.

Oink, oink. Snort.

Emma's jaw dropped. She shut her eyes, then quickly opened them again. She was still asleep—the nightmares continued. The biggest sow—eighteen hundred pounds if she weighed an ounce—peered up at her, beady eyes shining above a long snout.

Oink.

Dropping the coffeepot, Emma left the water running and fled the kitchen straight out the back door, the tail of her housecoat whipping in the wind. She dashed through the snow in her house slippers, yelling and flapping her arms, whirling occasionally to point at the house before she sprinted on. She ran down the lane and crossed the street, screaming. Heads turned. Eyes widened. Early morning errand runners gave the wild-looking woman clear berth.

"That crazy Emma Mansi," they muttered to one another.

Bursting into the sheriff's office, she breathlessly pointed at Sam and yelled, "Pig!"

Sam and Ken had both been scanning faxes while they drank their first cups of coffee, when Emma burst into the office. As one, the men turned to stare at Emma.

Holding the stitch in her side, Emma, round-eyed, repeated, "Pig!"

For a moment Sam glared at her. Color crept up his neck, and he fiddled with a pencil. He then calmly set his cup aside, refusing to meet her accusing gaze.

Ken stared at her coolly. "Pretty early in the morning for name-calling—"

"No! Pig!" She whirled, pointing to Ken. "You—pig!"

"Hey, come on." Sam shot her a dirty look. "Don't drag him into this."

She was hopping on one leg now, soggy slipper pulled up to her knee. "You don't understand. Pigs—lots of them—in my kitchen!"

Ken caught on first. "There're pigs in your kitchen?"

Emma nodded, trying to catch her breath. Her feet were two blocks of ice, her slippers encased in snow. "In my kitchen!"

Both men scrambled for coats. The three ran out of the office and piled into the cruiser and drove the short distance to the Mansi house with siren blaring. When they arrived, the back door was standing wide open.

Sam drew his pistol and Ken covered him. "Go back to the car and keep warm," Sam told Emma, "while we see what's going on."

"Be careful, Sam—they're huge! They could hurt you badly." She didn't know what a pig could do to a person, but anything that big must be dangerous.

Sam ducked inside, Ken backing him up. The men were gone a good five minutes before they returned to the cruiser.

"How did they get in there?" Emma asked, her eyes searching Sam's for information.

Sam glanced at Ken, then back at her. "There's nothing in there, Emma."

She gaped at him. "There's nothing—you're nuts!" She stormed out of the car, shoving past the two men, and into the kitchen, eyes searching for the pigs. The room was empty. The half-filled coffeepot lay askew in the sink. Coffee grounds spilled across the counter. Sam had turned off the faucet.

She searched the room frantically while Sam and Ken waited at the back door, arms crossed. "They were here a few minutes ago— when I came into the kitchen they were standing right there—" she pointed—"and right there. Look!"

One old sow had left a faint wet trail with her snout.

Sam and Ken exchanged looks before Sam reholstered his 9mm Glock. "Well, they're not here now," Sam observed.

"Maybe they've gone to Brisco's for breakfast," Ken joked in what Emma knew was an effort to lighten the situation.

Emma stared at the spot where the sow had stood looking up at her. The animal hadn't been fifteen feet away. She was certain of it. She hadn't been dreaming.

"Emma?"

Her gaze lifted to Sam.

"Are you okay?"

Running a hand through her hair, Emma suddenly realized her state of dress. Housecoat, slippers, no makeup, a virtual bed-head freak. Ken studied her appearance, and she had the feeling he was trying to decide how she had once so captivated his brother.

"I'm fine." Sighing, she cinched the belt on her housecoat tighter. "Sorry I bothered you." She lamely surveyed the empty kitchen. Pigs had been there earlier. Two of them.

Sows.

Two of them.

Big ones.

Sam came near and tipped her chin. "Try to get some rest today. You've had a lot on your plate lately."

"Thanks. But there were two sows in this kitchen fifteen minutes ago."

He smiled. "Get some rest. I'll talk to you later." He trailed Ken out the back door.

Two days later disaster struck again. Sam stopped by the house without calling first.

When Emma saw his face she knew something was wrong. "What is it?"

"We've got a problem," he said, tossing his coat over a chair. "I need coffee."

"Okay."

Emma followed him into the kitchen, where she poured him a cup of coffee. She sat down across the table from him.

"What is it?" she repeated. What could possibly have gone so badly wrong that Sam was acting like this?

"Ned did some investigating after he got the one offer on the house."

"Investigating?"

"Before a house can be sold there has to be a title search. With an old property like this that can take some time, so Ned thought he'd get a jump on the process. Didn't want any potential buyers to get cold feet in case a title search took a while."

"And?" Emma prompted.

"It seems the title isn't clear."

She blinked. "What do you mean?"

"Well, the abstract wasn't brought up to date, way back when your great-grandparents bought the place."

"And that means?" She was getting a bad feeling.

"That you don't really own the house."

"I . . . don't . . . own the . . . house?" Emma repeated.

"Nor did Lully."

"Nor does Emma." She was numb.

"Nor did your folks . . . or your grandparents."

"I don't understand."

"In effect, there's no record that your great-grandparents ever bought this place, so they couldn't will it to your grandparents, who couldn't—"

"I get the picture," she said grimly, thrusting both hands into her hair. "I get it but I don't believe it."

"Believe it. This property can be deemed abandoned property, and the city can take it over."

"And do whatever they want with it."

"I'm afraid so."

She closed her eyes. "There's got to be a mistake. I remember my parents talking about my great-grandparents buying this property. The city wanted them to buy the lot across the street, because of the cemetery, but my great-grandfather didn't like that piece of property because there were no trees. I know it was purchased legally."

His hand closed over hers on the table. "But we've got to prove it."

"We? This would fit right in with what you want, except there'd be no money from a sale."

"That was uncalled for."

He was taking a drink of his coffee when she looked up. "I'm sorry. I don't know what I'm saying half the time anymore."

"Lully meant for you to have this house; whether I agree with what you want to do with it is beside the point."

"What can we do?"

"The only thing to do is find a bill of sale or a deed proving your great-grandfather paid for this property."

"That's all?" Right now that sounded practically the same as climbing Mount Everest. Backwards. Or getting Ray to tell her Lully's password.

"That's all."

Emma put a checkmark beside the date on the counter calendar: November 26. Thanksgiving eve. Halloween had come and gone without incident. Emma had fully prepared herself to endure a night of childish pranks, but the evening turned out to be relatively quiet. She bought candy for trick-or-treaters, but none had shown up. Around nine-thirty she had turned out the porch light and gone to bed. Now it was November, and not only did she and Sam still have differing opinions on what to do with the house, she didn't even own the house. She'd searched every nook and cranny upstairs, and neither the deed nor the bill of sale could be found.

Snow fell outside the bookstore window, softly backlit by the streetlight. Last-minute shoppers ducked into Willis's Grocery for cranberries and whipped topping. Sighing, Emma returned to her work. She clipped the day's receipts together, dated the packet, and dropped it into a metal cash box, then closed and locked it. She could hear Elizabeth shoving boxes around in the workroom, doing some straightening before the holiday. Here Emma was in a bookstore about to call it a day, and she didn't want to go home. Everyone else would be home putting a turkey in the oven, rolling out piecrust, making those rich fruit, cream cheese, and nut salads that people ate only at holiday meals when everyone was allowed to splurge a little.

When she felt a plop of something wet hit her head, Emma looked up. "Elizabeth?"

"Yeah?"

"The roof is leaking."

Elizabeth stuck her head around the door frame, peering up at the ceiling. "Get a bucket," she said wearily. "If this keeps up all night, we'll have a flood in here by morning. I'll get the plastic sheets."

Emma got a pail from the bathroom and set it beneath the slow drip, then mopped water off the floor.

"Old roof should have been replaced years ago, but the landlord is so stingy he keeps patching it. Says it's got years of use left in it . . . yeah, and I'm twenty-five again," Elizabeth snorted, starting to spread heavy plastic sheets over books and bookshelves. "Years, my foot. It's gonna cave in on me one of these days."

Emma helped with the plastic before finishing the nightly closing chores. She snapped out the lights over displays and checked the lock on the back door, then carried Elizabeth's coat to her and shrugged on her own. They wrapped warm scarves around their necks before braving the cold night.

"Got plans for tomorrow?" Elizabeth asked, pulling on a pair of wool-lined leather gloves.

"Nothing. What about you?"

Elizabeth picked up the cash box. "Nothing. Warm a TV dinner, watch the Broncos play."

Sounded like Emma's usual holiday. Only she warmed a can of clam chowder, ate oyster crackers, and drank strawberry soda. She had the same menu every Thanksgiving. It made the day special.

"Why don't you come to the house?" Emma invited. "After all, it might be the last opportunity I have to invite someone there. I don't roast a turkey, and I have no idea how to make a pie, but I do open a mean can of clam chowder." Emma paused. "You're welcome to join me. We can watch the game together."

Elizabeth's eyebrows lifted. "You like football?"

"Love it!"

The two women laughed companionably and stepped outside into the falling snow.

"Isn't this lovely?" Elizabeth said, looking up into the sky.

Emma breathed deeply of the crisp air. Their words left puffs of steam in the air. The snow tires on passing vehicles beat a hollow sound against the pavement. Colorful candlelight twinkled from storefront windows, and icicle-shaped lights trimmed awnings.

"People decorate for Christmas too early," Emma said. "It takes the fun out of Thanksgiving when Christmas comes on the tail of Halloween."

Elizabeth had locked the store door when a sheriff's department cruiser drove by slowly. Sam was behind the wheel. He tipped his hat but kept on driving. Emma's gaze followed the car until it turned the corner and disappeared. What did Sam do on Thanksgiving? Spend the day with Ken and their mother?

"What can I bring?"

Emma forced her thoughts back to the moment at hand. "Nothing. Really. I meant it when I said my Thanksgiving dinner is always clam chowder and crackers with strawberry soda."

"Strawberry soda?"

"Yep." Emma grinned. "I adore strawberry soda, but I only drink it on Thanksgiving. It makes the day special. It's something Lully and I started doing after our father left."

She and Lully had made a production of the peculiar menu. Lully had liked sardines and cauliflower. Ever since that one Thanksgiving they'd given their traditional meals a try, they'd eaten their favorite things for the holiday celebration meal. The two of them would go to the store on Thanksgiving eve and shove the rattling cart down the aisles, gathering their bounty. Sardines, crackers, and cauliflower for Lully; clam chowder and oyster crackers for Emma, and two big bottles of the best strawberry soda they could afford. Then came the pièce de résistance—a package of Mallomar cookies. They ate the entire package on the way home. After the first such "celebration," Emma had thrown up beside the porch steps twice, so she took it a little easier the next year.

Snow melted in Elizabeth's hair as the two women walked away from the store. "Well, in that case, I'll bring my favorite thing. Pork rinds and cheese dip with snack crackers."

"Great," Emma grinned. "Come about eleven. We'll watch the Macy's parade, then eat and watch the football game."

"Emma, what are you going to do about the house?"

She'd told Elizabeth about the most recent hitch in plans. "Find that deed or bill of sale or letter, something that proves we actually owned the house all these years. Lully has to have it—she never threw away anything."

"Good luck," Elizabeth said, giving Emma a hug. "If I can help, just ask."

Emma did her shopping and went home to Gismo, feeling better about the approaching holiday, at least for the moment.

◈

Thanksgiving Day dawned cold and crisp with still a hint of snow blowing about. Elizabeth arrived at eleven with her pork rinds and cheese dip.

"Wow, I've never been in this house before," she said, handing her coat to Emma. "It's quite . . . something."

Emma laughed. "You're the soul of discretion. It's a pit. Nothing has been done to it in years."

"But, like you said, it has potential."

"You think so?"

"Yes, I do," Elizabeth said, her eyes roaming the rooms as she followed Emma into the kitchen. "This woodwork is wonderful. Cleaned and oiled it could be spectacular."

"I don't know. I tell myself something could be made of it but then, I don't know. I have such mixed feelings about it." She shrugged. "But then, I may have no choices."

"It will work out," Elizabeth said. "You'll know what to do when the time comes."

"I guess. I suppose I could have a yard sale next spring."

"Are you staying that long?"

"No," Emma admitted. "Probably not."

They watched the parade in silent companionship. Emma hadn't wanted to be alone this holiday, so spending it with Elizabeth was especially enjoyable. Their Thanksgiving meal was a great success, and the Broncos won the football game, so all in all it was a fun

day. When Emma told Elizabeth good-bye she realized she hadn't
thought about Sam or about the sale of the house all day, which
was a good thing.

A very good thing.

December arrived with a fresh snow. Emma stood at the kitchen
window, drinking a cup of coffee and wondering how it had come
about that she was still in Serenity nearly two months later, when
she'd planned to stay only a week, at most. The days drifted by
with little in the way of restoration toward the house. Emma
worked at the bookstore, slept, dug through boxes of papers so old
they crackled and broke apart in her hands, and kept in touch with
Sue and Janice by phone.

Snow was falling in earnest now. Fat, puffy flakes that covered
Ezra Mott's grave, frosting his gravestone. The graveyard actually
looked pretty with snow blanketing it, the tombstones poking up
like different-colored chess pieces.

Not many visited the graves. Most of the families were long
gone now. Ninety-eight-year-old Zelda Moyer still brought
plastic flowers to her husband's grave on Memorial Day and on
William's birthday, she supposed. Zelda was out there in the cold
this morning, shivering. Emma wanted to dash out with a blanket
or something. But she didn't. This was Zelda's time with her
husband.

If she and Sam had married and something had happened to
him after they'd been married sixty years, would she do the same?
Yes, she would. But then, she'd also thought they'd be married,
and she'd been wrong about that.

Emma sipped her coffee, remembering what her therapist had
said. Fear of abandonment. That's why she'd never made any kind
of commitment to a man. It sounded trite, but it was nonetheless
true. With every man she'd dated seriously, and there had been a
couple, she'd talked herself out of commitment. She'd listed pros
and cons, she'd tried to step out in blind faith, but in the end, fear

that the man would one day walk away made her break the relationship.

Irrational. Perhaps. But there it was. Every person she'd ever trusted, ever believed in, had turned away from her. How did anyone make that gamble? What were the odds of a man and woman living together for five years or ten, let alone sixty? The odds had to be astronomical. She was not a gambler.

The big grandfather clock chimed the quarter hour and Emma glanced at her watch. She had to hurry or she'd be late for work.

Elizabeth and Emma spent the morning packing, inventorying and shelving a book shipment. At lunch they ate sandwiches Elizabeth had brought.

"The roof didn't leak," Emma commented. "Well, not much."

"Lucky," Elizabeth returned, munching a chip.

Emma laughed. She liked Elizabeth and liked working in the store, even liked being in Serenity, for the time being, and she'd never thought she'd say that. In midafternoon she took a break from the bookstore and ran next door to Brisco's for a cup of hot tea. Elizabeth had used the last tea bag earlier, and Emma planned to pick up a sampler package of flavored teas at Willis's Grocery that evening on the way home.

Ned and Sam were sitting at the counter drinking coffee when Emma stepped into the café. Sam glanced up and smiled, but she went straight to the register. She hadn't talked to him in the past few days. She thought he might have stopped by to wish her a nice Thanksgiving, and then reminded herself she was an idiot. Why did the fact that Sam Gold spent Thanksgiving with his family upset her? Nothing Sam Gold did was of any concern to her.

"What can I get you, Emma?" Penny asked, turning from the kitchen pass-through.

"Two hot teas with lemon, please."

"Afternoon, Emma," Sam called loud enough for everyone in the café to turn and stare. "You're looking awfully pretty today." He had turned on the stool and sat with his back against the counter, grinning at her.

Her face flamed, and at that moment she could have strangled the sheriff.

Penny winked at her. "You ought to get his goat," she whispered.

Emma handed Penny the proper change. "I wouldn't know how."

She could hear his deep, masculine chuckle. He knew he was embarrassing her.

"I do." Penny leaned forward, whispering in Emma's ear.

"I–I couldn't," Emma murmured, her face flushing an even deeper red.

"Why not? He'd do it to you." Penny slapped a plastic lid on each cup. "Chicken."

Emma heard Sam and Ned talking in the background. Yes, he would do it without blinking an eye. She gave Penny a look and nodded slightly.

The waitress grinned and gave Emma a thumbs-up with a sly grin. "Go on. It'll be fun and give him a dose of his own medicine." She set the tea in a cardboard carryout tray.

"Thanks, Penny."

"No problem, Emma. Enjoy your tea."

Emma picked up the tray and walked past the register. When she reached the end of the counter she handed the tray to Ned, who stopped in midsentence and looked up in surprise.

"Hold that a sec," Emma said.

Then she clasped Sam's face between her hands and kissed him, long and hard. What started as a game found Emma enjoying this man's soft but firm mouth, enjoying it much longer than she'd initially planned.

Finally ending the kiss, she met his stunned gaze. Touching the end of his nose playfully with the tip of her finger she said softly, "You look rather nice yourself, Sheriff."

She collected the tray of tea from the openmouthed Ned. Striding toward the café door, she called back, "Now, you have a great day, fellows. Don't take any wooden nickels."

The café broke into applause and whistles. Face flaming, Emma left, closing the door firmly behind her. As soon as she was out of sight, she released a long breath of relief. Penny was right. That had been fun. In fact, it was really fun, and she giggled all the way back to the bookstore as she remembered the stunned look on Sam's face.

Then she sobered. It *had* been fun, but it had also stirred bittersweet memories. Though he'd been stunned, Sam had automatically returned the kiss. And that was one kiss she'd never forget. *Oh, Emma . . . you can't let yourself fall in love with Sam again.* She couldn't shake the sobering thought before it made her uncomfortable.

Elizabeth looked up as Emma entered the bookstore with the tea. She frowned slightly. "Something happen?"

Emma laughed. "Just a good joke," she said. "That phone will ring in a few minutes and I'll answer it."

"Then you'll tell me the joke?"

"Guaranteed."

Sure enough, Emma had barely had time to squeeze lemon into her tea when the phone rang.

Elizabeth's eyes danced. "You promised," she said as Emma picked up the receiver.

"Elizabeth's Corner."

"Emma!"

"Yes, Sam?" Emma twined the telephone cord around her little finger. She checked her watch. Four and a half minutes.

"What was that all about?"

"The kiss?" She grinned at Elizabeth's expression. "Why, I was just returning your compliment. You said I looked good, and I said you looked good."

"Right. Penny put you up to that, didn't she?"

"Penny who?" She heard a sound of irritation on the other end.

"Even if she did," he began and she held her breath, "I liked it."

She made herself breathe. "Me, too," she admitted, and then thought perhaps she shouldn't have.

"Maybe we should try it again, in a different place."

She laughed softly. "In your dreams, Sheriff." And in hers. What was she doing? This wasn't what she'd planned. "Hey." She changed subjects. "Ned thinks we should paint the cabinets when we paint the inside of the house."

"You still want to get into that?"

"Yeah," she wrapped the phone cord around her finger again. "I do. I know I'll find that bill of sale. It may take me forever, but I'll find it."

"You better find it before the estate goes to probate."

"I will. But it's like dipping a teaspoon into the Atlantic Ocean, the way things are piled and stacked in that house. I work some every day, but the mess only seems to be getting larger."

Sam's chuckle set off a tiny quiver in her stomach. She loved the sound of it.

"Any particular color schemes go with spiders? Coordinating shades, all one color, variegated?" Emma asked.

"Don't be fresh. Those spiders are long gone. Have you been down there to check lately?"

"Are you kidding? That's your part of the house." She grinned. "You're just a spider coward. Okay, it's too late in the year to paint outside, but we can paint inside. Maybe do a little wallpapering."

Hesitation came over the line. "Do you wallpaper?" he asked.

"I have. Once. Border."

"Great."

"Do you?"

"Wallpaper?"

"That's what we were discussing," Emma reminded him, having trouble keeping her mind on the subject herself. That kiss kept intruding into her thought processes.

"No," he said.

"Well—"

"What can you do, Emma?"

"Plant green things. You wouldn't believe what I could do. I could turn the house into a centerpiece for a botanical garden." Emma's vision flourished.

Sam's tone sobered. "You know, that old house has a personality of its own. I'm not sure it's wise to change it."

"It does, doesn't it?" The house had character, something new tract homes didn't have. She supposed it was like growing old. Few thought much about the elderly. But for Emma, new didn't always mean better. She loved the cubbyholes and the drafty window seat with its faded cushions in her old bedroom. The admission took her by surprise.

Sam hesitated, then, "Do you have plans for Saturday?"

"No. Why?"

"I'll pick you up and we'll drive to Durango for paint. We need to get started." Again, hesitation. "Ned thinks he has an older couple interested in at least looking at the house."

"Are you giving in? You said we couldn't paint. The ceilings are fourteen feet high. Scaffolding, you said."

"We'll buy a big ladder. We can at least start on the parlor."

And we'll need a big insurance policy, she told herself as she hung up the phone. She suddenly jumped up and down, shaking her hands wildly. He had given in to her—Sam had actually given in to her! Yet she felt rather foolish, painting a house when she didn't have proof it was even hers. Or spending money on a house that most likely would end up in rubble.

Sam hung up the phone slowly. Now what had he gotten himself into? Doing anything with the Mansi house was not on his agenda for any day. Did he think that painting a couple of the rooms would make a difference? Make Emma decide to stay in Serenity? If so, then he was a bigger fool than he thought.

He suddenly jumped in the air and clipped the heels of his boot. Hot dog. He had a date with Emma—an honest-to-goodness date, no professionalism involved. Just a can of paint, a paintbrush, a ladder, and a long Saturday afternoon. The house didn't matter, even if she could find the deed or bill of sale. He wanted her to stay in Serenity—and so what if he'd given in to her? He hadn't exactly—he'd just agreed to be more agreeable.

Man, he felt good!

"Yep, this place needs some work all right."

Jay Bennett had been the only person to respond to Emma's ad for someone to do general repairs around the house, which made her wonder if he wasn't busy because he wasn't good at his work or if he was just braver than most. She hoped it was the latter.

"What do you think?" Emma asked. "Can you do the work?" She wanted to sneeze. She'd been going through some boxes in a closet when the handyman arrived, and she felt like she'd been breathing dust for hours.

"I can do it," Jay said, rubbing his whiskered chin with one calloused hand. "But it'll cost."

She'd been afraid of that, but he was available. Maybe he hadn't heard all the stories about the Mansi house, or at least chose to ignore them. She had some concerns about the stories being true, considering the strange sounds she'd heard since being in the house again. She hadn't remembered the sounds a house made when it was old; she'd forgotten how the wind whistled around the corners and under the eaves at night.

"Can you give me an estimate?"

"Check the plumbing, electrical—you know that fuse box needs to be replaced?"

"No, I didn't."

"I'll put that in the estimate."

"Yes, do that," Emma murmured, almost seeing the dollar signs stacking up. She refused to consider that all this work might be for nothing.

"And that porch needs the step replaced, the others tightened up. Two boards in the porch. Nearly cracked my shin when I was checkin' that railin'."

"Okay." More dollar signs.

"Have to hand turn those little spindles," he said, pointing to the fan-shaped decorations that graced the corners of open doorways on the first floor. "And there's a couple on the front of the house that need replacin'."

His brown-eyed gaze darted into every corner as he walked through the living room, dining room, guest parlor, and into the kitchen. "Don't suppose you want to update those cabinets. Some glass doors would make a world of difference."

"I'll make a note of that, but I don't think it's the main objective right now. We'll paint them instead."

"Okay. Spindles, electrical, check the plumbing, replace that corner piece of molding in the living room, replace the splashboard and this faucet here in the kitchen." He tapped the faucet that kept leaking and sending water running across the counter all day. She'd taken to wrapping a tea towel around it and wringing it out three or four times a day.

"Please list each item separately so I'll know what I can have done."

"Sure thing. I'll have an estimate for you—" he rubbed his chin again—"day after tomorrow?"

"That will be fine. Drop it off at the bookstore, please. I'm there afternoons."

Jay tugged at the bill of his baseball cap. "Sure thing."

Emma walked the handyman to the door. "Thanks for coming."

"You betcha." He tugged the door open. "I'll add shaving the edge on this door to the list." Jay drove off in his battered pickup with the ladders on racks rattling as the vehicle disappeared down the lane.

"Just a few repairs," she murmured, kicking the door when it stuck again.

Sam stopped by the bookstore shortly after noon two days later. "Have you talked to Ned?" he asked.

Emma laid down the lamb's-wool duster she'd been using on

the bookshelves. "Ned never talks to me. He must think I speak Spanish only."

Sam pursed his lips. "Could be he's afraid you'll drag him down the street by the collar again." He grinned.

"Jay Bennett was here about the repairs. I'm afraid it's going to cost a fortune."

"We take one step at a time. I'll stop by a couple nights next week and help you go through some of the boxes in the basement. The bill of sale could be down there."

"Okay."

He smiled.

"Okay," she repeated. "So I don't refuse help when it's offered. Shoot me."

"I'd rather kiss you." The statement hung in the air between them until Jay Bennett entered the bookstore. "Got that estimate for you, Miss Mansi."

"Thank you, Mr. Bennett. May I look it over and call you?" Emma found it hard to concentrate on anything but Sam's offer.

"Sure thing." He pulled at the bill of his ball cap. "Sam."

"Jay. Good to see you. That cabinet you built for the office is working out great."

"Glad to hear it." He glanced at Emma. "I'll be on my way."

After Jay closed the door, Sam turned to Emma. "Jay is going to do the repairs?"

"Yes," her chin shot up as if daring him to say she was wasting money.

"Broootheeer. You must be loaded."

"With experience," she muttered.

"Jay will get the work done, but it will take months." With that parting shot, Sam left, leaving her to wonder why he hadn't stuck around to follow through on the kiss. . . .

She picked up the lamb's-wool wand and beat it against the wall outside the door, then attacked with vigor the task of dusting shelved books.

Elizabeth came in from the post office. "Was that Sam I saw pulling away from the curb?"

"I'm going to do some painting at the house; Sam is going to help."

"He is?" Elizabeth hung up her coat.

"The house is half his."

"Oh, yes, teamwork. That's nice." She looped her wool muffler over her coat. "What are you going to paint?"

"The parlor first."

Elizabeth almost laughed. "Sorry, but Emma, there are fifteen rooms! Rooms, I might add, that haven't been touched since 1902."

Emma had to smile in return. "Well, it's probably not been that long, but it's pretty bad. And the colors are . . . well . . . awful. The paper in my room is so faded it looks like the walls have been papered with grocery bags. I'd forgotten that it's always been that way."

Elizabeth handed Emma a red marker. "Be my guest. Go home and draw you some pretty flowers."

Sam picked Emma up in his SUV at nine o'clock on Saturday. Emma got into the warm vehicle, rubbing her hands together.

"Did you look at Jay's estimate?" Sam asked.

"Oh, yeah."

"And?"

"Most of the projects are doable."

"I'll split the cost with you."

"You don't have to do that."

"I know I don't." He looked at her and smiled. "But I want to."

The drive to Durango was beautiful. Called the Gateway to Mesa Verde National Park as well as to the San Juan Mountains and National Forest, the landscape was breathtaking. To the east was the Durango to Silverton narrow gauge railroad. Vallecito Lake was beyond that. The four-corners area was as picture perfect as tourist advertising promised. As part of Emma drank in the beautiful scenery, she was even more aware of the man beside her.

The paint department of the large home-improvement store was huge. The rack of paint chips offered twenty different shades of white.

"I want something subtle but within the colors of the era of the house," Emma said, reaching for a shade of pink.

"Thought Victorian houses had whitewashed walls."

"Some do—maybe ours won't." She picked up two shades of turquoise. "You've got to be kidding!" He picked up a butter yellow. "How about this?"

"I'd never find a border to go with that," she chided. "How about blue for the parlor?"

They quibbled over colors for an hour before settling on a pale peach and equally pale turquoise, though Sam grumbled he wasn't dipping a brush into the turquoise. Clearly relieved when they checked out, he quickly ushered her from the store.

"What's the hurry?"

"I'm afraid you'll change your mind again."

Emma laughed. Though they disagreed over everything, she'd enjoyed choosing the colors. She was sure they weren't entirely within the era of the house, but they'd definitely brighten the place and make it more appealing. And they were colors that fit into what she saw in her mind as backgrounds for the tearoom.

"How about lunch?"

"Sounds good."

They found a sandwich shop and settled into a booth near the window. They both ordered club sandwiches. Then, spotting the pie on display, Sam ordered a generous slice of French silk, and Emma settled on lemon.

"Have you been able to get into Lully's computer files?"

"Not yet."

"Lully wouldn't have jotted the password down somewhere? In case she forgot?"

Emma shrugged. "I haven't found anything. Of course, I haven't gone through all of Lully's personal things." She ran a fingertip around the rim of her coffee cup. "I haven't made myself do that yet. I've been concentrating on all of those boxes in the basement. I have no idea what's in the attic. It will take forever to go through everything."

It was midafternoon when they reached Serenity, and Sam stopped the SUV in front of the Mansi house.

"We can leave the paint on the porch," Emma said.

"No," Sam said, stepping out of the vehicle. "Too cold. Might freeze. Then I'd have to do all that paint choosing all over again."

The house, for once, wasn't blistering hot. She'd left some windows open in hopes of avoiding an inferno.

Impulsively, Emma stuck her tongue out at him and he laughed.

"There's still some daylight left," Sam suggested.

"You want to paint now?"

"No time like the present. But you're in charge of the turquoise stuff."

They painted the easiest room, the parlor, working together in companionable silence. Finally Sam dropped the roller in a paint pan and stretched.

"I'm through," he announced, twisting at the waist to stretch his stiff shoulders.

Peach-colored paint speckled his face and hair, splattered from the roller even with the splatter protector piece attached. Still, he looked so . . . appealing. She wanted to go to him, step into his arms—

No, she didn't have the right. No right at all.

Emma dropped her roller gladly. "I made chili this morning," she offered.

"Shredded cheese?"

Emma laughed, feeling suddenly very good about everything. He'd always liked cheddar on top of his chili.

"Of course."

"You're on."

Sam washed the rollers and pans at the outside faucet while Emma picked up drop cloths and pushed furniture back into place. They ate chili as they sat at the kitchen table. The dim, yellowed light gave the room a strange cast. How many times had she and Lully eaten a silent meal at this same table? How she wished she'd not treated Lully so cruelly. Lully had, after all, done the best she could—at least what she considered best for Emma. Mrs. Gold's actions had not been so warmly motivated.

"This is nice," Sam said, setting aside his empty bowl.

"It is, isn't it?" Emma returned, sipping her milk. "I'll take a good bowl of chili over steak any day."

His gaze traced her lightly. "I meant this. Sitting here with you, without arguing, without resentment."

Emma studied her nearly empty bowl. "I think I need to apologize to you . . . for a lot of things."

"You have nothing to apologize for."

She finally looked up. "I had a lot of anger. Still did even when I came back here."

She laid her spoon aside, carefully aligning it next to the bowl, then rubbing the almost indistinguishable initial cut into the handle with her thumb. "It's taken me a long time to get to this point, able to admit that I've been angry with you for far too long."

"You had a case against me."

"I thought I did, but I don't know." She released a long breath while staring at the discolored ceiling. "That was such a bad time, when I left here. I was a hopeless romantic, didn't think any further than—" She stopped there. "I didn't see the reality of things. We were too young, had no idea what we were doing."

His features had turned somber. "Hauling us out of that Motel 6 in the middle of the night was not the best approach. Too many people knew about it. Made your life miserable, and there wasn't a thing I could do about it."

Her voice had softened. "It was a very bad time for everyone. The whispered conversations that stopped when I went by, the open taunts. And we hadn't done anything. We'd just wanted to get married. Not even Lully would understand that nothing had happened, that we'd both decided to wait until we were married to . . ." She let the words trail off. "They wouldn't listen."

"I'm sorry, Emma. I failed you. I've lived with that knowledge since the day you left."

They studied one another for a long moment. Her gaze went to his mouth, remembering the kiss. How different it had been from fifteen years ago, how different from kissing anyone else. Sam was different from any other man she knew. Unique. One of a kind.

"I didn't intend to desert you, let you take the blame," Sam said.

"I was pretty hateful to you after—"

"You were hurt. So was I."

"Were you?" It was a question she had wondered about for fifteen years.

"Do you really have to ask that?" Sam asked softly, his eyes boring into hers.

She studied his face, seeing pain and sorrow etched in mature lines. "I guess I did."

"What did you think? That I could just walk away from you?" Sam asked.

"You did." Emma looked away.

Sam reached out and took her hand. "That wasn't exactly how it happened."

"It seemed like it to me." Emma pulled her hand away.

"I never got to explain to you what happened, what happened when I got home that night."

"No." Emma traced the pattern on the worn oilcloth on the table. "Maybe I never gave you the chance."

"You did, but I couldn't explain."

"Your mother must have made things difficult; she was pretty angry."

"And prepared to send me to military school the next day."

Emma looked up in surprise. "Military school? Why?"

The corner of his mouth turned up at the irony of that long-ago scene. "Because I lacked discipline."

She almost laughed. "You? Why, because you ran wild all over the country on your motorcycle, stayed out late every night, tried to marry Emma Mansi—who in their right mind would think you lacked discipline?"

He grinned. "So, she had a point. There was Ken to consider. She thought I was a bad influence."

"In order to keep you away from me and to keep Kenny from being corrupted, she was going to send you to military school?"

He nodded. "That's about it. Kemper Academy in Missouri. She filled out the application that night and had it all ready to mail. I guess she'd had the threat ready, and our running away was the last straw. Dad had even signed it. If I saw you again she would make good the threat. I knew that if I tried to see you, even to try to explain, someone would report it to her. She knew everything." He smiled. "Everything."

She frowned. "Everything?"

"She knew that we sat on the bleachers at games, held hands, kissed."

Emma felt her cheeks warm. "I didn't know," she said weakly.

"Would it have made a difference?"

"Yes," she admitted. "It would have."

"I wrote you a letter, Emma. Hand delivered it to Lully to mail to you."

"I didn't get it—either Lully didn't mail it or it got lost in the mail."

"Just so you believe me. I wrote the letter, explaining what happened. I loved you, Emma, but the thought of military school scared the dickens out of me at that time."

She smiled. "And now?"

"Now?" His eyes deepened. "What do you think?"

Thinking was something she tried not to do, not about him.

He toyed with his spoon. "My plan was to wait until you were eighteen. I'd be twenty-one and we wouldn't have to ask anyone's permission to do anything."

Emma's heart ached and tears pricked her eyes. "But, I left," she whispered.

"You left. Without explanation, without giving us another chance."

Only the dripping of the kitchen faucet broke the silence between them.

"I guess I never thought about what my leaving might mean to you. I thought . . . it wouldn't make any difference."

"It did," he said simply, without explanation.

"What happened after?"

"Lully searched for you. I talked to the sheriff, kept after him to have law-enforcement agencies look for you. But you'd disappeared into thin air, and he'd heard the rumors so he decided you were old enough to make your own choices. He didn't put forth much effort. You were gone for good. So, I enlisted in the Marines."

Emma bit her upper lip. She'd thought Lully hadn't tried to find her. "And then what?"

"When my hitch was finished I came back here. Dad was gone by then and mother's health was failing. I didn't know what I wanted to do, but the sheriff was retiring so I ran for his job. Not many people had my experience, so I won."

"Do you like your work?"

"I do. And if a teenager runs away, I'll do everything I can to find her."

She had to smile at his attempt to lighten the atmosphere but sensed he was dead serious. "The sheriff was right, you know. I couldn't stand all the taunts, the whispers, so I made the choice to leave, and I made sure no one could find me before I was of legal age."

He reached over and took her hand, his fingers linking with hers. Their gazes met and held. "We came so close, Emma."

She wanted to cry. "Yeah . . . so close, Sam." Close didn't matter, except with hand grenades and horseshoes.

"Did you go directly to Seattle?" he asked.

"That was as far as my money could take me."

"You went to school, and you've got a good job, one you like."

She nodded, smiling. "I always enjoyed puttering around with Momma's roses, so I decided to study horticulture and it was a good choice. I love my work."

He grinned. "Lully always said those old roses would bloom again."

"They will." She squeezed his hand.

"Never married?"

She caught his gaze and held it. "No. Didn't have time for relationships for a long time, then I wasn't that interested in anything long term. You?"

"No."

"Didn't find the right woman?"

"Lightning doesn't strike twice," he admitted softly.

Something inside her started to thaw—something she hadn't realized was frozen. As infuriating as he could be sometimes, she wanted to be able to go back, to be able to say she loved him . . . again. Just once.

He scooted his chair back from the table. "I'd better go. Have to check in with the office."

She walked him to the door and grinned when it stuck and he had to yank with both hands to get it open.

"This is on the list, isn't it?"

"I'll have Jay fix that first."

He stood with his hand resting on the doorknob, framed by the open doorway. "I had a good time today."

She smiled, tilting her head to one side. "Even though you don't like turquoise."

He bent then and brushed a kiss across her lips. Her eyes closed automatically, relishing the feel of his warm lips. He deepened the kiss, kissing her thoroughly.

"Even though," he whispered. Then he was gone.

Emma watched him drive away until the red taillights of his SUV disappeared into the darkness. "Oh, rats," she whispered. Now what had she done?

chapter
TEN

SUNDAY morning Emma woke to the smell of fresh paint.
Closing her eyes, she recalled the parlor with its new coat of peach
paint. She stretched sore muscles. She was tired but the room had
never looked prettier.

Snuggling deeper into the blankets, she turned on her side and
stared at puffy cotton-ball-sized flakes dancing around Ezra Mott's
tombstone. In the distance, church bells tolled their clear, musical
tones ringing over the sleepy countryside. It was a decidedly
comfortable sound. When she gathered sufficient nerve, she swung
out of bed and winced when her feet hit the icy floor. Double-
stepping to her slippers, she slid her toes into the chilly fleece. The
fire had died down in the woodstove, making the upstairs rooms
as cold as meat lockers.

Gismo moseyed in from the kitchen as Emma knelt in front of
the stove and wadded old newspapers. She tossed them into the
stove on a bed of dying embers and quickly slammed the iron
door. She heard a whoosh and saw through the sooty window
that the newspapers had disintegrated into charred pulp.

"Wood," she muttered and gently moved Gismo aside.

Stacking two big logs in the crook of her arm, she edged back
to the stove, trying to work the door open with a free index finger
while keeping the dirty wood away from her clean housecoat. The

largest piece slipped. She jumped, but not in time to prevent the heavy oak piece from bouncing off her slipper.

Yelping, she sucked in a breath and danced around before dropping to her knees. The other log rolled across the floor. Gismo barked and backed away, his eyes anxiously assessing the situation. Tears rolled down Emma's cheeks as she held her toe in both hands, afraid to look at it. The pain was excruciating. She had once dropped an iron on her toe and it had hurt less.

Rolling to her side, eyes closed, Emma held her foot, trying to absorb the pain. Gismo edged close, licking her cheek. She threw a hand up against the comforting assault, laughing and crying at the same time. The pain was so bad she got the giggles.

Crying and laughing, she tried to push Gismo out of the way so she could sit up. Only then did she hear the pecking on the glass at the front door. She got to her knees and peered out.

"Sam!"

Jerking her housecoat over her bare legs, Emma scrambled up and hobbled to the door. Brushing a tangle of hair out of her face, she pushed back the dead bolt. Sam stood there, Stetson in both hands, looking mildly amused.

"Hi," she managed, reaching out to unhook the screen. "I didn't hear you knock."

His gaze moved over her from head to toe, noting her disheveled appearance, and grinned. "You and Gismo taken to wrestling these days?"

"I was putting wood in the stove," she said, peering around a broad shoulder. "Where's your patrol car?"

"I walked over this morning."

"You're up early, aren't you?" She hitched the sash of her robe tighter. It was one of Lully's heavy wool sarong-type garments that served as a dress and sleepwear.

"Not by my standards."

It was early by anybody's standards. Not quite seven o'clock on a snowy Sunday morning. Most people would be rolling out of warm beds, putting on the coffee, and making the cold dash to find the newspaper on the front lawn.

"You're not going to church?"

"Mom's not feeling well. Besides, I go to church because I want to, not because I feel I have to." He grinned down at her.

"You—you weren't that interested in church . . . before."

"No. But a few years ago I discovered something missing from my life. God. I thought I could do everything on my own, but I was wrong." He shrugged. "Since then I've realized who God is and experienced what he can be to me. To everyone."

"I see." She didn't. Not really. But it was something she needed to think about. Lully had searched for God and seemed to have found him. And now Sam had too.

"Do you?" His eyes held hers, his face serious. "Lully and I talked about God, about how she'd found him. She worried about you," he said.

"She shouldn't have."

"Have you ever thought about God, about your relationship with him?"

She swallowed. "Some," she admitted. *Most of it since coming back to Serenity, to this house.*

"You're in my prayers," he said softly. "You have been for a long time."

Emma didn't know how to respond to that. This side of Sam was one she hadn't seen before, and she'd have to think about that. He'd seemed different, somehow, and she hadn't known what it was. Perhaps this was it. He seemed . . . content, at peace. She wished she could say that about herself.

"Now, let's see about this stove."

As Sam stepped past her, the aroma of Old Spice teased her nose. He shrugged off his coat and tossed it, along with his Stetson, onto the couch. He wore old jeans that were bleached almost white and a comfortable oxford shirt. Before yesterday, she hadn't seen him in street clothes since her return to Serenity. He looked very good in worn jeans. Very good.

Picking up the two dropped logs plus another from the wood box, he opened the stove door and stacked them inside, making sure to leave room between them for air circulation. Closing the door, he adjusted the damper.

"Got any coffee?"

"I was about to make a pot."

"Good."

Emma limped toward the kitchen, Sam following.

"What happened to your foot?"

"Dropped a piece of wood on my toe."

"Are you okay?"

"I'll survive." She filled the percolator with cold water and measured coffee into the metal filter.

He ran his fingers through his hair and leaned against the cabinet, watching her. "Didn't Lully believe in modern conveniences?"

"Apparently not." Emma plugged the pot into a receptacle. "Everything looks about the same. Except the refrigerator is new. The old one must have lain down and died. She probably let it lie there for a month, hoping it would get up and run again. Lully always kept the faith."

He chuckled. They both stood there as if neither one could think of anything to say. There had been a time when conversation between them came so easily the words would tumble over each other. But that was years ago. Words weren't so easy anymore. They both had changed.

His kiss was so much more potent, for one thing. Emma set the sugar bowl on the table. She couldn't think about his kiss. She had to keep a clear head, and kissing Sam wiped coherent thought right out of her mind. "What are you doing here so early?"

"I wanted to see how the paint looked after it dried."

A smile hovered at the corners of her mouth. "That couldn't wait until after nine o'clock?"

"Are you busy? Other than wrestling the dog?"

"No." She poured cream into a small pitcher and set it on the table. "Hungry?"

"Sure. You cooking?"

"Only if you like scrambled eggs and toast. I don't cook much."

"Scrambled eggs sound great."

He sat at the table while Emma dragged a large cast-iron skillet from the cabinet and lit a burner on the stove. In a few minutes she had assembled eggs, butter, a loaf of bread, and a jar of grape jelly.

Sam unfolded the newspaper he'd found on the porch and scanned the headlines. "Better spray some Pam in that skillet. The eggs will stick otherwise," he said.

"Thank you, Martha Stewart," Emma murmured. She checked the cabinets and found a can of cooking spray, which she held up for his inspection.

"That would do it. Bet you cook with Teflon pans."

"I thought everyone did." She sprayed the skillet and cracked the eggs into it.

Sam got up and opened the refrigerator and rummaged inside, coming up with cheese. Emma tensed when he reached around her, sprinkled a few small pieces on top of the eggs, and then took her hand that held a fork and blended the cheese into the eggs. "Makes them not so dry," he whispered in her ear, totally unnerving her.

Emma watched the cheese melt as she gathered her composure. Sam went back to his newspaper. She wanted him to kiss her again and called herself all kinds of fool for it.

Emma divided the eggs in equal parts on two plates and buttered whole-wheat toast. She set one plate in front of Sam and wiped her hands down the front of her robe. "That jelly looks old," she remarked.

"Have you checked the pantry? Bottom shelf. Lully usually bought clover honey to use in the winter," he said, laying aside the newspaper. He applied pepper liberally to his eggs.

"You seem to know a lot about my sister," Emma commented as she explored the lower shelf of the pantry. She emerged with a jar of clover honey.

"We talked," he said, reaching for the jar. "About a lot of things."

Emma poured two mugs of coffee and sat down. She didn't explore his statement. Lully had probably told him how disappointed she was in her sister, and Emma didn't want to hear that. She already felt enough guilt about her relationship with Lully.

As he ate, Sam picked up the paper again and started reading.

"Don't hog the sports section," she said.

He lowered the paper. "What part are you interested in?"

"Women's basketball."

He was clearly surprised. "You like basketball?"

"Women's basketball."

He thumbed through the pages and extracted the middle section and handed it over. She took it, passing him the toast. He handed her the cream. They ate and read, with only the occasional rustle of paper breaking the silence. She looked at him once, but quickly hid behind her part of the paper again, thinking that this was how it would have been if they'd married. Maybe after fifteen years their meals would be quieter because they would know that he took his coffee black, she liked cream, he read football, she followed the WNBA. The only difference would be that she wouldn't be so aware of his aftershave, or that his clean-shaven jaw was strong and clean-cut, or how the damp air made his hair curl.

Emma suddenly remembered her own appearance—no makeup, uncombed hair, bits of bark still clinging to Lully's ridiculous wool sarong thing. She looked a wreck, and she could feel sticky honey at the corners of her mouth.

She looked up to find Sam studying her, his chocolate brown eyes dancing with mirth. He slowly leaned forward and with the tip of his napkin wiped honey from her mouth. She could have melted, right here in her chair, melted and slid onto the floor in a puddle.

Gismo barked. Emma jumped as if she'd been shot. Sam's gaze went to the dog standing in front of the back door, growling.

"What's wrong with him?" Emma was grateful for the distraction.

Sam stopped her from going to the door with a chop of his hand. Holding a finger to his lips, he got up from the table and stepped to the window over the sink.

Gismo growled again.

"Shhh, boy," Sam soothed quietly.

"What is it?" Emma got up quietly to stand beside Sam.

Two figures stepped around the side of the house, huddled against the cold wind.

Emma frowned. "Isn't that Mayor Crane and Darrel Masters?" she whispered.

Sam nodded. "What are they doing sneaking around the house at this hour?"

"That's a good question. What are they doing sneaking around *any* house at *any* hour?"

They watched the two men cross the yard and disappear around the far corner. Emma and Sam tiptoed to the front of the house, where they watched the two men hurry across the front lawn and down the lane.

"They walked here?"

"Must have, or parked around the corner."

"If they wanted something, why didn't they come to the door?"

"If I know the mayor, he was snooping. But I'll ask and tell him to stay off private property."

"He probably thinks it's soon to be public property," Emma said.

"Well then, I guess he'll have to be reminded differently."

After breakfast, Sam and Emma attended church services together—which turned more than a few heads. Sam's mother was under the weather today and remained in bed. Emma liked sitting next to Sam, sharing a songbook. During the sermon he held her hand, his thumb caressing her knuckles absently. It was the first public show of affection, and Emma found she was comfortable with the subtle intimacy.

For lunch Emma made egg-salad sandwiches; they sat at her kitchen table and drank Cokes, ate chips, and polished off a bag of Fig Newtons. Then they painted for the rest of the day, working companionably. By evening they were bone tired but had made good headway on the dining room.When Sam left, he kissed her good-bye at the door, smiled as if he knew a secret, and walked out the door, leaving her wishing she knew what was going on.

Emotions were changing too quickly in their relationship. He kissed her like she'd never been kissed before, which, on the surface, wasn't a bad thing. But she was confused. She knew she still loved Sam, but what did he feel toward her? Dare she hope that his feelings were the same? The way he kissed her indicated he did. . . .

On Monday Emma finished work at the bookstore at six and bid Elizabeth good night at the door after they'd locked up. Emma decided to eat at Brisco's before going to the city council meeting at seven. She preferred the warm conviviality of the café to the yawning emptiness of the house.

The windows of the café were steamed over, reminding everyone the temperatures had dipped into the teens. Snowflakes swirled around Emma as she pushed open the door.

"Seat up front there, Emma." Penny waved the coffeepot at her.

Emma smiled at a couple of bookstore customers she recognized and slid into the front booth.

"English or American?" Penny called out.

"English," Emma laughed, ordering the tea she often drank over the decaf coffee she sometimes favored.

Emma drew a deep breath and scanned the busy restaurant, suddenly feeling very good about life. How nice it was to come into a restaurant and be known by name, by what she liked to drink, and to know something about the people. Was she finally overcoming her dubious reputation? Penny had two kids, Emma knew. She carried their school pictures under the clip on her order book. A boy and a girl she adored and a husband, a garage mechanic, who thought the world of her. Emma had seen him come in and drop a kiss on the top of Penny's head. A pang of jealousy bothered Emma at the memory.

"Here you go. Honey and lemon."

Emma smiled. Penny always remembered what she liked with her Earl Gray. This never happened to her in Seattle.

"We've got some good clam chowder," Penny suggested. "Homemade. Oyster crackers."

"Sounds wonderful," Emma said, slipping the menu back into the rack on the table.

"I'll be right back."

Emma poured steaming hot water over the Earl Gray tea bag and glanced around the café while her tea steeped. Good people here, she decided, in spite of the way more than a few in this room had treated the Mansi girls. She still held on to remnants of resentment, but even they were beginning to fray. So far everyone had respected her feelings concerning the house, and no one had approached her or even suggested a parking lot except Sam, who by stipulation of Lully's will alone, was obligated to tell her.

She ate her chowder with relish, occasionally returning the greeting of someone coming in or out of the café. She paid her bill a few minutes before seven, and prepared for the short, cold walk to city hall.

Penny grinned and rang up the sale. "Going to the council meeting?"

"I thought I would," Emma returned. The thought of another long night in the old house didn't appeal to her.

"Most everybody is. Everybody wants to know what's going on, and then rehash it here in the morning. Prime entertainment."

Emma laughed, as she was expected to, though she wondered how entertaining the council meeting would be. She'd never been to one before but understood that small towns like Serenity did things differently than large cities. "See you later."

Emma wrapped her muffler more tightly and pulled on her gloves as she left the café to walk across to city hall, which sat in the middle of the town square. The one-story building was square and plain, purely functional. She reached council chambers just as the meeting was ready to get under way.

Sam saw Emma enter the council room. Gazes shifted to watch her search the room. Immediately heads leaned together and whispered. He knew what that was about and felt a stab of guilt that he hesitated to beckon Emma over to sit beside him. He hesitated because Emma's indecision about the house, about staying in Serenity, had his own emotions bouncing back and forth like a Ping-Pong ball.

A part of him wanted—needed—to protect her. A part of him wanted to believe there was some reason for her to stay here. If God had a plan for them, Sam hadn't a clue what it was, and that made him ask himself even more often what he was going to do if, or when, she left again.

This time for good.

Could he take the chance that she could learn to love him again? Maybe. Didn't life consist of chances?

Emma saw Sam motion for her to sit beside him. She hesitated, not sure she wanted to prompt more gossip and speculation about them, but she needed the support of someone who knew what she was doing. He grinned at her frown of hesitation, as if he knew exactly what she was thinking. She hated that smug look on his face, but then even as a teenager he'd been able to read her like a book.

"Didn't know you were coming to council meeting," he said as she sat down. He helped her off with her coat.

"Did you ask the mayor why he and the banker were prowling around my house?"

"I did. Said they were checking out damage at the cemetery and cut through your yard for convenience."

"Do you believe him?"

Sam shrugged. "It's plausible."

She was going to repeat her question but the meeting was called to order by the mayor, who was flanked by the six councilmen at a long table in the front of the room. Mayor Crane tapped the microphone to see if it was on, and the sound assaulted Emma's ears. Why did everyone have to do that?

Old business was dispensed with quickly and new business announced. A couple of items were discussed, including the need for new sidewalks in a stretch of town that extended in front of Elizabeth's Corner. Emma heartily agreed that something needed to be done. She'd stubbed her toe on a raised slab a number of times. Once those two pieces of new business were covered, the mayor asked if there was anything else that needed to be discussed.

Drawing a deep breath, Emma stood. "I have a question."

The mayor looked surprised, his gaze darting from Emma to around the room as if he sought someone else with a topic that would supersede hers.

"What is it, Emma?"

His calling her by her first name irritated Emma; in her opinion, it diminished the importance of whatever she had to ask.

"What are the zoning laws for Serenity?"

"Zoning laws? Why on earth would you want to know about zoning laws?"

Emma frowned. "It's my understanding that there are no zoning laws, and I want to clarify that."

"But, why? Why would you need to know? Are you planning on staying here? starting a business?" The mayor looked as if he'd tasted something bitter.

"Everyone knows the house is for sale—or will be." She glanced down at Sam from the corner of her eye. "It's been a residence all these years—"

"I understood there was a problem with determining ownership of the house," the mayor said.

So, the gossip mill was going strong.

"It was a funeral home, a place of business, several years back," a councilman interrupted.

"It was," she responded. "And the bill of sale or deed will be found."

"Until it is," the mayor shrugged, "whether or not there are zoning laws is a moot point."

"It won't be when I get ready to sell the property. I need to know that if someone wanted it for a business there would be no zoning laws that would prohibit that." She glanced around the room, noting the frowns on several faces. "It's a simple question."

"Do you have plans for the property?" Darrel Masters asked. The town's banker sat on the council to the right of the mayor.

"I don't think that's anyone's business at this point," she said, trying to keep her voice from showing her irritation. "But, yes, I may have."

"What were you thinking about?" Masters asked. "Provided the abstract can be brought up to date. What sort of business? Another funeral home?"

"I'm not sure, at this point," Emma said. "But, again, that's my choice—and Sam's—and not an issue for city council."

"I don't want to start a funeral home," Sam hissed.

Emma nudged his knee. "Keep quiet."

"Or a tearoom," he reminded her under his breath.

The banker pursed his lips. "Well, I wouldn't want you to over-extend yourself."

Emma was incredulous. "How would I do that?"

Masters shrugged, exchanging a glance with his honor the mayor. "It's quite clear that you're not working, well, other than at Elizabeth's Corner, so funds must be short—"

Emma didn't know if she was more angry or more embarrassed by the ridiculous exchange.

"If—and I do mean *if*—that was any of your concern, I could assure you that I do have a good job in Seattle, one that is waiting for me when I return. And even if I were flat broke, it wouldn't be any of your business!"

"Now, Emma—"

She took a deep breath. "I asked a simple question. Are there any zoning laws in place that I need to be aware of when considering the sale of my family's house, which, by the way, is debt-free and you know that. If I needed money for a business I could use the house as collateral. I'm sure any bank in Durango would be glad to have my business." She pinned Darrel Masters with a steady gaze. "And don't bother to remind me that a bank won't loan on a title that hasn't been proven. I'll prove ownership."

Her statement was rewarded by the shocked look on Masters's face. The banker didn't like losing business.

"Back to my original question. Are there any zoning laws in place?"

The mayor's face was nearly as red as the banker's, and the other councilmen looked decidedly uncomfortable. The mayor cleared his throat and took a sip from a glass of water. Then he said, "Serenity has never felt it necessary to have zoning. We tend to regulate those things on our own."

"In other words, if I wanted to, I could sell to someone wanting to put a zoo on the property?" Emma pressed.

"Now, Emma," the mayor started, clearly alarmed.

The other councilmen sat up straight and glanced at one another.

"I'm not saying that I've accepted any offers."

Emma thought she heard a chuckle from Sam.

"Sam, don't you have something to say about this?" the mayor asked, clearly hoping for some sane influence from the sheriff. "After all, you own half the Mansi house."

"Well, like Emma said, no offers have been accepted."

"A zoo?" the banker asked.

"It doesn't matter," Emma said as she sat down. "But no zoning laws means I'm free to talk to those people who want to put in a nudist colony."

Sam seemed to suddenly feel the need to check the toe of his boot, and Emma was sure he was trying not to burst out laughing.

The mayor sat with a thud and then hammered his gavel as the buzz of conversation rose in the room. "Meeting dismissed."

Emma picked up her coat and strode from the council room, ignoring others' attempts to engage her in conversation, knowing Sam was close behind. The snow had stopped and the air had a crackle about it. Emma stopped in the parking lot of city hall.

"Let's get a cup of coffee," Sam suggested, nodding at the stream of people coming out of the building. "I want to hear some of the buzz that'll surely come from that little scene."

Emma laughed and turned toward the café.

"A nudist colony? Come on, Emma. You nearly gave Ruth Pierce heart failure."

"Gold!" Sam turned, as a red-faced mayor threaded his way out of the building. "Hold on—I need to talk to you."

Sam waited until the mayor approached. With barely a nod to Emma, the mayor pulled the sheriff aside. "What's going on?" Crane demanded.

"Going on where?"

"In there a few minutes ago. I thought you understood that the Mansi property goes to the city. Arrangements have already been made to move the cemetery—that cemetery and that eyesore of a house aren't doing this town any good. You get that woman to sign on the dotted line—and soon." Crane's face pulsated with rage.

Sam stiffened. "What woman?"

The mayor's eyes darted to Emma. "That crazy Mansi woman— you know who I'm talking about. The whole town's noticed how cozy the two of you have gotten lately, but need I remind you your job is on the line here?"

A muscle worked tightly in Sam's jaw. He stared at the mayor, lowering his tone. "Are you threatening me, Tom?"

The mayor backed off. His tone mollified. "We've been associated a long time, Sam. This is your town, and I know you have the citizens' best interests at heart. Why, the old folk have to take a bus or face a long walk to the doctor's office because there's no proper parking. Land developers are eyeing the property. Come election time, they're going to hold us both responsible—you more than me because you're half owner of that house! Where's your brain? This could be a smooth process, but you're making it complicated." Taking out a cigar, the mayor fumbled with a match and lit it. He drew on the smoke and then flipped the match aside. "Think about it. Both our jobs are in jeopardy because of that crazy—"

Sam's stormy look stopped him. "Look, Tom. Emma owns the house; my part is on paper only." His look hardened. "There's nothing crazy about the woman, and you come at me one more time with an idle threat and we'll see whose job's threatened." Sam turned on his heel and walked off.

Sam rejoined Emma, caught her arm, and steered her down the walk, picking up the thread of their earlier conversation. "So you like our council meetings?"

"That was the most absurd experience I've ever had!" Emma said, shaking her head. "What was that all about?"

"I don't know. I don't think I've ever seen the mayor or Darrel at a loss for words before. That's almost historic."

"It was a simple question, requiring a simple answer. Why all that hoopla? And for Darrel Masters to suggest I don't have the funds to start a business—"

"Do you?" Sam's scowl signaled her to swallow the words he apparently anticipated would spurt from her mouth. "Not that I have any right to ask about that, but if you're seriously thinking of opening a tearoom, finances are a big issue. And now that you've put Darrel in his place, he's not going to be very open to an application for a business loan."

"First, if I did think seriously about opening a business in the house, I wouldn't be going to Darrel for a loan. He's too prone to share information with too many people, the mayor included, if I don't miss my guess. I would go to Durango or somewhere else where they understand business ethics."

"Then you *are* thinking of staying?" His gaze caught hers and held.

"I don't know," she said finally. "I don't know what I'm going to do."

Seated in the café, they drank their coffee, carefully avoiding the subject of the future, watching and listening as people drifted in from the council meeting. There was, as Sam predicted, much speculation over whether Emma's comments about a zoo or a nudist group could in any way be taken seriously. Sam and Emma hid their smiles behind their coffee cups.

"Well, thanks for an entertaining evening," Sam said as they parted in front of the café, running the back of one finger down her cheek.

"You're welcome," she returned, wishing he'd kiss her again.

"When are you going to decide whether to stay . . . or go?"

"I don't know," she whispered. *Kiss me.*

"Soon," he said, then bent and brushed a kiss across her mouth. It wasn't enough, but it would have to do.

Emma watched him stride away, her nerves jangling. Sam Gold was an expert at putting her off balance.

When Emma arrived back home she wished she'd remembered to turn on the front-porch light that morning before she left. There was nothing so dark as a moonless night, and nothing so creepy as the huge, looming Victorian edifice against a black sky.

She made her way to the front door more by memory and habit now than by any light. She fumbled slightly with the lock. When she got the door open she was greeted with a blast of heat from the woodstove. Emitting a groan of impatience, Emma left the door standing open to let some of the heat out. She took her coat off and threw it over the arm of the couch. Gismo padded out from the kitchen to greet her, his nails clicking on the wood floor.

"Hey, Gismo. Wish you knew how to operate this stove. I'm tired of hauling in wood to have it burn up while I have the front door open to regulate the heat. It's ridiculous, but I cannot get this thing to work." She scratched his head. "You'd think Lully could have had some kind of other heat source put in, but then, she knew how to operate the stove."

Kicking off her shoes, Emma padded into the kitchen to fill Gismo's bowl and give him fresh water. She noticed the door to the basement was slightly ajar. She shoved it closed with a frown.

"Good boy, Gismo. I'm glad you didn't go down there. It's a mess." She shivered. Though she'd already gone through many boxes, many still remained. Then there were the attic and Lully's room.

Suddenly Emma's head ached. Too many things to do, too much of the past she still didn't want to confront.

chapter
ELEVEN

EMMA spread the last coat of hunter green paint on the shutters and dropped the brush into a can of thinner. Fourteen newly painted shutters lined the inside wall of the garage, ready to be rehung when weather permitted.

Ray Sullins, who had taken to stopping by the bookstore for the slightest excuse, had stopped by the house and found her contemplating the shutters one mild Saturday afternoon. He'd graciously offered to take them down for her when she said she planned to paint them. Emma wasn't sure he was up to the job, but his sincerity persuaded her to accept his help. He knew exactly where the tools were kept. Emma again was struck by Ray's familiarity with the house and its contents—even more surprised that Lully would allow the informality.

She stretched the kinks out of her back. The rest of the outside painting would have to either wait until spring or become someone else's problem. She stared out the garage window at the big house with its ornate corners and fan-shaped decorations on all the gables. Angles and curves and the steep pitch of the roof made any repairs a nightmare. Definitely a job for professionals.

Stepping back to survey her work, Emma smiled. Lully would have loved this color. Her sister had favored the dark and exotic.

"That's very pretty."

Emma started at the voice of Ray Sullins. The slim man was framed in the garage's doorway. Wind whipped the fringe of grayed hair that encircled his bald pate. Amber, narrow-set eyes, an odd cross between a gold and green, were fixed on her. A shiver crept up her spine. He unnerved her with his quiet approach and soft voice, yet she knew he was lonesome and missed Lully something terrible. He was like a lost pup, standing in front of the house at night and gazing toward Lully's window with a look of sadness.

Emma's heart ached for him. "Hi, Ray. Did you need something?"

Ray stepped into the shed, brushing down his windblown hair. The space suddenly seemed crowded, too close, and Emma stepped farther back into the lean-to. His gaze swept the shutters.

"You gonna put 'em back up?"

"Not today. Probably not until spring."

He nodded sagely. "Too cold."

"Yes," Emma agreed. She made herself relax, telling herself that Ray was interested in anything that happened at the house. She recalled the time he had walked through the front door calling Lully's name, as if he did it every day. He'd forgotten Lully was gone. When Ray found Emma in the kitchen, she was shaking from fright, and his face crumpled with grief. Then he had grinned and asked if she had any apples.

She gave him a shiny Delicious apple and ushered him back out the door, asking him to remember to knock next time he visited. His face registered his hurt. "Lully didn't make me knock."

Well, that was Lully's choice. Emma preferred to be alerted when she was about to be invaded. "I'm sure she didn't, but she's gone now," Emma had reminded him, keeping a gentle tone.

When she'd mentioned the incident to Sam, he said he'd talk to Ray, but he reminded her that Ray was harmless. He was childlike and had forgotten Lully wasn't in the house anymore. But from that point on Emma kept the screen door latched. She didn't need any more scares like that.

Now Ray was studying the shutters as if he hadn't seen them before. He bit into a shiny red apple, the juice running down his chin. Emma wondered if he'd gone into the house and chosen one from the bowl she had set on the kitchen table.

"What's you gonna do?"

"Do?"

Emma sighed mentally. She didn't want to be rude to the strange little man, but she didn't want him underfoot all afternoon either. She'd raked leaves from the flower beds last week and Ray had shown up. He watched a minute before offering to help. She agreed and then tripped over him every time she turned around. He was eager to help but too often "help" turned into "helpless."

"I'm going to take a nap."

It wasn't exactly a lie. She might. But then, she'd thought about starting to clean out the basement, looking through those boxes for the deed. She didn't need his "help" with that, and he'd surely insist on staying if she mentioned the project.

"Lully never napped," he said, taking another bite of the apple.

"Maybe not nap," she corrected, feeling guilty about the deception. His guilelessness unnerved her. "I might go to the basement and start sorting through old boxes. I don't know. I'll have to see what I feel up to."

Ray sent the apple core flying out the door. "I can help!"

Emma released a sigh. "No, Ray. Really. It's nice of you to offer but—"

His face lit with expectation. "I'm not doing anything. Nothing." He showed her his hands, palms out, as proof. "See? Through with the apple and ready to help."

Blither! Why had Lully been so insistent on telling the truth! If she could have lied she would have avoided the hassle.

Emma floundered for an excuse. Ray wasn't physically strong enough to carry heavy boxes up the steep stairs. Besides, she wasn't crazy about being downstairs alone with him.

A short siren burst drew their attention outside. Emma slumped with relief when she spotted the sheriff's cruiser parked in the drive. Sam got out and saw them, removing his hat and sunglasses as he approached. His dark hair glistened in the early afternoon sunlight. His gaze swept Emma and he smiled. "Ms. Mansi."

"Sheriff Gold."

Sam glanced at Ray. "Hi, Ray. I've been looking for you."

Ray's face brightened. "You have been looking for me?"

"Yes. Thought Mrs. Peabody could use some help carrying her groceries home. Looked to me like she bought a few more things than she intended to."

"I'll go help," Ray said, taking off down the lane at a fast clip. "I'm not doing anything."

Sam grinned at Emma.

She glanced up at him, then back at the quickly disappearing little man. "What?"

"Don't I get a kiss?"

Heat flooded her cheeks. Some men had more nerve than good sense. "Why?"

"Didn't I save you from an exasperating afternoon? I think that deserves a reward."

She had to grin. He'd read the situation correctly. "You're right. I didn't want to hurt his feelings. He has a good heart, I guess. But—"

"You'll have to thank old Mrs. Peabody. She really did need help. Now—" he leaned closer—"how about that kiss?"

"Sure. Tell Mrs. Peabody I'll kiss her the very first time I see her. Promise." She crossed her heart, then brushed past him.

He followed her to the back-porch steps.

"Want something to drink?" Emma called over her shoulder. Oh, she wished she'd taken advantage of that offer of a kiss, but he was being just a bit too full of himself right now.

"Why not?" He grinned in a way that said he knew what was going on in her head.

A blast of heat greeted them when they stepped inside the house.

"Haven't you learned to regulate that stove yet?"

"I know how, but it's not cooperating."

"You're in charge," he reminded, striding toward the front of the house. "You've got all the windows open!"

"Yes! Otherwise I'd be cooked by now!"

His chuckle irritated her. He could say that regulating that stove was easy, but she'd not found it so. Lately it was harder than ever to get it right.

"Come in here," he called out.

"I'm pouring your coffee! Don't be so bossy."

"Emma—"

"Oh, all right."

He could show her how to work the stove every day for a week, and she'd still have trouble with the vents and damper. Still, she went to the parlor, where Sam was kneeling in front of the stove, his face turned away from the blast of radiating heat.

"Come over here."

"I'm not sure I should."

"I'm harmless." He showed her his hands, palms out.

"Stop that," she scolded. "You sound like Ray." She felt bad for being so sharp. "He does try to help," she amended.

"So do I." Reaching for her hand, he drew her to the stove. "Look, the damper needs to be turned just so."

"I know what the damper is and that it needs to be set in the right position."

"Then why don't you use it?"

Emma gave him a withering look. "I'll bet you a chocolate cake you can't adjust it properly."

"A chocolate cake?" His brows lifted. "Fudge, with raspberry filling?"

"Three layer," she promised.

"Piece of cake," he mumbled, reaching for the wire knob.

He turned the knob. She waited. Nothing happened. He turned the knob again. Then again. Then with one finger he reached out and flipped the knob, which spun around crazily.

A bead of sweat rolled down his temple. He stripped out of his jacket and threw it on the couch. Dropping to his knees again he tested the damper knob gingerly, mumbling under his breath.

Emma perched on the edge of the couch, chin resting on the heel of her hand. "Having any luck?"

Without answering, he went to the window and jerked it up another inch. "There's something wrong with it."

"No kidding," Emma responded. "That's the last thing I would have thought of."

He shot her a sour look. "I'll call someone to fix it. Let the fire die down tonight so Jim can work on the stove tomorrow."

"You mean to tell me there's somebody in this town who specializes in stove dampers? The guy I called can't be here for another two weeks. Seems there's an epidemic of faulty dampers in Durango."

"Okay. So you already knew what the problem was."

"I might not be familiar with woodstoves, but I do know that when it's a hundred and five degrees in here all the time there's a problem."

He shook his head and she grinned back at him. "Let's drink our coffee before it gets cold," Emma suggested.

"In this heat? Not a chance." He pretended to come after her. Giggling, she took off toward the kitchen, slowing down when Sam gave up the chase.

"I'll see if I can get these vents loosened up enough to help with the problem," Sam offered, remaining in the parlor to work on the vents.

"Okay, but it's a losing battle, believe me. Did I tell you that I talked to Janice this morning?" she called over her shoulder as she walked through the dining room.

"Yeah? How is she?"

Emma had told Sam all about Janice when they had gone paint shopping and how she thought of the girl as almost family. The two were closer than Lully and Emma had ever been. "Still looking for a job. I hope she finds one soon—I don't want her discouraged."

Emma sailed into the kitchen and reached for cups and saucers in the cabinet, but a cup tipped and crashed to the floor.

"You okay?" He called from the parlor.

"I broke a cup!"

She started to the pantry for the broom, then remembered the dustpan with a brush that fit into its handle under the sink. She knelt to open the cabinet door and reached inside for the pan. But instead of feeling an enameled dustpan, she felt something slick. Something slick . . . and thick . . . and then it moved. She felt again, frowning. It moved again.

Shrieking, she jerked and fell backward, sprawling across the floor. She watched with horror as a thick coil of reptile slithered out of the cabinet, almost on her foot, then another length followed, along with a triangular-shaped head. The snake's head turned in her direction, its tongue flicking out. Hysteria choked her. Was the reptile poisonous? Would it strike her if she moved?

Another coil fell out of the cabinet, spilling over her foot. Nausea clawed at the back of her throat. *Please, God, don't let it come any closer.*

The snake slid off her foot, but lay, waiting. Somewhere in her mind a voice told her this was no ordinary snake. Certainly not the little garden snakes she was used to finding around the yard when she was a child. She'd never seen anything like this except in a zoo!

Mentally, she called Sam. *Help me!* But she was frozen. The snake lay perfectly still, except for its flicking tongue.

"Don't move a muscle." Sam's soft voice sounded from the doorway.

Choking back sobs, Emma couldn't have moved if her life depended on it. She was vaguely aware of Sam easing around to her right. He'd pulled out his revolver, prepared to shoot. *Shoot, Sam!* she silently urged. *Do something!*

The shot echoed through the house, shattering Emma's eardrums. The snake's head exploded, and Emma fainted.

When she awoke, Sam was holding her in his arms. For a

moment she didn't know why he was holding her so tightly. She lay with her head against his chest, held there by one big hand against the side of her face, her forehead pressed against his cheek. She heard his heartbeat, felt the strength of his arms, heard him saying, "It's okay, Emma," over and over in a gentle tone. She didn't want to move. She liked being here like this.

Then she remembered the snake and struggled to sit up.

"It's okay, Emma," Sam said again, more firmly. "It's gone."

"What was it?"

"A boa constrictor. A big one."

Emma shivered. Then she realized that they were in the parlor on the sofa. "What happened?"

"You fainted."

"I always faint at the sight of snakes falling out of my cabinets."

"At least you still have your sense of humor." He smiled, releasing her to sit up.

Eyes closed, she raked her fingers through her hair. "I've never been so scared in my life."

"I don't know where a snake that size would come from around here."

Her gaze met his. "Thank you," she whispered, remembering that he'd shot the snake.

Sam cupped her chin in his hand and leaned toward her, kissing her lightly. "How about that coffee now?"

Emma tried to relax while Sam reheated the coffee. Her heart was beating a mile a second. Had someone deliberately put the snake into the house—or worse, had Emma been living with it for days—weeks? She shuddered. "How did that thing get in here?" she asked.

"Who knows? Could have been here a long time, or you left the door open and it crawled in—"

"I don't leave the door open long enough for something like that to crawl in."

He sat down opposite her at the kitchen table. "Hey."

"Hey what?" She stared into her empty cup.

"We need to talk."

She groaned, "About the house? Come on, Sam. I've had it appraised—"

"I'm not talking about the specifics. I have a feeling you're not going to sell if the place brought a million dollars."

She smiled sheepishly.

"Don't think that so out of order," he warned. "Speculators are circling like vultures now, vultures with money in their pockets."

"Then what do you want to talk about?"

"A decision. A firm decision, and soon." His eyes darkened. "The mayor is hot under the collar; time-share people are ringing the phone off the hook. I can't take much more, Emma. You have to decide what route you're taking and stick with it. It's your decision."

She gazed at him. "Truly?"

"Truly."

"But I thought you wanted the parking lot."

"I still think a parking lot makes the most sense. I'd like to see the town prosper and grow. But I don't intend to fight you on the matter anymore. It's your home; the decision is yours. Let's try to make one before the town takes up arms."

She reached over and grasped his hand. Electricity flowed. "Thank you."

His eyes met hers. "I don't know what more I have to do to convince you that I'm not your enemy."

"Nothing—I know you're not, Sam. Just bear with me. It's my town too, you know. I want to keep the house, yet I want what's best for all concerned. There's Janice to think about . . . and your mother . . ."

Why did a simple will have to make life so complicated?

Mayor Crane occupied a ten-year-old, contemporary, ranch-style house on the outskirts of town, where an attempt had been made to create a housing development a few years earlier. The idea never quite worked out. Sam drove the cruiser down a street lit by an occasional streetlight, where only three houses lined the unfinished sidewalks. The place had a lonely, abandoned feel. But Thomas Crane still held hope for the development. Sam had to give him credit for persistence.

He agreed with His Honor on many fronts. He knew the town needed a new parking lot. They had to stay ahead of the times, or at least catch up. Their young people left as soon as they graduated high school, either to find jobs elsewhere or to attend college, never to return. There needed to be something to hold them here, something that wouldn't also bring pollution and urban sprawl. The mayor wasn't as picky, and the banker would loan money to anyone new coming into town. The corner of Sam's mouth turned down. Anyone, it seemed, except Emma Mansi.

He wheeled into the mayor's drive and parked. After ringing the doorbell he stood looking toward the mountains. He liked everything about Serenity, even the winters. He'd been one of the few who had returned to stay. But then, he enjoyed his job and being part of the community. He had responsibilities and some family. He had a good life here. Only one thing was missing—a woman he could love and trust, and children.

"Sam, how nice to see you!"

Vinita Crane, a petite woman, was a bird-watcher. She always reminded Sam of one of her subjects. At the moment she peered up at him with her bright blue eyes, her head tilted inquisitively to one side.

"Mrs. Crane. Is Buddy home?"

"Why, yes. He isn't in any trouble is he? I would be really upset—"

"No, not at all. I need to ask him a couple of questions."

"He's in his room. Come in, and I'll get him for you."

"Thanks."

Sam waited in a living room that was too full of furniture to be comfortable and too fussy for a man's taste. Somehow he'd never been able to picture the mayor in this room.

The Cranes' fourteen-year-old son, Buddy, slopped down the hall behind his mother, dragging his heels.

"Now Buddy, you answer all the sheriff's questions. Sam, would you like something hot to drink? The weather's bitter outside." She peered at him with sparrowlike eyes.

Knowing he'd not get a few minutes alone with the boy unless Vinita had something to do, he asked if she had any coffee on hand. She didn't, but allowed that she had instant. Sam hated instant—gave him heartburn—but it would buy him a few moments of privacy.

When Mrs. Crane had fluttered away toward the back of the house, Sam motioned for Buddy to sit. "I understand you have a new hobby."

Buddy pursed his lips and refused to meet the sheriff's eyes. "What new hobby?"

"You bought a boa constrictor a couple of weeks ago. About eight feet long?"

"Oh, yeah, I did. How'd you know?"

"Talked to Lloyd at the pet store this morning."

"Yeah?"

"Yeah."

"Lloyd's got a big mouth."

"Do you keep the snake in your room?"

"I was gonna." Buddy shifted, looking away.

"But you didn't?" Sam couldn't imagine Vinita allowing the boy to keep anything that size in the house, caged or not.

Could the boa have been stolen?

"Naw. Sold it. Mom wouldn't let me keep it—freaked out when she saw it and yelled at me to get rid of it."

"You sold the boa?"

"Uh-huh."

"When did you sell it?"

"Oh, a couple of days after I bought it. Found out it was hibernating. That's no fun. Lloyd didn't tell me that."

"Who did you sell it to?" Sam's internal alarm went off.

Whoever bought the boa could be the same person who was harassing Emma.

The youth shrugged. "I don't know."

"Bud, you know everybody in town."

"Guy had a ski mask on. I couldn't tell who he was. He was standing outside of school one day, and he asked if I had a boa. I said yes and he offered to buy it."

It was pretty cold outside; a ski mask wouldn't be unusual.

"Height, color of his eyes. Anything? Did he pay cash?"

Buddy shrugged. "He had brown eyes, I think. Tall, I think. Paid cash."

"Tall and brown eyes" eliminated a few people, but the description was too vague to be useful. Just then the front door opened, and the mayor whipped in with a blast of cold air.

"Sam." The mayor set his ever-present briefcase down inside the door and extended his hand, though his look was distant. "How are you doing?" He glanced at his son. "Any problem here?"

"None at all, Tom. I was asking Bud about the boa he bought from Lloyd and then sold."

The mayor frowned. "What's wrong with that?"

"Nothing. Except a boa ended up under Emma Mansi's sink, and I'm wondering who might have put it there."

Tom Crane looked genuinely concerned. "Someone put a snake in the Mansi house? Why?"

"We're not sure. If it was a prank to scare her, it worked. But it was dangerous too. I want to know who and how and why."

"Have you talked to the person who bought Buddy's snake?"

Sam shook his head. "Don't know who it is yet. Not a good enough description."

"Well that's a real shame." Tom turned back to look at his son. "You've told the sheriff all you know?"

"Everything," Bud declared, eyes shifting to his feet. "I don't know what he done with the snake."

"Well, that's not good, if someone put a snake in Emma's house, but I'm sure Buddy has nothing further to offer on the subject." He glanced at his son. "Have you finished your homework?"

"Not yet—"

"Then get to it."

The boy pushed himself to his feet and sauntered down the hall with his heels dragging, laces untied. The mayor frowned before turning back to Sam. He ushered him to the front door.

"Sorry Emma had a scare." His features sobered. "Have you talked sense into her yet?"

"Emma's got enough sense to make her own decisions."

Tom frowned. "You do recall our conversation the other night?"

"Oh sure. I recall the conversation." Sam slipped his hat on. "And I'm sure you recall my response."

"I'm not an unreasonable man. I won't push, within reason. One of these days she'll be ready to accept anything reasonable so she can get back to Seattle and her job. She does still have a job there—"

"Yes, she owns the place. Winter in a greenhouse is a slow time of year, I'm told."

"Sam, this is not an amusing matter. What if she should decide to sell to some flake and they turn that piece of property into a . . . a zoo or a . . . a nudist group—"

"She wouldn't do that to Serenity."

"How can you be so sure? She doesn't seem the least bit concerned about our needs."

"Maybe she's thinking more about her needs. The need to hold on to what she has left of her family."

"Well, I think she'd want all this settled so she could get on with her life. What was all that business about the zoning laws? She isn't thinking of putting in a business herself, is she? I mean, after all, Lully had that silly jewelry business, funny-looking stuff, but then those Mansi girls were always a little strange."

The mayor's attitude bothered Sam. "I don't see anything odd about them. Lully was talented and Emma's an intelligent woman."

"Well, you know what I mean."

"No, I don't. What do you mean?"

"Would Emma entertain a higher offer? I suppose we could come up with another twenty thousand."

"Money isn't a factor in her decision."

"Then for goodness sakes, what is?"

Sam shook his head. "You'd have to talk to Emma about that—"

"But you're part owner of the house. You have some influence. She should feel fortunate to get anything out of that place. Why, the land is the only thing that has any value. That snake probably escaped from whoever bought it and it was looking for a warm place to sleep through the winter."

Sam remembered seeing Crane and the banker snooping around Emma's backyard last Sunday. He wondered if the mayor wanted the house so badly he'd resort to dirty tricks like this. Sam asked, "Know anything about snakes, Tom?"

"Me? Nothing more than Buddy has talked about." He opened the door. "You let me know what you find out, about the snake and about the asking price, once you two settle on one." He didn't laugh. "Reasonable, considering the shape of the house."

The mayor's interest in Emma's house made Sam curious. "Do you know someone other than the town who's interested in the property?"

"Everyone. I've been getting a lot of calls from land developers. Time-share folks. Got a man coming down next week to talk to Emma—I'm sure you'll be included in the discussions."

"I'm sure I will be," Sam said.

The mayor pursed his lips in contemplation as he studied Sam's face. "You and Emma picking up where you left off fifteen years ago?"

Sam settled his hat on his head and stepped off the porch. "Thanks for the information, Tom. I'll get back with you."

"See that you do now." The mayor leaned out of the screen door. "And don't forget, you're a public official—your loyalty belongs to your job, not some old flame—"

Sam got into the cruiser and slammed the door. As he drove back to the office, Sam turned the conversations he'd had with Buddy and Tom over in his mind. Had Bud really sold the boa to someone? Or had he dumped it and made up the story for his father? The mayor had seemed to take Emma's scare in stride, more interested in the house than in Emma. Did Tom have something to do with the pranks played on Emma?

It didn't seem probable that the mayor would be involved in such pranks—after all, his job would be compromised if he were found out. But Sam wasn't ignoring anything at this point. Whoever was trying to scare Emma was succeeding. If getting the price of the house down to bargain basement was the motive behind the pranks, then he was afraid they were going to succeed. Spiders and snakes were seriously creepy things to most people—and possibly even dangerous. Pigs were a nuisance, but the incident had sure put Emma in a blue funk.

Sam was determined to find out who was responsible and why. Weird things were happening, and he was going to stop them.

Sam bumped into Emma at Brisco's that evening. She'd stopped off for a sandwich after closing the bookstore.

"Hi," he said, sliding into her booth across from her.

She already had a cup of tea in front of her; both hands wrapped around the steaming heat.

"Doing okay?" Sam said.

"As long as I don't think about that snake crawling out from beneath my sink."

Sam grinned. She had grit. The snake had thoroughly shaken her.

"Did you find out anything about how it got there?" she asked.

"Not much. Lloyd bought a couple of boas. I located one, but the other was an out-of-state purchase and I haven't found out yet to whom."

"Someone here in Serenity bought one?"

"It doesn't matter. I'm tracking them—"

"Sam, who bought a boa constrictor here in Serenity?"

"Buddy Crane for one, but he says he resold his within a few days and doesn't know who bought it."

"Doesn't know? How could he not know?"

"A man approached him outside the school not long after he bought the snake and paid him cash." She threw him a skeptical look and he continued. "He wore a ski mask. Bud couldn't give me a decent description."

"A ski mask?"

"It's winter, Emma. A ski mask wouldn't be unusual. Buddy thought nothing of it."

"And you believe him? Not that I'm saying he's lying, but doesn't that sound a bit fishy to you?"

"A little, but if Buddy sticks to his story, there's no way I can prove he's lying. I have to assume he's telling the truth and ask more questions."

"I know that. It's just—that thing really scared me. It could have eaten Gismo!" She shivered at the memory of the snake. How long had it lurked in the house? How long had it been under the sink? "Who's doing this to me, Sam? And why?"

He smiled at Penny as she set a cup of coffee in front of him. "It could be someone who wants the house and is willing to go to any lengths to get it. That's what concerns me now. The land is valuable, Emma. That's why it's important for you to make up your mind. Sell it or keep it, but I don't want to have to worry about you getting hurt."

She broke into a smile. "You'd really be worrying about me?"

He shook his head, turning away. "Just make up your mind, please?"

"So you think someone is trying to run me off. Is that what they tried to do to Lully—drive her out? In the past the pranks were harmless—never anything like spiders and snakes."

Sam shook his head. "I don't know, Emma. I only know you

need to be careful, not take any chances. I'll protect you with my life, but I can't be near you every minute."

She grinned at him.

"Keep your mind on the subject. This isn't a laughing matter," he said. "If anything happened to you . . ." He didn't finished the thought.

"You think whoever is doing this will try something else?"

"I don't know," he repeated. "Just be careful."

Sam paid the bill a few minutes later and walked Emma home. On the porch he held her tightly in his arms and whispered against her hair, "Call me if anything suspicious comes up. Anything at all."

"I will," she promised.

Sam waited while she let herself into the house. The lights flicked on.

Snow had started to fall. Emma was trying not to let the incidents get to her, but he knew she was more frightened than she wanted him to know. He mentally shifted his schedule so he could drive by the Mansi house more often to make sure no one was lurking around and to be available if she needed him.

"There's more to this than pranks," he muttered. "A lot more."

He vowed to find out what, exactly. Surely it was more than an infantile effort to lower the asking price on the house. Price wasn't a reasonable motivation—not with land developers in the game.

As he returned to his patrol car, which he'd left parked at the café, Sam wondered why Emma wasn't anxious to be finished with this business. What if she turned the house into a tearoom? What would she do then? Hire someone to run it? Then why make the investment unless she loved the town more than she admitted and planned to come back someday?

Or if she's falling in love with you again. That was the thought Sam wanted to hold on to.

She was confusing him. On one hand she wanted to leave Serenity and all its memories behind. On the other hand, she talked about laying down roots, opening a business, redoing her mom's rose garden.

Could she get past what she'd thought was his betrayal, his abandonment of her? Add to that the gossip and speculation and plain meanness of some people; could she get over those things as well? Sam didn't know, and he didn't know who was trying to run her out of the house.

But he meant to find out.

EMMA sat up, pitching the light afghan aside. The woodstove burned white-hot. She had fallen asleep again. Lately, she dropped onto the sofa after work to watch *World News Tonight* and often fell asleep before Peter Jennings gave the headlines.

She stirred when someone knocked on the front door. Why hadn't Lully installed a doorbell? That would be so much more pleasant sounding. Rolling off the sofa, Emma swiped a piece of hair into place and straightened the collar on her shirt.

Sam smiled down at her when she opened the door. "Hey."

"Hey." She gave her grooming effort another try. No lipstick, and her hair looked like she'd walked through a strong gale. "What's up?" Her pulse hammered, not uncommon when he was around.

He turned to look outside, his brown-eyed gaze scanning the fresh cover of powder dusting the ground. "I've borrowed a sleigh from a friend." He turned back to face her. "Want to go for a ride?"

She smiled, leaning against the door frame. An icy wind blew from the north, and the mere thought of an open-air ride brought goose bumps. Yet the man standing before her overrode Emma's common sense.

Her gaze traveled beyond the porch to the large sled behind

a frisky horse, who was blowing frosty vapors into the night air and stamping his feet. "It's so cold," she said.

"I'll keep you warm." He leaned closer, his eyes dancing with mischief. Emma suddenly found it hard to breathe. "How about it, Ms. Mansi? Want to go for a ride with the sheriff? I could, technically, take you into custody."

"For what?" she bantered. Both seemed reluctant to break eye contact. Something about the emotional current went dangerously far beyond the topic.

"Disturbing the peace."

"Whose peace?"

He looked away. "I plead the fifth." On the grounds that the answer could/might/would most certainly incriminate him.

She had to enter the same plea. "I'll get my coat." She put on the heaviest garment she could find in the front-hall closet. Lully's coat assortment varied, but the heavy wools were adequate for a cold Colorado night in an open sleigh.

Emma suddenly found herself looking forward to the excursion with childlike enthusiasm. A canopy of stars shone above their heads as Sam helped her into the sleigh. A bright moon illuminated the snowy landscape. Their laughter drifted over the mounds of crusted snow. Sam settled on the narrow seat, then reached for the heavy lap robe and tucked it securely on each end of the bench. His hand briefly brushed Emma and she closed her eyes, stuffing teenage adoration into its proper perspective. She was going for a simple ride with an old acquaintance. Big deal.

But it was a big deal.

Too big a deal for her to keep a handle on her emotions, especially with the way Sam's knee rested lightly against hers.

He picked up the reins and made a clicking noise with his tongue. The black mare started off, gaining momentum, taking the sleigh skimming over the frozen ground. One thing Emma could say with certainty: God had smiled on Colorado. The moon-drenched countryside flew past as the horse cantered over hill and dale, cutting wide paths through stands of tall aspen and fragrant pine. Emma's laughter left frosty trails as the years fell away and she was once more a young fifteen-year-old girl in love for the very first time. She clutched Sam's arm as the sleigh skimmed over fresh powder.

His gaze caught hers in the moonlight and he smiled, his gloved hands competently controlling the breathless ride. "Having fun?" he shouted as the sleigh took a harrowing turn, revealing a deep incline on the right side.

She scooted closer, realizing that she didn't care for heights. As a young girl these mountainous regions were home. Seattle had its mountains, but she had never been in a sleigh going lickety-split over such steep slopes. She nodded, holding his biceps tighter. "A little."

He squeezed her hand. "I'll take care of you."

That was exactly what Emma feared. Closing her eyes, she found herself thinking about God. Was he here, and was his Spirit living within her? Could she entrust him with her most secret need—the need to tear down the barriers and open her heart and become vulnerable again? Out here in this beautiful wilderness it was easier to believe. She felt her heart slowly begin to open.

Eventually Sam slowed the horse, and the mare trotted along beneath the full moon. He hadn't said anything in a while; they shared a comfortable silence.

Emma felt his arm brush the back of her neck, and she snuggled closer.

"Cold?"

She shook her head.

"Like the feel of my arm around you?" He chuckled.

She started to say no and pull away. He could be so confident of her at times—did her facial expressions broadcast to the world how she felt about this man? But the feeling of his arm, his warmth, the security of being with him stopped her, and she could do no less than admit the truth. "Yes," she whispered softly.

He reined the horse to a halt. Cold, snowy silence encompassed the sleigh. "Did you say yes?"

Nodding, she smiled and burrowed her head deeper into his arm's crevice.

He stood up, took off his hat, and shouted, "Hallelujah!"

"Lujah lujah lujah lujah lujah lujah lujah" the echo returned.

She laughed at his theatrics and pulled him down on the seat. "Stop it, you goose."

Grasping the back of her head, he pulled her toward him, lowering his lips to within a breadth of hers. "Do you know how long I've waited for you to say that?"

"That you're a goose? Goose, goose," she teased, tweaking his nose. "Stubborn goose."

He pulled her nose. "Mulish gander."

She pretended to be insulted. "Are you name-calling?"

He caught her closer, his eyes twinkling with mischief. "Are you going to answer my question?"

"No. It's too silly."

"Silly?"

She knew how long he'd wanted to make the admission; almost as long as she'd wanted to say it. Their eyes met and held in the moonlight. Then he gently lowered his head and kissed her—a full fifteen years' worth.

It was as if an emotional dam had burst between them and they were now swimming for their lives.

Three days passed without a word from Sam. Emma didn't know why he was suddenly making himself scarce—but then, deep down, she did. He had feelings and emotions like she did. Did he fear the past or, after the sleigh ride, was it the future that terrified him? They had dropped back into each other's life with the subtlety of a hand grenade. His feelings must be as tangled as hers, or was she only kidding herself? She hoped not, yet she wasn't prepared to think about anything further than the next day. They both needed breathing space, time to rethink the situation and admit that years ago they had lost something so precious, so worth holding on to.

Emma shook the reflection away and added nuts to the mixing bowl. Elizabeth had talked her into visiting the nursing home with her that afternoon. It seemed the residents of Happy Hollow looked forward to the holiday season and Elizabeth's banana nut bread. The job of baking all those loaves had become too much for Elizabeth, and she'd offered to pay Emma to help. Emma had declined the pay. She had discovered she liked doing things for others. She'd met Janice that way and the friendship was priceless.

Emma folded nuts into the creamy batter, wondering what Janice would do when she was on her own. She was a trusting soul. Janice had a strong faith in God—sometimes so much so that Emma envied her unwavering faith. Nothing seemed to shake it; with Emma, every little storm of life threw her into a sea of doubt. For the past few years, what little faith she had in a good God had floundered. And yet . . . there were people like Janice and Sue and even Lully, whose faith sustained them through so much. Perhaps if she, too, reached out to God, her own faith could sprout and grow. . . .

Guilt swept through her as Christmas carols floated from the radio. "'O holy night . . .'"

It was the season for hope and belief. Why couldn't she grasp onto the Lord and stay close to him?

Emma picked Elizabeth up around one o'clock, and the two women drove to the nursing home, chatting all the way. Christmas trees twinkled in the large complex, and carols floated through the one-story building as they entered.

Happy Hollow residents sat around in chairs and on sofas, reading or working puzzles; a few stared at the television screen. Emma and Elizabeth worked their way through the ensemble, shaking hands, greeting smiling faces with a bright "Merry Christmas!"

Later, they walked down the halls delivering packages of banana bread wrapped in red cellophane and tied with a large green bow.

Emma tapped at an open door, "Mr. Jones?"

An old man with a head full of snow-white hair lifted his hand feebly.

"I've brought you some banana bread!"

He nodded. "Just put it on the table."

Emma did as she was told, scooting aside pictures of grinning children and older couples to make room. "Merry Christmas!"

"Yeah—same to you." He closed his eyes and appeared to have drifted back to sleep.

Smiling, she moved to the next door, pausing when she read the nameplate: Edwina Gold. *Dear Lord, Sam's mother.* Emma knew she was here—did she think she could avoid Edwina forever? After all these years she was about to come face-to-face with Sam's mother.

She stood holding the colorfully wrapped Christmas bread, wondering if she should skip this room and have Elizabeth deliver the gift.

Coward.

That's exactly what she was: a coward. It was high time she grew up and stopped running. And there had never been a more appropriate time. Besides, she assured herself, Edwina probably wouldn't even recognize her after all these years. She took a deep breath and tapped on the door softly.

"Yes?" a voice answered.

"Merry Christmas, Mrs. Gold. I have a gift for you!" Emma chirped.

"Come in."

Emma walked into the room. A shadow of the former mayor smiled. The years had not been kind. She had to be what? Late sixties? She had seemed old, even when she and Sam were young.

"Hello, Emma. It's been a long time."

Emma covered her surprise. Edwina had recognized her immediately. Years ago the two women had barely spoken to each other, and their last heated parting shots had not exactly been Hallmark greeting-card material.

Emma set the bread on a nearby table and turned to leave when Edwina's voice stopped her. "Don't go."

She turned, feeling a chill race up her spine. "Can I get you something?"

"No." Edwina closed her eyes. "I'd just like to talk a few minutes, if you have the time."

Emma pulled a chair closer to the bed and sat down. "I can spare a few minutes." If the woman was going to take her to task about something that happened fifteen years ago, she wouldn't stay long.

Emma waited, smiling at the old woman in the bed. "Anything in particular you want to talk about?" She wondered if she should offer to crank up the bed. Edwina was lying flat, eyes closed.

"I haven't paid my respects since your sister's death." Edwina paused, seeming to struggle with the proper words. She looked up at Emma. "It's so sad when someone so young goes before her time."

Emma nodded, studying her hands. "Lully believed we're all given only so much time. Lully's time was all too brief."

Edwina glanced down at the thin blanket covering her wasted frame. "She's right. Nothing is by accident. I was surprised to hear the cause of death was a heart attack. Lully was thin, but she looked the picture of health."

Emma sensed the real reason for Edwina's invitation was about to surface.

"I'm sorry, Emma." Edwina's eyes brimmed with the silent need to be understood. "Actually, I have needed to say that I'm sorry for a very long time."

Silence filled the room. Emma heard the ticking of the clock in the hallway. Wind rattled the shutters at the windows. Carols drifted over the intercom.

"Sorry?" *Wow! What a woefully inadequate choice of words.* Emma pretended ignorance. "Sorry about what, Edwina?"

"About you and Sam. You were both so young. And foolish." Pleading turned to begging now. "You will admit that fifteen and seventeen were too young to get married, Emma. Surely you will admit that now that you're older."

Emma looked away. Did she admit that? *No,* her mind wanted to scream. *I don't admit that.* But deep in her heart she did; marriage at that age was a terrible risk. "I suppose so, Edwina." But it hadn't been a risk for her and Sam. They'd known exactly what they were doing. Emma was suddenly anxious to move—to do anything other than be with this woman who needed forgiveness. Emma wasn't sure she recognized the word anymore. Emma got up and walked to the door.

Edwina lifted her head to gaze at a picture of Christ and the lamb hanging on the wall. Emma realized it portrayed the same idea as the picture at home. Except in this picture, a ring of light encircled Jesus' head, and he held a lamb in his arms.

"I've always liked that illustration. It's comforting to know that when one of God's children goes astray he brings that child safely back into the fold."

Emma stared at the portrait. "Yes. It is, isn't it?" Gone astray. God brings them safely back into the fold. The idea was nice.

"I handled the situation all wrong." The older woman dropped her head to the pillow. "So wrong. How many times I've wished I could live that day over."

The conversation had turned personal again. Wrong? Edwina was saying she was wrong? Talk about too little too late.

Sighing, Mrs. Gold looked at Emma. "Not long after you left town I had a heart attack."

This woman—this iron Trojan when she was mayor of Serenity—was so different now that Emma could hardly connect the two women. "I'm sorry—I didn't know."

Edwina waved the polite response aside. "I was luckier than Lully. The illness gave me time to think, to reevaluate my life, my children's lives. I had an epiphany, I suppose you could say. When my husband died suddenly and then I had a heart attack a few months later . . . I came to understand that not one of us is ever self-sufficient. None of us can stand by our own strength. Only God can sustain us . . . but we have to reach out to him. He's there to pick us up when we most need him. Like the lamb, we need his protection."

The two women were silent, letting the words settle between them. Emma heard the sincerity in Edwina's voice, wanted to believe that fifteen years did make a difference. But she didn't believe it. She appreciated the apology, but it came too late.

Edwina reached over and touched Emma's arm. Her fingers were cool and papery. "I know you can't find it in your heart to forgive me. I don't expect you to—fifteen years of bitterness can't be erased with a single apology. I see it in Sam's eyes every spring when the anniversary of that attempted elopement rolls around. I hear it in his voice when your name is mentioned. Don't think I've gotten off scot-free, Emma. I've paid. Dearly. For fifteen years I've watched Sam back away from first one relationship, then another, because nobody else was you. Simple as that."

She met Emma's eyes and continued. "Simple as that. The others weren't you. My son would deny it with his dying breath. But I know. I know." Pain filled her features. "There is no greater heartache than to know that you've hurt your child irreparably. I can never give Sam back those years. Never. But I can apologize and let you know we've all suffered from what I believed at the time was the only way the situation could be handled."

Unshed tears brimmed in Emma's eyes. She didn't have trouble buying the admission; hadn't she done the same thing with every man she dated the last few years? Now she recognized the pattern of defeat. They were all good, decent men for the most part, but they weren't Sam, never could be Sam.

"I'm sorry, Edwina. Maybe in time—"

"I don't demand that you forgive me," Edwina acknowledged. "But I know this: the Spirit that is within God's children can do what we can't. We are given the power of his Spirit. You can't forgive on your own, Emma. But through God we can do all things." She flashed a hint of a smile. "I'm not asking you to like me—only to forgive the sinful nature that exists in each of us."

"Oh, Edwina . . ."

Emma rose from her chair and took the old woman in her arms. Why did the circumstances have to be so hurtful? Now she might actually feel pity for the woman—losing a husband, sons growing up and leaving home. Years of resentment were hard to overcome, yet there was no reason for Emma not to forgive. What was past was in the past, where it should remain. Christmas was a time of new hope, and it had been a long time since Emma had felt this much hope.

Before she left Edwina that afternoon, Emma felt as if a huge anchor had been lifted from around her neck.

Emma buttoned her coat and huddled deeper into the wool lining as she and Elizabeth left Happy Hollow Assisted Living late that afternoon. Visiting with Edwina had left her restless. For an hour afterward, she took deep breaths, willing herself to be calm. She admitted to herself that she was too old to hold a grudge. Grudges took energy, and lately Emma wasn't up to the fight.

Emma drove Elizabeth home and then stopped on the way home to pick up a few gifts. She supposed the holidaylike atmosphere at the nursing home affected her more than she thought. The weathered, kind, smiling faces had made her realize how ungrateful she was for the things she had: health, youth—basically her whole life ahead of her. Last Sunday after church, Ray Sullins had given her an orange and a candy cane, and had wished her Merry Christmas. *I miss Lully*, his eyes silently told her.

I do too, hers said back.

She purchased a pair of butternut-colored calfskin gloves for Elizabeth. As she passed the men's department, she had the insane urge to buy something for Sam. The impulse wouldn't go away after several moments of browsing, so she bought the most impractical thing she could find and still call it a token remembrance: a pair of gold cuff links. She knew that it would take Houdini to find a shirt that required cuff links these days, but the gift couldn't be misconstrued or considered intensely personal.

She had the present wrapped, and then stuffed it into her shopping bag. Who knew? She might decide not to give him the gift after all.

It all depended on whether he gave her one. Ho, ho, ho.

Snow fell in blowing sheets as she carefully drove home with her packages. Thoughts of Edwina's admission, the weather, and impatient Christmas shoppers left her tense. She felt close to tears and for what rational reason? Some long overdue apology? She was like a pathetic love-starved orphan who, when given an ounce of pity, sought a pound.

Climbing her front-porch steps, she stomped snow off her feet and inserted the key into the lock. Four inches of fresh snowfall covered the barren ground. The thought of putting up a tree crossed her mind, and she wondered if she was losing it. She was alone, living in a mausoleum and considering putting up a Christmas tree? She chuckled humorlessly. What was wrong with her tonight? Christmas lights, Santas ringing bells on street corners, carols saturating the air—it was enough to make the meanest Scrooge experience a fit of melancholy. She opened the door and a blast of heat knocked her back a step.

Entering the foyer, she shrugged out of her coat and trailed a wet slick of snow into the kitchen, where she heated a can of soup and later watched *Entertainment Tonight*. When several Oreo cookies and a piece of banana-nut bread failed to improve her mood, she paced the old house, going upstairs to check on Gismo, back downstairs, flipping through television channels.

Around eight o'clock, she put her coat back on and went outside. She traipsed to the shed and got a shovel, determined to clean the walk. Halfway into the project, she realized it was hopeless. Snow was falling faster than she could shovel.

Self-pity engulfed her.

She crossed her arms and stared at the picturesque landscape, biting her upper lip. This stunk. All around her, families settled in for the night—relatives who loved and cared for each other. Christmas was around the corner and she didn't even have a tree up. There was not even a wreath or eggnog or cute little sugar cookies cut in shapes of Santa Claus and bells to brighten her holiday.

She bent down and grabbed a handful of snow, forming a tight ball. She stared at the lump, feeling tears roll down her cheeks and off the tip of her nose. Leaning over, she began to roll the small ball into a bigger one. Gradually the lump grew much larger. Within fifteen minutes she had the base of a huge snow-man. She worked with intent now, rolling the midsection, then the upper torso. By now the snowman was three inches taller than she was. She trudged back to the shed in deepening drifts and retrieved a stepladder, so she could heft the unsightly fat head onto the shoulders.

Racing back into the house, she begin grabbing things: a woolen scarf, a carrot from the crisper, a man's hat she found in the closet. Dad's? Buttons—she needed black buttons. She located the items in a sewing basket next to a chair in the parlor.

She flew out the front door with the armload of items. Twenty minutes later she had created a rather unusual-looking snowman. Her hands were red and numb because she'd discarded gloves an hour earlier, but Mr. Snowman had two tree limbs for arms and scraggly branches for fingers. Studying her creation, Emma was reminded that there was always someone worse off than she was.

As she stared at the funny-looking bulk with black-button eyes and a carrot nose and wearing a hat, she realized two things: she was losing her mind, and that was the ugliest snowman she'd ever seen in her life. Ten red M&M's formed a smiling mouth. He looked pathetically happy—the exact opposite of Emma's present mood. She wondered if God ever looked at man in the same way. Sometimes unhappy with what he saw. Often sad and heartsick with what he'd created in love. Did he look at her that way?

Hot tears swelled to her eyes. She had dug a big hole for herself over the years and had systematically filled it with despair, self-pity, and more despair. Was that how she intended to spend the rest of her life—wallowing in the muddled sea of what-could-have-been and poor-me? That was exactly what she'd been doing, was still doing. But how could she stop? Self-defeat wasn't what she wanted in life.

Slowly, deliberately, one hand closed around the shovel, and then she grasped it with both hands. Lifting the heavy implement over her head, she brought the steel down, knocking the ugly snowman's head off with one swift blow. The M&M's mouth smiled grotesquely up at her from the snow-packed ground, carrot nose askew, one button eye dislodged from its socket.

She brought the shovel over her head again. And again. And again until tears blinded her. She slammed into the mounds of snow over and over and over, trying to empty herself of the pain that besieged her. Lully was dead; Sam's mother was sorry. What did it matter? What did anything matter?

Sinking to her knees, she buried her face in her hands and sobbed, releasing the pent-up tension she'd lived with since the morning of the phone call informing her of Lully's death. *No, Emma, you've lived with bitterness and resentment longer than that—it started years before the phone call.* This one she couldn't blame on Lully.

As snow came down around her, Emma cried out to God to ease the awful hurt and let her heal. *Fifteen years, God. Isn't that enough?*

If he loved her, truly loved her as he did the lamb that had gone astray, surely he would allow her to begin to heal. It wouldn't happen overnight, but it could happen. For the first time Emma allowed herself a wish. She wished for forgiveness for her own sins of blaming everybody and everything else for her years of resentment and self-pity. She felt so ashamed. Her childhood hadn't been the best, but other people didn't grow up with perfect surroundings and they managed to go on. Deep down, she knew real healing would come only when she turned loose and allowed God to handle what she thought was unachievable.

She turned her face up, letting the wet snow mingle with her tears. "I'm fighting and holding on to something that I can't control, Lord. My past is impossible for me, but you have said that you are willing and able to take this from my hands. I ask that you take it and make me stronger in the process."

Christmas *was* the season for hope and new beginnings; grudges took too much effort to maintain.

Rolling to her back, Emma stared at the sky. She had to find a way to forgive. Edwina said it was impossible for human beings to forgive on their own; only God's Spirit within them could do that.

Perhaps it was time Emma searched for that Spirit.

A WEEK later, Christmas dawned gray and dreary. Unable to even pretend to sleep, Emma walked into the kitchen a few minutes before six o'clock. The long day stretched ahead of her. Elizabeth had invited her for dinner in the late afternoon. Emma had promised to bring a salad and dessert, but her heart wasn't in the mood for gaiety. In the past, holidays—especially Christmas and Thanksgiving—had been days to get through.

Emma plugged in the percolator, then went into the living room to add wood to the stove. Her gaze fell on the two personal gifts wrapped in colorful paper: the calfskin gloves and the gold cuff links. They were the first personal gifts Emma had bought in fifteen years. She usually gave Sue and Janice a box of Fannie Mae chocolates for Christmas, but that was hardly personal. Sue was her employee and friend, and Janice wasn't allowed to have personal items other than essentials.

She stuck a couple of sticks of wood on the fire and shut the stove door. The repairman had been there and finally the stove worked. Her eyes fell on the cuff links again. She had no idea why she had bought them except that it felt good. *As if you'll be around to see him wear them, ninny.* She had talked to Sam at Brisco's briefly only once since their sleigh ride. He had sounded casual and not at all on pins and needles like she'd been, wondering if their date and the kiss had meant anything. She rubbed her arms when shivers assaulted her. Sam Gold still had the power to make her feel giddy.

She moved to the front window and looked out. A blanket of snow covered the ground. Fog shrouded the top of the Rockies. All over America small children would be waking up, throwing covers back, bounding into the living rooms, and squealing with delight when they saw what Santa had brought. Nintendos, wagons, bicycles, sleds. Dolls and play ovens and baby strollers with miniature curly-headed plastic infants. Tired parents would be wreathed in smiles as they watched the chaos.

This was her first Christmas truly without Lully. She and Emma hadn't celebrated the holiday together in fifteen years, yet this morning Emma clearly felt her sister's absence. The two of them hadn't made much of a family. Tears blinded her and she turned away, going back to the kitchen for coffee.

Sam stopped by as she was making breakfast. "Merry Christmas," he said, handing her a gaily wrapped box. His features sobered. "I know today is going to be hard on you."

Pulling her robe collar closer, she admitted, "I didn't know if you would have time to stop by today."

He frowned. "For you, I'd make time. Kenny and I are splitting shifts. He's working this morning and I work this afternoon."

"Can you come in?"

"Sorry." His face assured her he'd like nothing better. "But I have to visit Mom, and then it will be time for my shift." He leaned in and gave her a brief kiss. "How's my girl this morning?"

"I'm not your girl."

"How's my grouch this morning?"

She smiled. "Wait here a minute." She returned with his gift, relieved it was nothing that proclaimed "I love you."

He grinned. "I didn't know if you'd remember me or not."

"Oh, I remember you, Sam Gold." She leaned against the door frame, shivering.

He bent and kissed her on the lips this time. "I hope I'm never far from your thoughts. Bye—call you later."

The house screamed its silence after he left. The old mansion seemed so empty today.

At ten-thirty, Emma climbed the stairs and walked down the long hallway. Pausing in front of the second door, she bit her lip and turned the knob. The scent of candle wax and incense was stronger here. Emma's eyes scanned the room. Lully was everywhere. A worn nightgown hung on a peg outside the closet door as if she had momentarily stepped out of it. The bed was rumpled and unmade. Shoes littered the floor. Socks and hosiery had been flung here and there. A thick coat of dust layered the small dressing table, where there were jars of creams and blushes and tubes of lipstick with lids missing. Lully loved to experiment with cosmetics.

Emma meandered about the room, touching everything, experiencing Lully's presence. A small, framed picture sat on the nightstand. The image was one of Lully and Emma when they were very small—maybe four and seven. A birthday cake sat in the middle of the table with one candle burning. Emma didn't know whose birthday they were celebrating. Both girls wore a smile, and the shadowy image of a man's arm lurked in the background. Dad. Mom must have taken the photo.

Opening the drawer, Emma shoved the picture inside and closed it. She had to do something with Lully's personal effects. She had avoided the task as long as possible. Christmas Day wasn't appropriate for endings. It was a time for beginnings, and Lully would understand that Emma had to begin somewhere.

An hour later she had lugged six large boxes up from the basement and had begun filling them with Lully's things. Emma had nowhere to keep them, so they would go to the Salvation Army, where someone could use them—pay them back for all the years they'd kept Emma and Lully in clothes. She emptied the closets and drawers and then turned to the dresser. Memories cut sharper now. Lully's slips and underwear. Nightgowns—a small packet of lavender sachet to keep the intimate apparel smelling sweet and fresh. Sweaters—blue, light green, red—were in the bottom drawer. Emma carefully folded each garment and tucked them into a box.

When the dresser was empty, she scooped up makeup, lotions, brushes, and creams and dumped them into an empty shoe box. She added the carton to the other items.

She stripped the worn spread off the bed, then the sheets and pillowcases. The mattress cover came next. Everything was put in a box. Emma was crying now. She yanked the heavy drapes down, coughing as dust swirled up her nose. The hardest part of losing someone is removing his or her presence. It was so final.

Emma stared through the window at the gravestones, alone and forlorn in the snow. Was this what life was all about? she wondered. You live and then you die. You end up in a cold piece of ground covered with snow, with only an occasional visitor to remember you.

Dropping to the side of the bed, Emma bawled—racking sobs that made her nose run and her eyes red. She hated this. Her counselor had told her about the "outer child," the part of one's personality that loves to play martyr. The outer child has a favorite feeling: anger. The child feels only anger. The outer child tests the people it looks to for security—to the limits.

Oh, Sam. Is that what I've been doing? She was trying to fill a hole with countless reasons why her childhood shouldn't have happened to her. She had thrown herself in that hole and dared life to try and move her.

When emotion subsided, she wiped her eyes and nose, and opened the nightstand drawer. She removed the photograph gently, laying it on the bed. She would take it home, put it on her bedside table, and try to remember the good years. The years when she had felt safe and warm and protected, the years the Mansis had been a family. And she'd remember the idyllic months when she had loved Sam Gold and he had loved her back.

Emma was about to shove the drawer closed when she saw a

small journal at the very back. Picking it up and opening it, she felt almost guilty when she recognized Lully's handwriting. About to close the book, she paused, wondering exactly what Lully had thought in the last days of her life.

She turned to the first page. It only took a second to realize this wasn't a daily journal. After flipping through several pages, Emma understood that Lully wrote only about events that touched her deeply. Toward the front there were several pages dedicated to the search for Emma after she'd left home fifteen years earlier. Tears rolled down Emma's cheeks as she read how afraid her sister was that something awful had happened to Emma, about how she had prayed that Emma was all right, that God would keep her safe.

I was safe, Lully. I thought you didn't care. I was terrified at the time, but I didn't know how to pray—not really. I didn't have you there to pray for me.

Emma returned to the beginning and read. There was an entry on the day their mother died, and one when Dad left. On one page, Lully spilled her fears about how scared she was to be handed the responsibility of her twelve-year-old sister—would Family Services learn they were alone and take Emma from her? There were a few notations about how frightened she felt when the kids played mean pranks on them, when they sneaked around the house and vandalized the cemetery.

One passage in the later pages caught Emma's attention.

I found Mommy's Bible today—the one we used to read before Daddy left. She'd underlined a lot of her favorite passages, and I wondered why the words hadn't meant anything—or were of no particular significance at the time I read them. One of the passages is about the lost sheep—the one in the picture that Emma loves so much. I don't think Emma understood the importance of the portrait—I know at the time I didn't. But I do now as I write this; the lost sheep is us, Emma. You and me. Everyone but God has abandoned us—yet Jesus was and still is there to gather us back into the fold. I wish—oh, how I wish—I had been old enough or wise enough to tell you that we are loved, Emma. Deeply loved by a Shepherd who watches over us even if the world doesn't care. How I wish I'd understood. How I wish I had swallowed my stubborn pride and taken you to church like you asked every Sunday morning. But I hated the stares and the whispered innuendos. I'm not a witch. Maybe I'm different from most people, but no two of us are created alike. They shouldn't have taken their hatred out on you. You were a little girl forced to live a lie. I knew Daddy wasn't coming back. I didn't want you to lose hope—that light that stayed in your eyes for years. I'd watch you sit on the porch and watch the road until it got so dark you couldn't see anymore. I wanted to tell you the truth, but lying—keeping your hope alive—seemed so much more humane.

Emma's eyes blurred as she turned the page.

I met a nice man today: Ray Sullins. Ray's different, like me, but so kind, so gentle. He wants to help me with my jewelry but I told him no, that he shouldn't come around. People will talk. Like they don't anyway. Someone dug up Marietta Higgsby's tombstone and put it in our front yard last night. The Higgsby family was deeply upset and accused me of sorcery—like I'd will a tombstone in my front yard! Anyway, Ray is simpleminded. He's not handicapped, just simple in mind. He told me he has the mind of an eight-year-old, but he seems so much wiser. He's a gentle man. Maybe a friend.

Another entry a week later:

Ray comes by every day now. We work on jewelry and I baked him a peach pie last night. He said no one had ever baked him a peach pie—not just for him. We sat on the porch and held hands until the moon was high in the sky. I don't know what the neighbors think, but I don't care. God knows my heart—and Ray's. We aren't lovers; we're just good friends. Emma, it feels good to have a friend. I think often about you and Sam Gold. Sam stops by occasionally and brings me something. Maybe a half gallon of chocolate mint ice cream, other times a new plant to put in my garden. The other night I was lying in bed thinking about you and Sam, and the Lord laid it on my heart that I was wrong. Wrong to stop you from going after love. You were young and so was Sam, but I'm coming to realize that youth—or simpleminded people—can make it if they try hard enough. Emma, I have something I need to tell you, something

I should have told you a long time ago. Sam wrote you a letter shortly after you left and asked me to send it to you. He didn't know where you were. I told him I would, but I didn't. It grieves me now to think about my selfishness, but at the time I thought I was protecting you. I don't know what the letter said; I didn't read it. I threw it away. I threw your life away, Emma. Please, please forgive me. And please don't hate me. Sam is a good man. I know that now. He would have found a way to take care of you. If only we knew then what we know now. . . .

Emma put the journal aside and wept brokenly for all the lost years. For what she and Sam *should* have had. She could literally feel her heart softening toward Lully, forgiveness trying to penetrate the hardened wall. When she regained control of her emotions, she picked up the journal again.

The next entry made Emma's blood run cold:

I've been feeling poorly lately, so Ray made me go to the doctor. I hate doctors; they plain scare me. Not by what they do, but by what they might find. Anyway, he did find something, and Ray had to take me to the hospital for tests. He was so good to me—stood there the whole time and held my hand and kept reassuring me everything would be all right. Sometimes I think his eight-year-old mind can see things that I can't. Seems my heart is weak—something happened at birth that's caused it to wear out faster. Maybe that's why I was always so tired when we were young. The doctor gave me lots of pills and said I wasn't to exert myself at all. Ray is taking good care of me. He cried last night, said he was afraid of losing me. I don't want to abandon him; I know what that's all about. And like us, Ray has no one.

Emma reached for a fresh tissue and blew her nose. She felt guilty, as if she were intruding into Lully's most private thoughts, yet she was powerless to lay the book aside. Had her sister realized that one day Emma would be reading these words? Had she left the journal to cleanse the wounds between them? It would seem so by the way she sometimes addressed Emma in the entries. Emma read on, pausing to reread the next passage.

I'm getting weaker now. Ray denies what is clear: no amount of medicine is going to help me, and transplants are hard to come by. We wait each day for the phone to ring, but it never brings the message we're hoping for. Some nights I have to sit up all night because I can't breathe lying down. My heart hurts. Literally. I long to pick up the phone and call you, Emma, to hear your voice. I think the sound would be nice and comforting to me, but then I see Ray and his uncontrollable tears and the worry that lines his face, and I realize I can't do that to you. When I'm gone you will experience another loss, but you won't have to watch this slow and agonizing death. I love you, my dear sister. I can't remember; have I ever told you that? Forgive me. Youth sometimes forgets the important things. We might have gotten the short end of the stick in life, but I know without a doubt our reward waits for us. If possible, I will be standing at the gates of pearl waiting for you when God brings you home. There we will never feel alone again.

The entries each got shorter as Lully's heart weakened. The handwriting got spidery. One was in a childish block style that Ray must have written for her.

LULLY LOVES YOU EMMA.

Then one final entry two days before Lully's death:

I can't leave you the legacy of a normal life; I can leave you something more precious. Find it, Emma. Look with all your heart.... It's in the house.... It's in your heart.

The paragraph ended with:

Lord, please don't let me give up yet. I don't understand why or what's happening to my body, but draw me even closer. Fill me so full of the knowledge that you are carrying me during this struggle that what's happening doesn't matter. Allow me to be a shining example of your love ... no fear. Just a quiet rest in knowing that soon I will be running through golden meadows, laughing and playing like a child again....

Holding the handkerchief under her nose, Emma reread the final passage, obviously written with Lully's last strength. "Something more precious . . ."

What? Emma looked up, holding the journal to her breast. What had Lully left when she had nothing but the house and a few impersonal items?

Emotionally unable to continue, Emma laid the journal aside and left the bedroom. The task was turning out to be more painful than she had anticipated. Why had she let so many years go by without contacting Lully? Pride? Fear? Anger? She wasn't sure even now. She'd thought for the longest time that when Lully hadn't come looking for her that she had abandoned Emma, too. The journal proved Emma wrong. Lully had looked for her and found her. Then she had let her assert her independence with the hope and a sister's prayer that she would come back. She never would have—Emma suddenly realized she never would have come back if not for Lully's death. Serenity held too many memories for her, too many broken promises.

She walked into the kitchen, intending to bake an apple cake to take to Elizabeth's when she discovered that Lully's cabinets were void of spices. She had forgotten she had used the last of them to make the banana bread. It was Christmas Day—where could she get cinnamon and nutmeg? The café. Brisco's Café was open until one o'clock for the locals who gathered for coffee and donuts every morning, holidays included, or for families who enjoyed having breakfast together. Christmas Day was no different. Emma could borrow a few spices from Thelma Earls, the owner. Hurrying to the front closet, she slipped into a heavy coat and put on a warm hat.

Ten minutes later she entered the small café that smelled of coffee and fresh Danish. Mostly men, drinking coffee and swapping small talk, filled almost every table in the town gossip hall. Womenfolk were home basting the turkeys and mashing potatoes, shooing young children from underfoot.

Thelma looked up when the door opened, her beefy face flushed by the heat. "Ms. Emma. Merry Christmas!"

Emma nodded, pulling off her gloves. "I need to ask a favor, Thelma."

"Sure thing, sweetie." Thelma set the glass coffeepot aside. "What can I do for you?"

"I need to borrow a little cinnamon and nutmeg."

"Can handle that," Thelma assured her. She disappeared into the back room and started dumping spices into paper cupcake linings.

Emma took a seat at the counter, smiling pleasantly at the occasional man who noticed her. She spotted a man sitting by himself, his Danish untouched. After a while, he laid aside the paper he was reading, and picked up his hat and briefcase. He approached the register, glancing at Emma.

"Thelma will be right back. She's getting some spices for me."

He nodded.

She studied his profile. She didn't know him, but that didn't mean he was new in town. So much in Serenity had changed in the last fifteen years. Probably visiting a son or a daughter for the holiday.

Jay Bennett laughed and got up from his table. Bidding the men a Merry Christmas, he walked toward the register. When he spotted Emma he grinned. "Well, if it isn't Ms. Emma Mansi."

Emma smiled. "Merry Christmas, Jay."

"I'm ready to do the rest of those repairs any time you are."

"That's great, Jay. We'll start again after the holidays."

Jay laid his bill on the counter with a couple of dollars. "See you in the morning, Thelma!"

"Have a good day, Jay!" Thelma called from the back room.

The man still standing at the register waiting to pay turned at the mention of Emma's name. When the door closed behind Jay, the man said, "Ms. Mansi?"

Emma looked up.

He extended a well-manicured hand. "Oscar Wellman." When the name didn't register with Emma, he went on to explain. "I'm with Shangri-La Developers in Denver. I'm visiting a relative here for the day, but I'm also in the area looking for potential land investments—this is quite a stroke of luck. I have your sister's name on my list." He paused and cleared his throat. "I planned to talk to her about possibly selling the house."

A land developer. Emma shook hands with Mr. Wellman. "I'm sorry. My sister died a couple months ago, and I haven't decided what I plan to do with the house."

"No?" The tall, well-dressed man in his sixties cocked a dark brow. "Please forgive me. I was under the impression that the house would be for sale immediately. I bumped into Tom Crane and Darrel Masters at a convention last week and they were speculating on buying the property themselves—for a parking lot? Now it would be a shame to tear down a historical treasure." Oscar rubbed his chin pensively. "I'm quite sure my company could keep the house intact but build around the perimeter—make all the time-share units rustic—it is the house bordering a cemetery, right?"

Suddenly Tom Crane's actions of late took on a sinister note. It seemed that the mayor and Darrel Masters *had* been snooping around the house, itching to get their hands on the property for a municipal parking lot. "It is, but it isn't for sale," Emma answered.

"So odd," he murmured. "Very puzzling. I heard that other sources are also interested in purchasing the property. This area—so close to Durango—is ideal for time-share development, and if it's a matter of money, well, let me assure, you my corporation has deep pockets. They will give you above and beyond top price for the property, should you decide to sell."

Tourists were the last thing the people of Serenity wanted. The town had remained small because of people's preference to do so. Tom Crane knew the residents' regard for privacy—surely Mr. Wellman had his facts wrong.

"I'm sorry, Mr. Wellman." Emma stood up to take the package Thelma was now holding over the counter. "My house is not for sale."

She started to pay and Thelma waved the gesture aside. "May have to borrow off you one of these days. Merry Christmas!"

"Merry Christmas." Emma prepared to leave, and Oscar Wellman followed her out the doorway. "Ms. Mansi." He fell into brisk step with her. "I don't mean to be rude, but am I to understand that you alone own the house? I was given to believe that Sam Gold is co-owner."

"He is, but he knows I don't want to sell the house."

"I understand there's a slight technicality concerning the deed, but—"

"Slight," Emma said. "Only slight, and it will be cleared up soon. But the house still won't be for sale."

"Well, now, perhaps you should talk to Mr. Gold. He didn't seem as adamant when I spoke with him yesterday afternoon."

Emma whirled. "You spoke to Sam?"

"Yes, late yesterday afternoon. I presented an offer and he said he would consult you. I must say, your refusal to look at the contract surprises me. The offer Shangri-La has made is above generous, and I warn you, you won't be able to match it anywhere else. The owner of Shangri-La used to live in Santa Fe, and his heart is here in the Durango area."

Emma swallowed back a sharp retort. How dare he imply she was being selfish to keep the house from a land-grubbing speculator? She couldn't trust Shangri-La to keep their word. They'd bulldoze the house to the ground and build new units. Some young designer would move the cemetery headstones and plant azalea bushes on Mom and Lully's grave.

"Perhaps this has all been too sudden for you. The death of your sister, the memorial. I know how that can be—I buried my mother less than a year ago. Tom indicated that you're still in shock, and that's only natural. Your sister was so young." He paused, reaching out to take her arm.

"Tom Crane?"

"The mayor—yes. He and Darrel, of course, want the parking lot, but my company would be a better choice, Ms. Mansi. In time, perhaps you will come to realize what is best for all concerned. Tom says Sam believes that it's best to sell—"

"Sam believes?" Her eyes narrowed.

"Well, he is co-owner—"

Whirling, she walked back to the restaurant and opened the door. Patrons glanced up as she threaded her way through the narrow aisles to the back table where the mayor and Darrel Masters were sitting. Slamming her hand flat on the chrome tabletop with a smack that resounded throughout the room, she said quietly, "I own that house. Sam will get half the proceeds *if* I ever sell or he will be paid half *if* I decide to keep it. Either way, gentlemen—" she leaned closer—"the house is *not* for sale to you or you or—" she turned and pointed to Oscar Wellman, who was now standing in the café doorway, mouth agape—"him. Understood?"

The mayor and Darrel nodded wordlessly. A piece of egg dangled from the mayor's fork that was lifted halfway to his mouth.

Taking a deep breath, Emma straightened. "Thank you, gentlemen. Merry Christmas."

Her cheeks burned as she walked off, head held erect. Brushing past Mr. Wellman, who still held the door open, she sucked fresh air into her lungs. Her knees trembled. She was accustomed to confrontations and she didn't like them. But someone had to put a foot down, and it was high time she let the people of Serenity know that they weren't going to push her around like they had Lully.

Slamming her front door shut, Emma strode to the living room and picked up the phone. The line rang three times before a woman answered. "Hello?"

"Hi—is Sam there?"

"Yes?"

"This is Emma . . . Emma Mansi."

The woman's voice warmed. "Emma. How nice to hear from you after all these years. Betty Higgins—Sam's neighbor? I cooked a turkey for the boys and a few side dishes—you know men. Ken and Sam would have eaten a cheese sandwich and called it Christmas."

"I'm sure Sam and Ken are very appreciative. May I speak to Sam?"

"Yes, I'll get him—have you had your dinner? You're welcome to come and eat with us. I know Sam would—"

"Thank you so much, but I've promised to eat with Elizabeth."

"Oh . . . well, I understand. Perhaps another time. Soon?"

"That would be nice."

Emma tapped her fingers on the cord impatiently as she waited for Sam. She imagined a "few side dishes," including dressing, sweet potatoes, green beans, Jell-O salad, mashed potatoes and gravy, cranberry sauce, a pumpkin and a pecan pie—

Sam's voice came on the line. "I was thinking about you. I didn't know if you'd want to come over here for dinner or I would have asked. What's up?"

My temper. Emma drew a deep breath and said as calmly as she could, "It is *my* house. I don't care what Lully said in that ridiculous will, the house is *mine,* and I'll find that deed if it takes me a hundred years. This house is the only thing I have left of my crummy, rotten life. I hate the house. I wish I never had to see it again but I'm not selling it. You understand? I'm *not* selling it!" Her voice caught with emotion. "Do you understand?"

After a moment of silence Sam said, "You hate the crummy, rotten, falling-down-around-your-head house, filled with spiders, snakes, pigs, and God knows what's next. It's the only thing left of your crummy, rotten life, and you hate it and all the painful memories it brings, but you're not selling it for any amount of money."

"That's right." She sniffed.

"I got it. Anything else?"

"You can tear that contract up from Shangri-La Developers right now!"

She heard him lay the phone down and come back a minute later. The sound of tearing paper came across the line. Deliberate ripping.

He picked up the receiver again. "Anything else?"

"Do not entertain any further ideas of selling my house. If I sell it, which I won't, I'll give you half."

"And if you don't sell it?"

"I'll still pay you half—but I might have to make payments to you."

"Sounds like a deal."

"Okay?" He was okay with it?

"Okay."

"You'll leave me alone and let me do what I want with the house?"

"Do I have a choice?"

"No."

"Okay."

"And please tell Mayor Crane and Darrel Masters to stay off our property. For some reason, I think they may be in on this charade—the spiders, the snake. Those pigs."

"Mayor Crane and Darrel Masters?"

"No, those pigs—the ones that I found rooting in the kitchen a couple of weeks ago—although if what I suspect is true, Crane and Masters are swine, too. Trying to trick me out of our house so they can build a parking lot."

"*Our* house?"

"*My* house. You know what I mean."

Sam changed the tone. "Did you like your present?"

She softened. "I loved it. Thank you—you have beautiful taste."

"It's just stationery. Thought you might remember to write when you go back to Seattle."

"Okay. Did you like your gift?"

"It's my favorite one this year. Gold cuff links. Thanks."

"I hope you have a shirt that you can use them on."

"Hey, it's my lucky day—I do. Thanks."

"Okay then. We're clear once and for all on the house?"

"Clear as a bell."

She slammed the receiver down; his calmness infuriated her.

How could he be so composed when her whole life was an incomprehensible mess!

"You hung up on him?" Elizabeth set the turkey in the center of the table and stood back to admire the beautifully browned bird. Candles lit the festive red tablecloth and sparkling china. The shop owner had gone to a lot of trouble, Emma realized. And her efforts were well rewarded.

"I know it wasn't a nice thing to do." Emma took a sip of eggnog, wandering to the twinkling tree. Ornaments from years past festooned the blue spruce. Memories of Elizabeth's life nestled among the fragrant pine and shiny tinsel.

"Then why did you do it?"

"I don't know—Sam can be so nice one minute and so detached the next. Everything I demanded he agreed to. Just like that. 'Okay. Anything else? Sounds like a deal. Do I have a choice?' He ripped up the contract without an argument."

"Did you want a knock-down-drag-out fight?" Elizabeth asked.

"Of course not." Emma set her cup on the lamp table. "I want some emotion from the guy."

"And you don't see his feelings in his eyes?" Elizabeth shook her head. "Everybody else does."

"That's nonsense—and it's not fair to Sam to imply that he cares a wit for me. The whole town is accusing him of being partial to me, pampering me so I won't give in and sell. It isn't right. He's caught between the devil and the deep blue sea."

"Defending him now?" Elizabeth returned to the kitchen and came back carrying a bowl of sweet potatoes with marshmallow topping. A moment later she brought out string beans. "The man's in love with you," she said, arranging the serving bowls on the table. "The beans are from my summer vegetable garden."

Emma turned slightly at the remark. Somewhere between "defending him now?" and "the beans are from my garden," the conversation had taken a serious turn. "Excuse me?"

"Come now, Emma. You're not sightless. Surely you see the way Sam looks at you, the little things he does for you—driving by your house at least six or seven times a day—in a town like Serenity where the biggest thing that happens is the kids playing pranks in the cemetery?"

"That's why he drives by so often. To prevent the pranks."

"Kenneth has a car. Why doesn't he drive by?"

"Maybe it isn't his territory."

"In Serenity?" Elizabeth hooted. "Sam and Ken take care of the town; they don't designate territory."

Elizabeth returned to the kitchen for the green salad. Emma stared out the window at fading daylight. The days were short this time of year. It was barely four-thirty and the streetlights were blinking on one by one. Bare branches tapped the frozen window-panes.

"The man's in love with you." Elizabeth's words rang in Emma's ears. *Oh, if that were only true*—Emma caught her wishful thoughts. If that were true, it would mean nothing. She had been down that rocky path before. Sam was wishy-washy. She couldn't trust his declarations of undying love. She wasn't fifteen and starry-eyed anymore, and she knew the hurt love could bring. Emma knew people could change; she had changed, grown up. Now she was able to recognize fact from fiction. A serious relationship between her and Sam was fiction. Steven King fiction.

"Here we are." Elizabeth set the salad on the table and motioned for Emma to sit down. The two women sat across from each other on one end of the long table. Twelve place settings and cut-glass goblets graced the holiday table.

"You must think me eccentric, but I always set the table for twelve. You never know when you're entertaining angels unaware."

Emma smiled. She'd never once thought of angels eating turkey and dressing with them.

Elizabeth reached for Emma's hand and bowed her head. Emma followed suit. "Father, we thank you for this beautiful day when we recognize the birth of your Son, our Savior, with grateful hearts. Such a gift cannot be repaid or even given proper thanks. We bow humbly in your presence, Father, grateful for the bounty before us. Forgive us for the ways we fail you. Open our eyes to your grace that surrounds us daily. We are blessed, truly blessed, this day. Amen."

"Amen," Emma whispered.

Elizabeth picked up the bowl of potatoes and handed it to Emma. "He is in love with you, you know."

Uncertain of her meaning, Emma said quietly, "Who? The Lord or Sam?"

"Both," Elizabeth said. "Both, you silly girl."

Emma balked at sudden tears. Then why was Sam trying to run her out of town? She hadn't considered the possibility before now, but hadn't Oscar Wellman huddled with Sam and come up with a contract? Sam had torn the contract in two, but would he have mentioned it if Oscar hadn't told her first?

Ohhhhh. She scooped up a forkful of beans. *The dirty rat.*

Emma was still steaming over her argument with Sam when she opened the front door around ten o'clock Christmas night. Gismo greeted her in the foyer and she scratched his head and let him out. A few minutes later, he was scratching at the door to come back in.

Emma threw herself onto the couch and stared at the picture of Christ holding the lamb. Sam said God cared about her, but then Sam didn't care or he'd never have talked to the developer. But he'd torn up the developer's offer without an argument. Her head was spinning. "What does it mean?" she asked the picture, but, of course, there was no answer.

She curled up on the couch, wishing someone would give her the answers. Then she spied her mother's Bible on the side table. She hadn't looked at it since coming back, but Lully had read it every night when they were young. In her journal she'd written of the comfort the Bible had brought her, especially in the last days of her life.

Almost without thinking, Emma picked up the worn book. The leather cover was cracked at the edges, the pages clearly thumbed. She opened to the first page where births and deaths were listed. Lully. She had to record Lully's name inside, below their mother's name. *Was Dad still alive? Leave the date of death blank.* Reaching inside her purse, she drew out a pen and very carefully wrote Lully's name and the date of her death. Tears stung her eyes. There was such finality in that small act.

She thumbed through the pages, seeing passages underlined, clearly passages that meant something to their mother, and others perhaps to Lully. A yellowed piece of paper fell out of the back of the Bible, and Emma picked it up, pushing Gismo aside while reading a passage from Psalms. Before shoving the paper back into the Bible, she glanced at it.

It took a moment for the writing on the paper to register. Then her loud whoop of joy sent Gismo running for the kitchen. She'd found it! The bill of sale. Written in spidery hand, Jeremiah Stout stated that he'd sold a piece of property with a four-room house on it to her great-grandfather.

Sam. She had to call Sam. Before she even thought, she dialed the sheriff's office. Sam answered on the first ring.

"Sam! I didn't think you'd be in the office on Christmas night!"

"I said okay. The house is not for sale. And a sheriff is never off; don't you know that?"

"I found it! I found the deed!"

"You did? That's great."

"It was in Momma's Bible all along! It's a handwritten bill of sale. This proves this house belongs to us!"

His tone softened. "I'm glad for you, Emma. I'll talk to Ned and get the abstract update started."

When she hung up, Emma danced around the room and Gismo ventured out of the kitchen. "I don't have to sell the house!" she told him. "They can't make me sell it or take it away from me!"

It was only later that she wondered why it had been Sam she wanted to tell first about the bill of sale. Sam with whom she wanted to share her joy.

Well, he owned part of the house, she reasoned. *It was natural to share the news with him first.*

Of course, her conscience said.

"Of course," she repeated. "Only natural. Don't try and make anything out of it."

chapter
FOURTEEN

THE DAY after Christmas—could there be a more lackluster day? Emma had been so excited about finding the bill of sale she hadn't slept a wink. She could hardly wait to show Mr. Crane and Mr. Masters that precious piece of paper. There would be no doubt in anyone's mind that the property was hers and that she had every right to either keep it or sell it.

But what difference did it make?

She and Sam were still at odds over what to do with the house. Although Sam seemed willing to give in about selling the house, his mother's plight still nagged her conscience.

And the whole town was at odds over the house now too. She'd overheard two women arguing at the market this morning. One said that Emma was perfectly within her rights to keep the house— after all it was almost a town monument. The other rather heatedly threw a head of lettuce in her cart and said they needed a parking lot a lot more than they needed a historical monument, and she had the calluses on her feet to prove it. All the bill of sale confirmed was that the town didn't have the right to take the property.

Emma sorted through the remains of Christmas papers and ribbons. She carefully unwrapped and set on the mantel the Hummel collector's plate that Elizabeth had given her.

"Ride into Christmas" depicted a rosy-cheeked boy riding his sleigh through the snowdrifts of Christmastime, clutching his lantern and carrying a Christmas tree.

Her hand paused. She couldn't fall in love with Sam, not again. It had taken years to get over him—she wouldn't put herself through that agony again.

His mother had told her that for some reason he couldn't make any serious commitments. For Pete's sake, he was thirty-four and still single. Was it because of her? Could it be?

And what about you, Emma Mansi? You're thirty-two and single. What does that say about your commitment tendencies?

It's not the same, she argued with herself.

It's exactly the same. It seems that every time you or Sam come close to committing to another person, you each get cold feet.

You don't know that for certain.

Yes I do.

Annoyed over her argument with herself, Emma picked up two cardboard boxes and headed upstairs, armed with a club, a flashlight, a broom, a dustpan, and large garbage bags. She still had much of the attic and the entire basement to clean. Items would have to be shipped to Seattle, thrown out, or put into storage.

She reached the top of the stairs and walked to the overhead door twenty feet from the stairway and yanked the chain. A short set of rickety steps rattled down.

The attic always made her think of Clark Griswold in the movie *National Lampoon's Christmas Vacation,* where he'd been accidentally locked in the attic while his family and in-laws took off for a day of Christmas shopping. The Mansi attic was a replica of the Griswolds': boxes, battered furniture, old trunks, discarded lamps, even an old Victrola. And cold. Extremely cold. Emma rummaged in an old trunk and put on two moth-eaten sweaters, a pair of heavy, insulated hunting pants, and a Denver Broncos ball cap before tackling the job.

She worked through the afternoon, sorting through boxes and trunks. Old broken toys, kitchen junk, forty-year-old bank statements she pitched. Some of the better clothing items were set aside for charity, and others were thrown in a box for trash. At times she found herself sitting cross-legged on the cold rafters, looking through old picture albums, laughing and crying. Her school pictures were a disgrace. In one her hair looked like a heinous rooster tail; in another she was grinning with two missing front teeth and a gap on the bottom row.

Lully's third-grade picture was sidesplitting. The collar—big collar—of her dress was tucked in on one side. Her hair escaped a barrette, and she must have had a cold that day because her nose was beet red from constant wiping. This was serious family black-mail material—if she had a family. The sudden impact of that thought devastated her. She had no family; she was completely, utterly alone.

"Oh, Lord," she whispered. Tears rolled into her mouth and she swiped them away. "I am so scared."

Why? I am with you.

She swiped at her eyes and glanced up. Imagination, that's all it was. Her imagination had created a voice in her mind, a voice saying exactly what she wanted—desperately needed—to hear.

Why do you doubt me?

"I don't doubt you—not really." Emma looked around, glad there was nobody in the attic to hear this. Maybe she was going crazy—no, she didn't hear an actual voice. It was more like a thought or a feeling, a sense of presence. She'd had many silent conversations with this whatever-it-was, but she'd always consid-ered it her own thoughts talking back to her. Now she knew it was God's voice.

"I . . . haven't talked to you much since Lully used to read the Bible to me."

I know. I've missed you.

This is nuts. Emma put the albums in a box and set it aside. She worked for a few more minutes, then paused, listening to some-thing deep within.

Do not be afraid. You are my child, and I care deeply about you.

"I . . . love you too," she whispered, realizing finally that she truly did. "I'm sorry, God—I've been mad—mad at you." Her voice caught and her eyes closed. "All these years I've been furious with you," she sobbed. "Because of Mom—then Dad. Leaving Lully and me to make it on our own. Why, God? Why do you make some people's lives so perfect and others—?"

Someday you will know—in my timing.

"Oh, God." She knelt, weeping. "Please forgive me."

I forgave you, for everything. I hung on the cross.

Bringing her hand to her nose to stop the flow, Emma bawled. She was sitting in the attic talking to God. And he was talking back.

She surely had lost her mind. Scrambling to her feet, she started pitching boxes through the attic opening. They landed with a thud at the bottom of the attic steps. Box after box dropped, one breaking open and the contents spilling into the hallway.

She crawled over the rafters and reached for several mid-size cartons wedged in the very back corner. When she opened the first one, she frowned. The box contained feathers and colorful beads. Packages and packages of ornamental beads of several sizes and colors, of shells and pearls. As she opened each box she discovered tools suitable only for making fine, delicate jewelry.

Lully's jewelry supplies—but how? She glanced at the attic opening.

How did they get in the attic? Lully had made the strange, exotic looking necklaces and earrings until the day of her death. Part of a necklace was lying in her lap when they found her, the other part grasped in her hand. Her workbench was downstairs. Emma hadn't paid much attention lately, but that first night she'd noticed that some of Lully's finished jewelry, materials, and tools were on the bench.

Setting the boxes aside, Emma puzzled over the find. Had someone boxed up the supplies since Lully's death to get them out of the way? Who could have done that? Sam? Ken? Ray Sullins?

Shoving the ball cap to the back of her head, Emma grunted as she tried to move a trunk that must have had an old Buick in it.

Dragging the trunk to the edge of the stairs, she decided to leave it there until she could get help.

"Don't even think about it."

Emma started at the sound of Sam's voice. Peering down through the opening, she saw him standing in a jumble of boxes at the foot of the ladder.

"Hey." She was more than surprised to see him.

"Hey. What's going on?"

"Sam, you wouldn't believe what just happened."

"What?"

"God . . . it was . . . I could have sworn . . ." How could she tell him she had made peace with God? That she'd actually talked to him—well, not talked to him exactly, but she'd heard that still small voice people talked about? Would Sam understand? "I . . . just had a talk with God."

He smiled. "I talk to him several times a day."

She cocked her head. "Are you serious? You're not making fun of me—don't think I'm some kind of weird fanatic because I talked . . . with him?"

Sam's features sobered. "I don't think you're a fanatic. You seemed close to God when you were younger. What happened, Em? What made you turn away?"

Emma sighed as she sat down at the edge of the opening. "I don't know—I was mad at him for so long, Sam. Furious, actually. Because of what he'd done to me and Lully."

"He didn't promise a perfect world—not down here," Sam reminded.

"I know." She sat for a moment lost in thought.

Finally Sam asked, "What are you doing up there?"

She snapped back to the present. "What does it look like? I'm cleaning the attic. How did you get in?"

"Walked through the open front door."

Emma frowned. "The front door was open?"

"Wide open—I figured open windows were no longer enough; now you've gone to opening doors to cool off."

Emma shook her head. "I didn't open the door—I haven't been out of the house this afternoon."

Sam shoved his hat to the back of his head and frowned. "Maybe it's one of those spooks next door. Anyway, I wanted to tell you I called Ned. He'll get things moving on the abstract."

"Thanks. I appreciate that." She studied him, silently acknowledging what a good friend he could be. "I'm sorry I yelled at you. And on Christmas Day."

"You were upset. I hadn't had time to tell you about the new offer from Wellman's company. Guess I don't have to now. You made your point pretty clear." His gaze skimmed her appreciatively. "What's that you're wearing? Looks great on you."

Her cheeks turned pink. Two moth-eaten sweaters, camouflage hunting pants, and a ball cap? Did he have to point that out? Somehow he always found her looking like a rag bin. She gave him an I-don't-want-to-hear-it look. "While you're here, can you help me with this trunk?"

He grasped hold of the ladder and climbed up into the attic, his eyes scanning the mounds of boxes. "What are you going to do with all of this stuff?"

"Give it away, throw it away, take a few things back to Seattle with me." Frowning, she picked up a medium-size box. It was heavy, bound with masking tape, and marked EMMA. Suddenly, Emma asked, "You didn't box up Lully's jewelry-making stuff, did you?"

"No. Why?"

"Because someone did. There're four boxes over there all containing her jewelry paraphernalia."

"You didn't clear it out of the house?"

"No, I didn't."

"Strange."

"Real strange." Her front teeth worried her lower lip as she studied the box with her name on it. Family trinkets? Some of her old clothes left from childhood? "I found Lully's journal. She knew she had a heart condition. So did Ray. Maybe—

maybe in those last days she didn't feel like working so . . ."
She paused, not wanting to think about Lully growing weaker
every day.

"Maybe you're right. I'm sorry she didn't let anyone know she
was ill."

"She didn't want me to know, didn't want me to be here to see
her like that."

Emma blinked away the burn of tears. She looked at the box she
was holding. What had Lully left that she thought necessary for
Emma to keep? Lully was a pack rat. She kept everything from old
records, which were surely collectors' items by now, to camping
equipment, to Dad's old set of wooden golf clubs, Grandma's old
dishes, a garden plow, and a galvanized washtub. Nothing had
been thrown away in thirty years.

Emma struggled to rip the tape off the box. Sam calmly took out
his pocketknife and neatly cut across the binding. "Thanks," she
said.

"My pleasure." Their eyes met and held for a long moment.
Emma finally looked away for fear he'd hear her heart hammering
its way out of her chest.

Emma carefully folded back the cardboard flaps, and her jaw
dropped open. Money. Piles and piles of neatly banded hundred-
dollar bills lay in the box that had once held a dozen bottles of
Palmolive dishwashing liquid.

Sam let out a low whistle. "There must be hundreds of thou-
sands of dollars here."

Emma looked up, eyes stricken. "Who does it belong to?"

"The box says Emma, doesn't it?"

"But it couldn't be for me—we've never had this kind of money.
Lully and I nearly starved the years we were together."

Sam reached into the box and lifted out a stack of money.
Emma had never seen that much money in her life—not even at
the bank when she made deposits. He put the money back, then
withdrew a small piece of white paper and handed it to Emma.

Emma read it out loud:

Dear Emma—

*If you're reading this, then you know it's too late for me to say this in person.
I love you, dear sister. And I am so sorry we wasted all those years when we
could have been close and loving and a real support for one another. I don't
blame either one of us—that emotional baggage will drag a person down
every time. I hope you'll get rid of your baggage; life is way too short to live
in emotional pain.*

*I believe we make our own bad luck by simply not trusting in God. Faith.
That's the answer, Emma. Have faith, and everything will fall into place, as
it should. As I feel myself getting weaker, I realize more and more that God
has a plan for our lives. We weren't put here to just fill space, and when our
time is up, it's over. Nothing we do will change that. So we need to walk in
faith even when the road is darkest.*

*The money is my legacy to you. I hope it brings you great happiness. It's
from my jewelry business—I must admit my happiness came from making the
jewelry, sharing beauty with others. The money meant nothing. I have lived
a frugal life. I liked it that way. No fuss. The other legacy, if you haven't figured
out by now, is Sam. Don't let him get away again. I will see you on the other
side, little sister. And we'll be a real family this time, I promise.*

Your loving sister,
Lully

P.S. The password to my files is simple: Emma.

Tears streamed down Emma's cheeks as she looked deep into
Sam's eyes. "Oh my, you've got to love that woman," she whispered.

Sam was in the back room of the office, going through a box of
old files, when he heard the phone jingle. Ken picked it up. "Sheriff's office."

"What are you up to this morning, Lloyd?" A moment later, Ken
called out, "Sam? Lloyd Smith wants to talk to you."

Sam emerged from the back room carrying a box of files he set on Ken's desk. "Go through these and see if there's anything there we need to keep." Picking up the receiver, Sam said, "Yo, Lloyd. What's happening?"

"Got a little piece of news I thought you might be interested in. About the snake."

"The one we found in Emma's house?" Sam pulled up a chair and sat down.

"The same. The mayor's boy was in this morning—I told you Buddy Crane bought a boa a few weeks back?"

"Yeah."

"Buddy was in about an hour ago. We got to talking and I asked him how the snake was doing. He seemed real reluctant to talk about it. He browsed the store an hour before he bought a parakeet and a cage. I was ringing up the sale and teasing him a little— you know, like how's that boa going to get along with the bird— that kind of stuff. Buddy wasn't laughing—seemed kinda nervous, actually.

"Well, you know me, I never shut up. Got to querying him about the snake and how his folks liked having it around? You know Ms. Crane—she's squeamish about those slugs on the walk at night, always out on her front porch with a box of Morton salt, knocking the poor critters off one by one. Mass murder."

Sam chuckled. "I've seen her."

"Well, anyway, the more I talked, the more Buddy squirmed until he finally blurted out that he didn't have the snake anymore.

"'Don't have the snake anymore?' I sez. 'Where in the world is it? A snake that size is mighty hard to pawn off on anyone.' Well, then Buddy gets this real sheepish look on his face and admits the snake got hold of him one night and scared the stuffing right out of him. Early the next morning, he got it into a tow sack and drug it to the cemetery and let it loose. Then he admitted he ran like the devil himself was chasing him."

Sam sat up straighter. "Let it loose? He told me he sold it."

"Then he was lying. That boa musta been wandering through

those tombstones for a week or two before it somehow got into Emma's kitchen. This time of year critters are looking for warmth, and you know that old Mansi house is loose as a goose. Coulda crawled in anywhere."

"Thanks, Lloyd. Thanks a lot."

"Sure thing."

That accounts for the snake, Sam thought. Sam hung up, sitting for a moment to let the news digest. Emma hinted the other day—teasingly, but he had taken it seriously—that she thought he might be trying to run her out of town.

The accusation stung. The only thing Sam Gold was guilty of was loving Emma Mansi. If it weren't for Lully's death, chances are he would never have seen Emma again, but instead she had been put back into his life full force.

He raked his fingers through his thick hair. If she didn't love him, how was he going to live with that knowledge? He loved her too much to live in this town day after day, seeing her . . . hearing her laughter. If she kept the house and turned it into that tearoom, she would eventually move back. He knew Emma. She was going to ask her friend Janice to come to Serenity and run the shop. If Janice were here, she would eventually convince Emma to move back to Serenity. That's when Sam would leave. He'd resign as town sheriff and move farther north. Wyoming, Montana—anywhere but Serenity, where he would be forced to see her frequently, knowing that she didn't love him.

But somebody *was* trying to run Emma out of town. He had his suspicions but needed to investigate further. Too many suspects wanted the Mansi property for various reasons: municipal parking lot, land speculation, even for a historical monument—the Veterans of Foreign Wars were talking about wanting the house for a bingo hall. But no one, he thought, would terrorize Emma to get the house, and yet strange things continued to happen.

"Should burn the eyesore to the ground and be done with it." Sam slammed his hand on the desk and got up.

Ken glanced up from the box of files. "What's wrong now?"

"Buddy Crane turned that boa loose in the cemetery several weeks back. Got scared of it and let it go."

"It must have been looking for warmth when it got into Emma's house."

Burying his face in his hands, Sam let out a breath of frustration. "I'll go tell Emma."

"It should make her feel better—or maybe not. She won't sleep a wink from now on, thinking about critters crawling into her house."

"Maybe she shouldn't." Sam reached for his hat. "The boa presence has been explained, but that still leaves the other incidents."

Ken shook his head. "Serenity hasn't had so much excitement since Helen Bennett got her hand caught in that wringer washing machine."

Sam left the office, slamming the door behind him.

Winter's coming; I can feel it in the air. I can smell the pungent scent of burning leaves. On days I feel up to it, I take short walks to the end of the drive to see the pumpkins in the far fields. They look so round and fat and golden sitting in the sun. I wish you could have known this side of Serenity, Emma. You would find peace here, as I have. The colorful leaves surround the tombstones and the whole area reminds me of Joseph's coat—so colorful, so beautiful. Today, everything looks so beautiful, so surreal. I know soon I will meet Ezra Mott, Emma, and I'm so excited—

Emma whirled when she heard the back screen door open and close softly. Frowning, she laid Lully's journal aside and quietly stood up. Ray? She didn't call out. No one had permission to enter the house without her knowledge.

Perhaps it was the wind. A bitter wind blew from the north, rattling January tree branches.

Creeping out of the bedroom, she walked softly along the carpeted hallway until she reached the top of the stairs. She peered over the railing, staring into the foyer. Footsteps shuffled softly through the parlor, but she couldn't see the intruder.

Putting her foot on the first step, she eased down. One step. Then another. Fear rose to the back of her throat. Should she go back to the bedroom and call Sam? If he wasn't there, Ken could come—

Someone was in the kitchen now. She could hear noises— faint . . . croaks?

She stepped down two more stairs. She was still too high to see the kitchen door.

Croak. Croak. Croak

Bullfrogs.

Someone was putting bullfrogs in her kitchen.

Steam rose from the top of her head, and she forgot common sense. Bolting down the rest of the stairs, she snatched a heavy umbrella from the stand and burst into the kitchen swinging.

Frogs—at least twenty of them—sprang about on the linoleum. *Croak, crooak, crooooak.* Their bulbous throats ballooned. Emma screamed and hopped back as one of the slimy reptiles sprang at her.

A movement caught her eye. Distracted now, she focused on the intruder at the back door. "Ray!"

Ray tried to pull the door open, fear flooding his face. His child-like wails filled the kitchen. Emma pitched the umbrella aside and tried to comfort him.

"It's all right, Ray . . ." Her thoughts were mindless, disjointed nothings. Frogs hopped all over the kitchen counter, the table, the stove, the top of the refrigerator. What was Ray doing here with frogs?

"No! Let me go! Ray's scared!"

"Ray, come here."

He bolted out of the kitchen, openly terrified, sobbing as he dashed through the front parlor, into the foyer, and out the front door. Sam was coming up the walk. He jumped and sprang aside to keep from being hit.

Emma bounded out of the house and down the steps. "Stop him!" she shouted.

Sam turned and started down the lane in pursuit of the simple-minded man.

Donny Coleman's Camero rounded the corner on two wheels, peeling rubber on the asphalt. The car raced closer, Donny gunning the accelerator and laughing at the boys in the backseat.

"Ray!" Emma screamed when she saw what was about to happen.

"Ray!" Sam bellowed. "Stop!"

Sobbing, Ray raced on blindly. When he came to the end of the lane he kept running, straight into the Camero's path. The car hit him, throwing him up over the windshield, his body glancing to the left side.

Tires squealed as Donny stood on the brakes; the sports car slid for two hundred feet before coming to a stop. The gangly youth crawled out from behind the wheel, his face ashen.

Emma ran down the lane. Tears streamed down her face as she gently lifted Ray's head and cradled it. "Why didn't you stop— we called to you." A sob caught in her throat. Blood covered Ray's face, and his left arm rested at a grotesque angle.

"Don't be mad at me," Ray murmured.

Emma hugged him tightly, feeling a strong bond. Lully had loved this simple, childlike man. He had been her friend. But why? Why had Ray tried to scare her out of her own house?

Emma held him tighter as tears rolled down her cheeks. Sam was on his two-way radio, calling for an ambulance.

Ray opened his eyes and met Emma's. "I did it for Lully. Didn't want anyone to take Lully's things." His eyes widened with sincerity. "Lully's good. Lully loves me. I protect Lully."

"Oh, Ray." Emma's heart sank. "It's been you doing these things? You put the spiders and snake—"

"No snake!" Ray shook his head violently. "Snakes scare me. No hurt you—never hurt you. You're Lully's sister. I never treat Lully like others do. Don't want you to sell Lully's house—she'll be gone

forever if you do." Blood gushed from his nose. In the distance
a siren wailed. "You can have Lully's money—she wanted you
to have it. It's in a box . . ." His voice faded as he began to lose
consciousness. "All of it . . . didn't want you to sell Lully's house."

Emma looked at Sam through a veil of tears. "Oh, Sam . . . Ray's
been the one—"

Sam rested his hand on her shoulder as she cradled the injured
man. Emma felt strength, love, and grief through Sam's gentle
contact. "I haven't wanted to alarm you, but I had my suspicions
that he was involved in the pranks in some way. During my investigation, I started thinking about Ray and Lully and his devotion
to her."

"Why didn't you say something?"

"I had no proof, Emma. Ray is simpleminded—I didn't feel
you were ever in any real danger, and until I could get concrete
proof regarding Ray's activities, I had nothing to go on. But it all
makes sense now. Ray's loyalty to Lully had no end. In his mind,
he couldn't stand to see any part of Lully disturbed, the house
included. I first began to suspect Ray when those pigs appeared
in your kitchen."

"I still don't know how he did that."

"Ray is good friends with Joe Stills—one of the largest pig farm-
ers in this area. After the incident, I checked with Joe, and he said
two of his best sows were missing that morning for a few hours. I
don't know how Ray managed to do it, but I knew without a
doubt he was the culprit. I just couldn't prove it."

Emma shook her head. "I knew, in his way, he loved my sister,
but such childish pranks . . ."

"In many ways he is a child." Sam's hold on her shoulder tightened.

The ambulance arrived. Emma insisted on riding with Ray to the
hospital. The injured man was whisked into the emergency room;
a team of doctors and nurses inserted IVs and put an oxygen mask
over the little man's face. Ray's injuries were grave—so grave the
doctor told Sam and Emma if they were praying people, they'd

better start right now. They sat in the waiting room, holding hands, praying for Ray's recovery.

Late that afternoon Ray was moved out of Intensive Care. His injuries were serious, but he would recover. Emma stayed with him throughout the long day. Ray opened his eyes once and smiled at her. Lully had been fortunate enough to see through the simple, naïve mind to a deeper, more profound man who had captured her heart. Emma didn't know why, but she forgave Ray for the pranks he'd pulled. She covered his hand, careful not to disturb the IV tubes, and cried like a baby.

"I hid Lully's money so no one would find it," Ray whispered, his fingers closing over Emma's tightly. "In a box—I took good care of it for you."

"Thank you, Ray." She needed to tell him that she had found it, but there was so much more she wanted to thank him for. "Thank you for taking care of Lully. You were the only family she had."

A smile formed on his features. "We had each other. And God. Lully taught me all about God and how he loves me. I was hoping I'd get to go be with God and Lully." His eyes fluttered closed. "But I guess God doesn't want me yet. For the first time in my life, I was going to be like everybody else." His eyes fluttered open again. "I'm sorry about the frogs. I wanted to scare away whoever wanted to buy the house."

"But you scared *me*, Ray." In his naïveté he didn't realize the house had never been for sale. "Did you put the spiders in the basement? Do you have a key to the house?" Of course, he had a key to the house. Lully had given him one.

"No. Those boys—Donny and Brice—did it. They took my spiders and said they were going to buy some more somewhere. I didn't want 'em to take the spiders. But they did. They weren't the bad kind of spiders. They wouldn't hurt nobody. I kept them in my room in a fish tank. They were mine. They never bothered anybody. I kept Harry—" He grinned. "Harry was my favorite. I kept him in a box in my pocket when I polished the floors at the nursing home. He liked the sound of the floor buffer." He shook his head. "Now they're all dead."

Emma cringed when she thought of all the elderly residents of Happy Hollow, blissfully unaware of Ray's pet, and her heart pounded at the thought of spiders scampering in and out of their rooms during the night.

Sam came to the hospital around seven o'clock. He and Emma sat outside the doorway in a small waiting area, watching the tears and fears on the faces of families visiting other patients.

"You need to rest," she told him at eleven. She knew he had put in a full day. He had nodded off twice, jerking awake when someone spoke loudly or a cart rattled down the hall.

He shook his head. "You go home. I'll stay and I'll call you if anything changes."

They argued about it, Emma insisting that Sam needed his rest more than she did. She could catnap in the chair and he couldn't. He had to be at work at seven, and she didn't. In the end, Emma won out.

She walked downstairs with him, through the dimly lit antiseptic corridors. The hospital was settling into its nighttime routine. Meds were given, family members staying overnight with patients settled into the uncomfortable lounge chairs beside the hospital beds, listening to the bleeps and blips and swooshing of the machines.

Pausing at the emergency entrance, Emma reached up and touched Sam's hair. So dark and curly. The gesture was oddly comforting. Life was so fragile. One minute you were here; the next you were gone. Maybe the answer was to grab hold of life and make the best of it, live for the moment, for the day . . . while looking toward an eternity with God. She didn't know, but maybe . . .

Sam smiled wearily. "You will try to get some sleep?"

"I promise." She smiled back. They stared at each other for a long moment. In his eyes she saw need. She knew hers reflected the same message. "I found a note in Lully's journal about the letter. You brought it by and asked her to send it, but she didn't. She destroyed it. She thought at the time she was doing the right thing, but in the end she recognized that was a mistake. She told me she thought we could have made it."

He shook his head, sadness in his eyes. "Too little too late."

She reached out and hugged him.

He remained stiff, unyielding. "I need to know, Emma. Are you going to leave Serenity?"

She nodded. "I'm going to call Janice and ask her to move to Serenity and run the tearoom with Elizabeth. I think she will. Elizabeth will move the bookstore to the house."

He looked away. "Then you've made your decision?"

"Just now, Sam. Just this moment I realized I have to go back for a while. Here, with you, I can't think straight. And the town is at each other's throats about what's going to happen to the property, and will they have a parking lot. It's my town, too, and like you, I don't want to see it torn apart by conflict. Money isn't everything. Sure, we could hold out for a king's ransom if we wanted, but we would be taking advantage of friends and neighbors. I don't want that and I know you don't. I'm thrilled to know that a few are on my side, and they still welcome a Mansi in town. But I have to have some space—room to think and pray and care for my business that I've severely neglected. I've been on my own for so long that the thought of letting you back into my life overwhelms me. It has to be right, Sam. This time it has to be right." She gazed at him longingly. "I want to stay; please just give me a little time to adjust to all these new, frightening emotions."

"If I say, 'Yes, take as long as you need,' will you come back?"

"Of course—I promise. And this time I'll write."

His laugh was humorless.

"Honest." She realized her voice was shaky. "I even have beautiful new stationery to use. And there is e-mail, you know. We'll never be farther than a keyboard away."

Her heart was breaking. Why couldn't she trust? God had given her another chance with Sam. Why couldn't she take it and run?

"But I won't leave until Ray is better."

Sam's eyes softened. "You know . . ."

She touched her finger to his lips. "I know, but I'm going to pray that God will change my heart—clear all doubts. Make his will so clear that even I can see it."

"Don't blame yourself about Ray, Emma."

"I don't."

And she didn't. She'd frightened Ray, and he ran. Hers was a natural reaction to finding someone planting bullfrogs in the kitchen. Never in her wildest accusations had she suspected Ray as the culprit. The mayor, Darrel Masters, someone from Shangri-La Developers, Buddy Crane, and, God forgive her, even Sam—sweet Sam. How could she have suspected the man she loved of wanting to harm her? But never Ray.

Snow was falling outside, whipping wet blizzardlike flakes. Sam pulled the fur collar of his jacket closer and settled his hat brim lower. "I'll be back around five."

"Okay."

He started out the door, and Emma suddenly found herself running after him. They both stopped just outside the emergency entrance. They stepped aside as two ambulance attendants ran by, wheeling a stretcher.

Sam turned to look at her. She hesitated . . . and then slowly walked into his arms. For a moment he held her lightly as if he wasn't sure what to do; then his arms closed around her. They stood, swaying, holding on to each other as snow blew around them. His breath was warm against her ear.

Finally, she pulled back, kissed him lightly on the mouth, and whispered, "Thank you."

"For what?" His voice dropped to a husky timbre.

"For . . . do I have to have a reason?"

"No ma'am. Not today, not ever." He pulled her back and kissed her long and thoroughly. When their lips parted, he touched her nose briefly, and walked into the snowy night.

chapter
FIFTEEN

EMMA refused to press charges against Ray. His pranks had been basically harmless, and other than having the wadding scared out of her, Emma had suffered no lasting effects.

The house was hers. Sam accepted the decision like the man she knew he was. She wanted to love him full out, without reservation. She did, in her heart. But she didn't trust her rocky emotions enough to walk into his life fully. Not just yet.

Thursday afternoon Emma looked up to see Sam standing in her living room doorway, arms crossed, hat tilted rakishly back from his forehead. She had packed the remainder of the boxes to be shipped. The moving van was coming tomorrow morning. Emma had a four-thirty flight to Seattle.

"Hey," she greeted.

"Hey." He eyed the mound of boxes. "You're really going."

She wrapped a picture and carefully laid it beside her purse to be gate checked. The portrait of Jesus and the lost sheep would have a place in her apartment.

"When's Janice coming?"

"This weekend." Emma taped a box marked Storage and set it aside. "You'll like her." *You'd better not like her too much*, she found herself adding silently. "She and Ken might hit it off. They're both about the same age—both single," Emma said aloud.

"Ken works in a jail; Janice lives in one."

Emma made a face at him. "That's not fair. She's had a real knack for getting involved with the wrong man. It's a gift with her."

"And you want her to hit it off with my brother?"

She whacked him with the end of a dish towel and he grinned. Catching her by the arm, he sobered. The room suddenly got deathly quiet.

"Don't go."

"Sam—"

"I mean it, Emma. Don't go." He pulled her closer until their noses were nearly touching. The scent of his aftershave nearly did her in. "From the moment I let you go that day, I have regretted it. I should have fought for you, Emma. God knows I loved you enough. But I was young and foolish and Mom was having a fit and Lully was beside herself—"

"You could have told them, argued harder that maybe we were young but we knew what we were doing—"

"I could hardly tell my mother to shut up, Emma. And you didn't talk to my mother, the mayor, that way."

"I was sorely tempted a few times, believe me." She pulled away, sullen.

"Well, I tried too, but—" He took off his hat. "Face it, Emma. We were too young fifteen years ago. I didn't have a job or a future. If we had married, chances are we wouldn't have made it. My folks wouldn't have supported us and Lully couldn't have."

"You were relieved to get away from the crazy Mansi girl. Admit it." All the hidden accusations, accusations she thought were long set to rest, spilled out.

"That's not true. I loved you. I still love you. I've never stopped loving you. A day hasn't gone by when I haven't thought of you, wanted to pick up the phone and call."

A sob caught in her throat. "We could have made it, Sam. There are lots of young marriages that make it."

"There are lots that don't, too. Maybe we would have; maybe we wouldn't have. I've argued with myself a million times. We'll never know. But we're two different people now." He reached out and pulled her back into his arms. "Older, wiser, with a few open wounds, but we could make it this time, Emma." His eyes softened. "We could make it."

Biting her lip, she pulled away and turned her back on him. It hurt; it hurt so bad and she knew he was hurting too. What he'd said was true, all of it. Chances are, they wouldn't have made it, not with such a rocky start.

"I knew where you were, Emma. Lully told me when I came back to Serenity. I thought about coming after you. Day after day, year after year. But I didn't because I blamed myself for not fighting for you in the first place, and I knew you blamed me too. I knew you were filled with bitterness, the kind that doesn't go away unless a person works at it, and I didn't figure you had been working at it.

"Lully and I visited a couple times a week. She loved you, you know that now. She regretted her part in the breakup. Any time she heard from you she'd come to the jail and read your letter to me. I knew you worked in a greenhouse and you loved what you did. I knew you hadn't married." He approached softly and gently tucked a lock of hair behind her ear. "When Lully left the house to both of us, you know what she was doing?"

Emma shook her head. "I didn't at first; I thought she'd lost her mind, especially when she said I'd find my real legacy here. When I found the bill of sale I thought that was it; then when we found the money I thought that's what she was referring to. But she was referring to us. By leaving the house to us, we would be forced to deal with each other. Forgive one another."

"Pretty smart lady."

"I don't know, Sam. I don't know."

She'd thought about this a zillion times, dreamed about Sam saying he loved her, suspected deep down in her heart that he still did, yet in the far recesses of her mind doubt still loomed, waiting to devour her. Could she ever trust him with her heart again?

Could God heal all wounds? He had to, or even now they would not be able to make it. And the last thing Emma wanted was a failed marriage.

"Think about it," Sam cajoled.

She wiped at sudden tears. "I'll . . . pray about it." She realized by the mere choice of resources how far she'd come. Eyes softening, she took his hand and held it for a very long moment. "Miracles do still happen."

He bent and kissed her lightly on the mouth. "I believe in miracles. I've waited fifteen years for one; I can wait another few weeks."

"Who said anything about weeks—"

He kissed her soundly this time. "Days then."

"Oh, honey, I'd give it serious thought if I were you. Sam's such a good man." Elizabeth pointed the movers toward another box in front of the house. Emma was storing everything until she could decide what she wanted—not wanted, because she knew what she wanted. But she had to be certain this time. Emma mentally rechecked her list to be sure the house was empty of Lully's personal effects.

"I will think about it, Elizabeth. I promise." There'd been nothing else on Emma's mind since yesterday and the moment Sam had asked her to stay. But events were moving too quickly. The movers were here; she had a flight in three hours. She couldn't decide her whole life in twenty-four hours.

Emma's thoughts turned to Janice. Since Janice was being released from the halfway house and needed a place to stay, Emma had invited her to live in the Mansi Mansion. She would help Elizabeth set up shop, and eventually, Emma hoped, be Emma's assistant in the tearoom venture. "Janice will be here on a ten o'clock flight Saturday morning. I told her you would meet her at the gate. You'll need to take a placard—"

"I won't need a placard. We'll recognize each other. You said she's about your age, blonde hair, clear blue eyes, petite—pretty as picture."

"She's too pretty. That's why she gets in trouble." Emma turned to face Elizabeth. "Look after her, Elizabeth. She's a great gal, really. But she picks the wrong man every time."

"Won't be easy to pick the wrong man here. There're not that many young and single. Sam and Ken, Nick Pierson and—"

"Sort of steer her away from Sam, okay?"

"You mean until you think this thing through."

"Yes. Elizabeth, I'm working on this!"

"Humph. Well, I'd pick up my pace a little if I were you. There're plenty of single women out there who've got their eye on Sam."

"As long as it's just an eye I'm okay."

"You have Sam here. And now Janice."

"I have Sam and Janice here." Emma heaved a sigh and handed the mover another small box. "And Gismo." In spite of her intentions, Emma had fallen in love with the mutt. "Janice will take him home with her when she gets here tomorrow."

"I'm glad to keep him." Elizabeth rubbed the mutt's nose. "We get along fine, don't we, boy?"

Gismo gave a doggy grin.

"Well, you're loaded now, so I guess you can pretty well do as you please until your flight." There had been over a half million dollars in the cash box. Most of the money she'd immediately put into stock investments, with some going toward getting the house in good shape. She had seen a lawyer yesterday and donated money to the town for a municipal parking lot. It wouldn't be on the Mansi property, but it would be close enough to ease the town's parking problems. The lot would be named in honor of Lully. Sam's part of the house—she'd given him an inflated price, of course—would take care of Edwina as long as she lived, even if that were to be one hundred. The land speculators and time-share vultures could fly a kite. Serenity was just that: serenity, and the folks didn't need a tourist invasion. She supposed it was bound to happen someday. *But the crazy Mansi girls won't be responsible*, she thought with a grin.

Sam didn't know about his part of the settlement or the parking lot yet. Emma asked that her actions not be revealed until the plane lifted off for Seattle.

Two-thirty. Emma lifted the front-room curtain and peeked out. Sam still hadn't been around. The moving van had left thirty minutes ago; her flight was in two hours. Where was a cop when you needed one?

Picking up her cosmetics case, she took a final walk through the house, checking to make sure everything was completed. Memories that were once painful were now only reminiscences— some pleasant, some not so pleasant. Just like any other house. Life at this old house hadn't been all bad. In the early days when Mom and Dad were here, they had been a family. Life had seemed normal.

Lully once said that God had a plan for everyone. Emma's plan had been a little rocky so far, but if God had a plan for her, she was now willing to acknowledge it. And she was now willing to acknowledge God, for who else could have brought her through the storm? She was optimistic about the future, though no clear sense of direction had surfaced. But she supposed that's the way it should be. If she could know what she'd face in the future, she might never have the courage to skip into it with competency.

Well, it was time. Picking up her purse and the picture of Jesus holding the lamb, she went out the front door and locked it. She would be back more often; she'd promised herself that. No more running away. This was home, like it or not, and the idea of the combined bookstore and tearoom excited her.

Few air travelers clogged the airport when she arrived. Emma returned her rental car, checked in, and walked toward her gate. On the way, she stopped in a gift shop and bought *Vanity Fair* and *Home and Garden* magazines. Inexplicably, the thought of returning to Seattle did not excite her—not like she'd thought it would. Sam's face, his words, still rang in her thoughts: *"We could make it this time, Emma."*

If God had enabled Moses to part the Red Sea, couldn't he make a way for her and Sam to forge a successful marriage together here on earth? Of course he could, Emma realized. He still worked miracles, big and small.

She emerged from the shop, looking both ways to see if she could spot a tall, dark, curly-haired sheriff in the crowd. There was none. She proceeded to the gate. Why hadn't she accepted Sam's offer to stay? There was nothing holding her in Seattle. She could always sell the business and turn a good profit. There wasn't a man in Seattle whose occasional company she wouldn't gladly forego. She'd miss Sue, but Janice would be in Colorado. A tearoom. She envisioned roses climbing trellises and blooming outside the tearoom windows. Perennials of every hue brightening the multiple flowerbeds she and Sam would . . .

She and Sam?

Visions of her mother kneeling in the warm soil, tending the roses, flashed through her mind. Her mother had always hummed as she worked, her dainty hands sifting the soil with loving care. Emma could bring those roses back to life—she could make them even more beautiful than Momma's—a visual tribute to the woman who loved blooming roses. To the Mansi women: Lully, Mom, and Emma. Now wouldn't that be ironic.

The tearoom would be beautiful—maybe not profitable, but money was no longer an issue. And she would take care of Elizabeth and the bookstore until her dying day. The thrill of holding old hardback books in her hands—pages that had endured the ages, passages that other eyes had read—was grand. Slick new paperbacks served a busy world, but they couldn't replace antiquity.

If she moved back, she could spend more time with Janice, possibly help her get her life straightened out. Ken and Janice. Emma grinned. The two names fit like oil and water.

She mentally ticked off the pluses as she entered the gate area and waited for the boarding call.

Behind the security check, Sam Gold stood by the window watching the woman he loved. Emma looked small and lost sitting in the nearly empty C-Gate One waiting area.

Why had he let her walk away again? He'd kicked himself for letting her go the first time, and now he was letting her get away again. But he couldn't force love; he'd found that out over the years. Until Emma gave herself to their relationship, he wouldn't budge. Sometimes you're lucky enough to find that one right person; sometimes you're not. Sometimes you go through life searching and hoping and looking, but it's never a true fit. Sam didn't want that for his life.

Thirty-four was pushing the scale a little. He had to stop looking for Emma in every woman; he had to stop hoping. She was boarding a plane in five minutes. She'd be back, but that would be more agonizing than seeing her leave this time. In the future she'd be leaving over and over again. To have her so close—but yet so far away . . .

If she loved him, she would make the declaration. He'd made his; he'd thought it through and the answer hadn't come out the way he'd liked, but she knew where he stood.

Yet she needed time.

Time.

How long was time to her? To him it was a million years, standing here, his throat tight with emotion. What could he do to make her stay? to make her realize that they belonged together? Should he swoop into the waiting area like a deranged lover and demand that she stay? make a fool of himself in public, and in uniform? If that's what it took, he'd gladly make the sacrifice, but Emma was a tough nut to crack. He'd misjudged her once; he wasn't going to make the same mistake twice. If she loved him— and she did, he saw it in her eyes every time she looked at him—

then she would have to convince herself he was trustworthy. He saw it in her eyes . . .

"Ladies and gentlemen, we are about to begin boarding flight 597 to Seattle. First-class passengers and those with children or needing extra time . . ."

Emma turned and peered over her shoulder at the waiting room. Her eyes traveled to the coffee shop across the way. *Oh, Sam, if you loved me you'd be here. You'd demand that I stay.*

"All passengers, please have your boarding passes ready."

Emma stood up, searching the main pedestrian area. It was time for her to board. Passengers hurried by to catch other flights. Biting her lip, she closed her eyes and whispered, "I know I've been foolish, dear God, but please let him come. Please don't let me walk away from the only man who had ever loved me unconditionally—"

I love you unconditionally.

"I know—I'm sorry—I mean here on earth."

That's better.

"Rows fifteen through twenty-five can now board."

Emma glanced at her ticket. Blither. She was row twenty-four. She had to board now. Picking up her cosmetics case, purse, and picture, she started down the Jetway, tears blurring her eyes. She turned around abruptly and bumped smack into a fellow passenger. Murmuring an apology, she turned back around and kept walking.

He's not coming. He's not coming.

Sam watched Emma disappear through the doorway. A grown man didn't cry, especially a county sheriff, but he knew one who was about to set an embarrassing precedent.

Moving back to the window, he put his hand flat on the glass, as if to touch her one last time. His eyes scanned the small windows of the departing plane. He could see figures moving down the aisle, passengers straining to push overloaded luggage into cramped overhead bins. He saw Emma take a seat by the window at the back of the plane. He stared at her, trying to get his fill. It wasn't possible to plug the empty hole she'd left in his heart. He turned his head, wiping his eyes on his sleeves.

Backing away from the window, he sat down. He wouldn't leave until the plane took off, until he saw the jet stream fade into the distance. Only then would he accept that she was gone.

The clerk stood at the passenger desk, counting tickets. The door to the Jetway closed, and a pretty attendant locked it.

Sam stared at his boots. They needed a good polish. There were traces of mud from yesterday's snow. Moisture blurred his vision.

Inside the plane, Emma put her earphones on, leaned back, and closed her eyes as the flight steward closed the first-class drapes. She looked out the window, not wanting the other passengers to see her cry.

The wheels of the Boeing touched down at Seattle-Tacoma International at 6:14 P.M. The big tires squealed down the tarmac, engines reversing thrust. Passengers remained seated, seat belts intact until American flight 597 taxied to the gate and parked.

Emma unbuckled her belt and gathered her personal belongings. She waited until the door was opened and passenger rows systematically filed out. She felt drained. Emotionally unstable and downright out of sorts. Why had Sam not tried harder to stop her from leaving? Why hadn't he just once chosen to fight for her? All at once she realized that this was what she had been waiting for, this was what it would take for her to fully trust him, trust his love. For him to fight for her—now. Only this would undo the wrong he had dealt her in the past. And he hadn't come through.

The rows slowly emptied, and Emma stood up and maneuvered

through the narrow aisle. Emerging from the Jetway into the terminal she stopped short. Standing at the gate, arms crossed, Sam stared at her. Her jaw dropped.

"As I was saying," he said calmly as she approached, "we can make it this time, Emma. I'm not taking no for an answer."

Her heart suddenly flipped a somersault. Passengers bumped into her, jostled and stepped on her toes, but she stood rooted to the floor, staring at the man she loved more than life itself. She finally salvaged her voice. "How . . . ?"

"I bought a ticket. It cost me first class but it was worth it." He frowned. "If that isn't love, I don't know what is."

Warmth began to creep through her, slow and sweet and so wonderfully exhilarating. He hadn't let her go this time. This time he'd come after her. *Thank you, God.*

Clearing her throat, she said softly, "Um . . . that thing you said about we could make it this time?"

"Yeah?" Sam took both her hands, ignoring the rude travelers shoving their way through the terminal.

"Well you see . . . I have this gaping hole inside me that I—"

He stopped her. "Me too." His eyes adored her as they stood facing each other, the future—their future—hanging in balance. "I think we're going to start filling holes with love and acceptance instead of anger and resentment—with the understanding that God has given us the opportunity to choose how we fill the hole. With gratitude for the good times—because we've had those too, Emma. With conscious effort we can fill in those holes and move on."

For the briefest of moments, the world stopped for Emma. There was only Sam—the way it had always been. "Yeah . . . well . . ." She sighed, licking a salty tear with her tongue. "We're going to have to buy awfully big shovels."

A smile touched the corners of his eyes. "I'm sort of partial to hardware stores. What about you?"

"I hate hardware stores." A sob caught in her throat.

"Fine. We'll buy them elsewhere. The point is we buy them. Right?"

"So right," she conceded. "The tearoom . . . I could make something of that, Sam. Like us, it could be good—really good."

"Roses will bloom again for you, Emma. I promise."

Sam lifted her off her feet and swung her around in a bear hug. "Oh, Emma, I thought you had left me a second time," he whispered. "I told God I couldn't bear it again."

Laughing through a veil of tears, she pressed her mouth to his ear. "God is so faithful. He never leaves us. It's taken me fifteen years to discover that. If you're asking me to marry you, I accept."

He kissed her hungrily, making a spectacle in front of the two amused airline employees.

"I love you, Emma Mansi," he whispered between frenzied snatches of kisses.

Playfully grasping his ears, she drew him nose to nose. "This time it's for keeps."

Their gazes locked. In the depths of his eyes she saw everything she needed to know. Emma didn't need any more assurances.

This time it was for keeps.

A Note from the Author

Dear Reader,

Roses Will Bloom Again is my first HeartQuest novel in a contemporary setting. The book has been in the works for some time, and I am delighted to finally tell the story of Emma and Sam. So often while I was in the process of writing this story I thought of how my life parallels Emma's and how often I have to rein up and allow God to work freely in my life. Emma felt that life had dealt her a raw deal, and she had a hard time believing God loved her. She blamed everyone for wrecking her life, and she retreated into a "safe," sterile world that was only an illusion. Although God promises that he has nothing but good for us, some days can look kind of bleak, can't they? Emma was *so* certain God had forgotten about her that she forgot to trust.

But God doesn't forget any of us. What Father could forget his child, even when she finds herself in the middle of trials and troubles? Like Emma, I've discovered I can't possibly know the good the Lord has in store for me, for his grace and love know no end if I will trust—trust until it hurts and the Lord has an opportunity to work in my life.

I hope your trust, like Emma's, was deeper by the time you read the last page of this story. God is good—all the time. All the time, God is good!

Talk to you again real soon.

In his name,

Lori Copeland

About the Author

Lori Copeland has published more than fifty romance novels and has won numerous awards for her books. Publishing with HeartQuest allows her the freedom to write stories that express her love of God and her personal convictions.

Lori lives with her wonderful husband, Lance, in Springfield, Missouri. She has three incredibly handsome grown sons, three absolutely gorgeous daughters-in-law, and three exceptionally bright grandchildren—but then, she freely admits to being partial when it comes to her family. Lori enjoys reading biographies, attending book discussion groups, participating in morning water-aerobic exercises at the local YMCA, and she is presently trying very hard to learn to play bridge. She loves to travel and is always thrilled to meet her readers.

When asked what one thing Lori would like others to know about her, she readily says, "I'm not perfect—just forgiven by the grace of God." Christianity to Lori means peace, joy, and the knowledge that she has a Friend, a Savior, who never leaves her side. Through her books, she hopes to share this wondrous assurance with others.

Lori's other books include the Brides of the West series (*Faith, Hope, June,* and *Glory*); *Child of Grace; Christmas Vows: $5 Extra;* and the Heavenly Daze series, coauthored with Angela Elwell Hunt (*The Island of Heavenly Daze, Grace in Autumn,* and *A Warmth in Winter*).

Lori welcomes letters written to her in care of Tyndale House Author Relations, P.O. Box 80, Wheaton, IL 60189-0080.

TURN THE PAGE FOR AN EXCITING PREVIEW
FROM LORI COPELAND'S NEXT BOOK

RUTH

BOOK #5 IN THE BEST-SELLING
BRIDES OF THE WEST SERIES
ISBN 0-8423-1937-9
AVAILABLE FROM
TYNDALE HOUSE PUBLISHERS
FALL 2002

chapter
ONE

EVERYONE had gotten involved in the after-wedding festivities. Tables covered in lace tablecloths and adorned with bouquets of dried fall flowers were set up outside in front of the church. A large wedding cake festooned with a tiny bride and groom stood amidst the decorations. An air of festivity blanketed Denver City as fiddlers tuned up.

Well-wishers descended on the happy couple as Ruth drifted away from the confusion. She'd be back to extend her best to the new Mr. and Mrs. Jackson Montgomery when things settled down a bit.

Oscar Fleming caught her eye, and she smiled back distantly. For the last few days the crusty widower had been on her trail. There had to be fifty years difference in their ages if there was a day, but that hadn't stopped Oscar. He smiled, winked, and showed a set of brown teeth worn to the gum every time he could catch her attention. Ruth stiffened as the old fellow sprinted in her direction.

"Afternoon, Ruthie!"

Ruth mustered a polite smile, her gaze darting to the marshall, who was watching the exchange with a self-satisfied grin. "Good afternoon, Oscar. Lovely ceremony." She tried to side-step the old codger.

"Hit was, hit was." He blocked her path, grinning. "Thought maybe I'd have me th' first dance."

"Oh," she said, her gaze swinging toward her friends Patience and Mary, but they were both helping a group of women set food on the tables. They were too busy to pay heed to her silent plea for help.

Oscar held out his scrawny arms. "How 'bout it, Ruthie? You and me cut a jig?"

Jig, indeed. Ruth swallowed, drawing her wrap tighter as she tried to manufacture a plausible excuse. She glanced up when a hand wrapped around her left arm. Dylan McCall politely interrupted. "Now, Ruthie, I believe you promised *me* the first dance."

Though weak with relief, Ruth seethed. *Ruthie.* How dare the conceited brute call her that? Still, it was a chance to escape. She stiffly accepted his proffered arm and mustered a friendly smile. "Why, I do believe I did, Marshall." She smiled her regrets to Oscar. "Will you excuse us?"

Oscar's grin deflated, his chin sinking down to his chest. "Maybe later?"

"Of course," she conceded. *Much, much later.*

As the couple strolled off, Ruth pinched Dylan. Hard.

Though he winced, Dylan kept a pleasant smile pasted on his face . . . and pinched her back.

"Ouch!"

She jerked free of his grasp and flounced ahead, pretending to ignore him. The very *nerve* of Dylan McCall acting as her rescuer!

His masculine laugh only irritated her more. "Admit it, Ruthie," he called. "You welcomed the interruption!"

Ruth's face burned. "Not by the likes of you!"

He paused, chuckling as she marched to the punch bowl. Picking up a cup, she dunked it into the bowl and drank quickly, unfortunately stringing red liquid down the front of her best dress. She dropped the cup and swiped at her bodice, then felt punch oozing through her right slipper.

Her temper soared. It was Dylan's fault. He made her so mad she couldn't think straight. From the corner of her eye she saw Dylan politely tip his hat and ease into the crowd.

"Oooooph!" Ruth sank into a chair, steam virtually rolling from the top of her head.

Forever. Whew. Dylan threaded his way through well-wishers, pausing to speak to the ladies. Lily and Harper bloomed under his attention, but his mind was on the ceremony that had taken place earlier.

Forever. That made a man break out in a cold sweat—at least, a man who liked women but didn't care to tie himself down to any particular one, only one, for the rest of his life. Not unless he was planning to die tomorrow.

He'd been accused of breaking women's hearts, and he had broken his fair share, he supposed. They could be as pretty as ice on a winter pond or ugly as a mud dauber, and he'd allow them a second glance. Dylan didn't judge a woman by the way she looked on the outside. He'd learned long ago that the outside didn't mean beans. He'd told someone once that when he met the right woman he'd marry her, but deep down he knew he'd never see the day. There wasn't a *right* woman. Not for him. There were just . . . women. Women all softness and pretty curves, but inside they weren't worth his time. Sara Dunnigan had taught him that. Women were out to use a man, use him up for their own purposes. Well, he had *his* own purposes, and they weren't to share with any woman.

The married women turned to watch him walk away, leaving Lily and Harper tittering. Dylan was aware of, but neither welcomed nor resented, the attention. A woman's naïve notice made him feel in control. He could always walk away, and he intended to always be able to do just that.

The receiving line had begun to thin as he approached the newlyweds. He shook hands with Jackson. "You're a lucky man."

The sincerity in his tone wasn't entirely contrived. Jackson *was* lucky. Glory was the one woman who could tame the wagon master, and Dylan wished them luck.

Jackson grinned down at his bride. If ever there was a happy man, Montgomery fit the bill today. "It's your turn next, McCall!"

"Don't hold your breath, Montgomery."

Dylan leaned in and kissed the bride lightly on the cheek. Glory blushed, edging closer to Jackson. Beaming, Jackson drew her close. "That's my girl. Beware of wolves in sheep's clothing."

Dylan lifted an eyebrow. "Me? A wolf?"

"The worst," Jackson confirmed with a sly wink. "Knew that about you right off."

The two men laughed.

The new Mrs. Montgomery frowned. "Jackson—"

Throwing the marshall a knowing wink, Jackson took his wife's arm and steered her toward another cluster of well-wishers.

Dylan milled about for a while, exchanging expected pleasantries and hoping he could leave soon. Events like this weren't his cup of tea. He spent the majority of his time alone, which he preferred. He spotted Ruth talking with Mayor Hopkins, her cheeks flushed, eyes aglow, laughing up at him. She'd never looked at Dylan that way . . . but then, he supposed a woman like Ruth wouldn't. Men like him were loners. They had to be. Keeping the law was a dangerous business. Ruth, even with her independent streak a mile wide, would avoid a man like him, as well she should.

Dylan had stepped onto the sidewalk when Pastor Siddons threaded his way through the crowd toward him. "Marshall McCall! They'll be cutting the wedding cake soon. You won't want to miss that." The pastor beamed. "Etta Katsky makes the best pastries this side of heaven."

Smiling, the marshall acknowledged the invitation. The whole town was friendlier than a six-week old pup. It was a good place for Ruth and the other women to settle.

The two men stood side by side, watching the festivities. Arthur Siddons's pleasant face beamed. "Nothing like a wedding to make you feel like a young man again."

Dylan refused to comment. His gaze followed Ruth as she moved through the crowd. He'd never seen her smile like that, laugh like that, so happy and carefree. Pastor looked up at him, a sly grin hovering at the corner of his mouth. "Right pretty sight, wouldn't you say?"

Dylan had to agree. "Ruth's a fine-looking woman. All the girls are."

Art nodded. "Mother was just saying how nice it is to have young blood in the town. Tom Wyatt and his boys are low-down polecats. We've known that for years, but I have to say the devil was taken by surprise this time. Had it not been for you and Jackson, those six young women would be working the mines right now, without a hope for the future."

Dylan bristled at the thought. "The Wyatts ought to be strung up by their heels."

"Yes, many agree. But Wyatt's not done anything he can be legally prosecuted for. We know he promised the women husbands, but in a court of law he'd say the women, the orphanage, and Montgomery misunderstood. He would eventually set them free, once they worked off their debt to him. But considering the wages he'd pay, that would take a mighty long time. It isn't the first time he's used deceit to gain mine workers. Brought eight women out last year, and one by one they escaped. Found one this spring." The reverend shook his head. "Poor woman didn't make it."

A shadow crossed the marshall's features. "I thought once that Jackson and Glory had met the same fate."

"Yes, Jackson and Glory were lucky to survive their ordeal." The pastor beamed. "Wouldn't have, without Glory's common sense."

"No." Dylan's gaze found the laughing bride and groom. "She's quite a woman."

Art nodded. "Colorado's a rough territory. A man can freeze to death in just a few hours." Sobering, the minister's gaze rested on Mary, who was smiling up at Mayor Rogers. The couple seemed to be enjoying each other's company. "Now, there's the one I worry about. The poor thing coughs until she chokes. Won't be many men who want to take on such a responsibility."

Dylan agreed. Mary's asthma would make it difficult for her to find a husband. His gaze shifted to Harper and Lily, who were busy setting out platters of golden brown fried chicken. Harper was so independent and quick-tongued it would take a strong man to handle her. Lily would do okay for herself, and Patience wouldn't have any trouble finding a husband. She was the looker of the bunch.

His attention moved back to Ruth, who was now conversing with a tall, lanky man who looked to be somewhere in his late twenties. The couple made a striking pair. The young man's carrot-colored hair and mahogany eyes complemented Ruth's flaming tresses and wide blue eyes. But Ruth was going to be trouble for any man who took her on. She was as prickly as a porcupine—and as quick to raise her defenses. Made a man wonder what was inside her. No, not him, but some man; some good man looking to settle down.

Patting his round belly, the pastor chuckled softly as he followed Dylan's gaze to the couple. "They make a fine-looking pair, don't they? Conner lost his wife a couple years back. Fine man, Conner Justice, so young to lose a mate. Lost Jenny in child-birth . . . baby was stillborn. His wife's death was mighty hard on him. Conner is only now coming back to community socials."

Dylan's gaze narrowed. It appeared to him that Conner Rogers was recovering quite nicely. He was certainly enjoying Ruth's company. The sound of Ruth's lilting laughter floated to him, a sound he hadn't heard very often. She was enjoying herself for the first time since he'd met her.

Well, good for Ruthie. Conner Rogers maybe needed a new challenge, and the fiery redhead would certainly provide him one.

The pastor patted his belly again. "Well, I hear a piece of that cake calling my name." He stuck his hand out to Dylan. "Guess you'll be moving on?"

"I have to be in Utah by the end of the month."

"Worst time of the year to travel."

"I'm used to it." He preferred better weather, but when he'd decided to help Jackson deliver the brides to Denver City safely, he'd known his delayed travel would probably mean encountering bad weather. It wouldn't be the first time he'd been inconvenienced, nor would it be the last.

"Take care of yourself."

Dylan smiled, his gaze involuntarily returning to Ruth and Conner Rogers, while the pastor wandered away to claim his piece of cake. Ruth looked like she was having a fine time.

"Well, I am, too," he told himself, but right now he couldn't have proved it.

Visit www.HeartQuest.com for lots of info on
HeartQuest books and authors and more!

www.HeartQuest.com

CURRENT HEARTQUEST RELEASES

- *Magnolia,* Ginny Aiken
- *Lark,* Ginny Aiken
- *Camellia,* Ginny Aiken

- *Letters of the Heart,* Lisa Tawn Bergren, Maureen Pratt, and Lyn Cote

- *Sweet Delights,* Terri Blackstock, Elizabeth White, and Ranee McCollum

- *Awakening Mercy,* Angela Benson
- *Abiding Hope,* Angela Benson

- *Roses Will Bloom Again,* Lori Copeland
- *Faith,* Lori Copeland
- *Hope,* Lori Copeland
- *June,* Lori Copeland
- *Glory,* Lori Copeland

- *Winter's Secret,* Lyn Cote

- *Freedom's Promise,* Dianna Crawford
- *Freedom's Hope,* Dianna Crawford
- *Freedom's Belle,* Dianna Crawford
- *A Home in the Valley,* Dianna Crawford

- *Prairie Rose,* Catherine Palmer
- *Prairie Fire,* Catherine Palmer
- *Prairie Storm,* Catherine Palmer

- *Prairie Christmas,* Catherine Palmer, Elizabeth White, and Peggy Stoks
- *Finders Keepers,* Catherine Palmer
- *Hide & Seek,* Catherine Palmer
- *English Ivy,* Catherine Palmer
- *A Kiss of Adventure,* Catherine Palmer (original title: *The Treasure of Timbuktu*)
- *A Whisper of Danger,* Catherine Palmer (original title: *The Treasure of Zanzibar*)
- *A Touch of Betrayal,* Catherine Palmer
- *A Victorian Christmas Keepsake,* Catherine Palmer, Kristin Billerbeck, and Ginny Aiken
- *A Victorian Christmas Cottage,* Catherine Palmer, Debra White Smith, Jeri Odell, and Peggy Stoks
- *A Victorian Christmas Quilt,* Catherine Palmer, Peggy Stoks, Debra White Smith, and Ginny Aiken
- *A Victorian Christmas Tea,* Catherine Palmer, Dianna Crawford, Peggy Stoks, and Katherine Chute

- *Olivia's Touch,* Peggy Stoks
- *Romy's Walk,* Peggy Stoks
- *Elena's Song,* Peggy Stoks

COMING SOON (FALL 2002)

- *Ruth* (Brides of the West #5), Lori Copeland
- *Autumn's Shadow,* Lyn Cote

- *A Victorian Christmas Collection,* Peggy Stoks

HEARTQUEST BOOKS BY LORI COPELAND

Faith (Brides of the West #1)—With the matrimonial prospects in her little Michigan town virtually nonexistent, nineteen-year-old Faith—along with her two sisters, Hope and June—answers an ad for mail-order brides. Before she knows it, she's on her way to Deliverance, Texas, determined to make a success of her marriage to wealthy rancher Nicholas Shepherd. But from the moment she arrives in Deliverance, sparks begin to fly between Faith—a strong-willed tomboy—and her prospective husband—a man with a pretty strong will of his own! Then there's Liza, Nicholas's mother, who is anything but thrilled that his son has chosen a mail-order bride. And after a string of wedding postponements and a slew of interfering circumstances and people, a union between Nicholas and Faith begins to look less and less likely.

In the meantime, Faith and Nicholas are beginning to care for one another—but is their matching stubbornness destined to forever put up a barrier between them? Best-selling author Lori Copeland gives you a lighthearted story of romance and faith in this first book of this historical romance series.

June (Brides of the West #2)—Like her sister before her, June leaves her Michigan home to embrace her future as a mail-order bride: partner and helpmate to a young Washington State pastor. But from the start, nothing works out as June expects. Caught up in her fiancé's vision for an elaborate tabernacle that would befit God's glory, she soon learns that not everyone approves of the plan. Most opposed is the hardheaded Parker Sentell, who secretly favors supporting the bedraggled group of orphans in the local orphanage. June's friend Samantha and her aging aunt run the orphanage, and June finds the orphans a natural outlet for her generous, nurturing spirit. But the two projects seem incompatible, and June finds herself faced with difficult choices—choices that challenge both her faith and her heart. A lighthearted story that illustrates God's faithfulness even when we don't understand his plan.

Hope (Brides of the West #3)—Mail-order bride Hope Kallahan is not amused when her stagecoach is waylaid by a bunch of bumbling outlaws. The feisty beauty is puzzled by the oddball in the group—the disarmingly kind Grunt Lawson. She doesn't know that Grunt is really Dan Sullivan, the government agent sent to infiltrate the gang on what was supposed to be his last assignment. Together, Hope and Dan learn that no matter what happens, God works everything together into a plan that's bigger and better than all their hopes and dreams.

Glory (Brides of the West #4)—On the run from a no-good scoundrel, Glory reluctantly joins a wagon train of mail-order brides heading for Denver City. But what if her secret endangers them all? And the way the handsome wagon master makes her heart do flip-flops is just plain befuddling! As if five mail-order brides weren't a big enough handful, now Jackson has a fiercely independent young woman to look after—one who makes his job all the harder by insisting she doesn't need help! Jackson suspects otherwise . . . and his heart soon insists that this feisty beauty deserves the lion's share of his attention. As Glory's past unfolds, both Jackson and Glory learn important lessons about God's faithfulness—and the strength of their growing love.

HEART QUEST

OTHER GREAT TYNDALE HOUSE FICTION

- *Safely Home,* Randy Alcorn

- *Jenny's Story,* Judy Baer
- *Libby's Story,* Judy Baer
- *Tia's Story,* Judy Baer

- *Out of the Shadows,* Sigmund Brouwer
- *The Leper,* Sigmund Brouwer

- *Child of Grace,* Lori Copeland
- *Christmas Vows: $5 Extra,* Lori Copeland

- *They Shall See God,* Athol Dickson

- *Ribbon of Years,* Robin Lee Hatcher
- *Firstborn,* Robin Lee Hatcher

- *The Touch,* Patricia Hickman

- *Redemption,* Karen Kingsbury

- *The Price,* Jim and Terri Kraus
- *The Treasure,* Jim and Terri Kraus
- *The Promise,* Jim and Terri Kraus
- *The Quest,* Jim and Terri Kraus

- *Winter Passing,* Cindy McCormick Martinusen
- *Blue Night,* Cindy McCormick Martinusen
- *North of Tomorrow,* Cindy McCormick Martinusen

- *Embrace the Dawn,* Kathleen Morgan

- *Lullaby,* Jane Orcutt

- *The Happy Room,* Catherine Palmer
- *A Dangerous Silence,* Catherine Palmer

- *Unveiled,* Francine Rivers
- *Unashamed,* Francine Rivers
- *Unshaken,* Francine Rivers
- *Unspoken,* Francine Rivers
- *Unafraid,* Francine Rivers
- *A Voice in the Wind,* Francine Rivers
- *An Echo in the Darkness,* Francine Rivers
- *As Sure As the Dawn,* Francine Rivers
- *Leota's Garden,* Francine Rivers

- *Shaiton's Fire,* Jake Thoene